Arthur Wollaston Hutton

Cardinal Manning

Arthur Wollaston Hutton

Cardinal Manning

ISBN/EAN: 9783337261375

Printed in Europe, USA, Canada, Australia, Japan

Cover: Foto ©Andreas Hilbeck / pixelio.de

More available books at **www.hansebooks.com**

CARDINAL MANNING.

CARDINAL MANNING

BY

ARTHUR WOLLASTON HUTTON, M.A.

Ecce sacerdos magnus, qui in diebus suis placuit Deo et inventus est justus.

LONDON :

Methuen & Co.

1894

Richard Clay & Sons, Limited,
London & Bungay.

PREFACE

WHEN invited to undertake a Memoir of Cardinal
Manning I was at first reluctant to do so, fearing lest
my point of view would at once alienate from me a
numerous body of readers whose sympathy and good
will I ought to secure. But on reflection I saw that
this ought to be no real obstacle, since I could speak
with some personal sympathy of his life as an Anglican,
of his anxious period of transition, and of his work
within the Catholic Church, surrounded as it was by
an atmosphere with difficulty apprehended by those
who have had no experience of it. Personally I
cannot claim to have known him very well, for I only
met him on two or three occasions after I was first
introduced to him in 1876 and before 1883; and after
that date I did not see him to speak to until 1890,
when I re-introduced myself to him, on the occasion of
my having undertaken to write this book, and found,
to my surprise, that he quite remembered me, and
was ready to talk freely and fully on personal matters.
Of course I do not claim that he approved or authorized
my writing his Life. As I was leaving he said with
a smile, "You cannot expect me to godfather your,
book"; having earlier in the conversation asked me

not to publish anything until after his death. Nor
did he then, or later, supply me with any substantial
information; but he cleared up sundry points on which
I should have been at fault without his assistance;
and I wish to put on record here my vivid impression
of his kindly, courteous manner, his dignity, earnestness,
and patience.

My book is thus almost wholly compiled from
materials open to all who will take the trouble to
consult them. I am aware that my numerous extracts
from Manning's own less accessible writings, from
the comments of others upon his career, and even
from newspaper reports, lay me open to unfavourable
criticism; but I shall not complain if my critics also
admit that my book is thus made better. It would
have been easy for me to have written, at equal or
even at greater length, an account of Manning's
life that should have excluded all such quotations;
but the work would not then have had the character
of authentic biography. Such a study from a competent hand has no doubt its value, when a trustworthy and full memoir has already appeared that can
be appealed to as an authority. But in Manning's case
no such work exists, nor is likely to exist for many
years to come. His biographer cannot refer to the
familiar and luminous pages of an *Apologia* to illustrate
his points. He is at liberty to assume very little previous
knowledge on the part of his readers. What therefore
I have here attempted is in the main a chronicle in
brief, showing precisely what Manning said and what
he did at such and such a time, and further what was
thought and said about him by observers on the spot.
I have not of course excluded all reflections of my own

on what I relate; but, on the whole, I leave my readers
free to form their own conclusions. It is not less true
of biography than, as Macaulay said, of history, that
it is contained in its most authentic form in newspapers. A vast amount of valuable matter is daily
buried in our newspapers; and in resuscitating, always
with acknowledgment, a few fragments to illustrate
Manning's career, I think I have done my readers a
service.

My thanks are due to numerous friends who have
contributed advice and information; but more especially
to Mr. John P. Anderson, the courteous and indefatigable
Clerk of the Reading Room at the British Museum, to
whom is due, substantially, though not in its present
form, the full bibliography which will, I hope, give a
special value to this volume. I also owe it to Mr.
Anderson that I could make good use of the few and
short visits I have been able to pay to the Museum
myself. To Mr. H. Whitehead I am indebted for a full
and accurate collection of facts, involving prolonged
and laborious researches there, which I could not have
spared the time to undertake; and I have also found
very serviceable the two collections of letters which
Mr. Wilfrid Meynell has put forth in *Merry England*.
I trust that the book will be found to illustrate fairly
and with sympathy the progress and consistency of
Manning's career; and so, until a full and authorized
biography has been published, which can hardly be for
some years to come, may be accepted as a tribute to a
life that must, on the whole, be accounted noble and
memorable.

PREFACE TO THIS EDITION

THE issue of this Memoir as a volume in the series of ENGLISH LEADERS OF RELIGION, gives me the opportunity for making sundry corrections. My thanks are mainly due to correspondents for these corrections, and in one or two cases to the writers of press notices. To the great majority of the latter I am under an obligation for their friendly and considerate criticisms, though in very few cases did they add anything to what was already contained in the book, while in some instances it was clear that the writer had read no further than the preface. To the essay of one critic, however,—that contained in the *Quarterly Review* for July, 1892—I wish to call special attention, as it contains much fresh and interesting matter, which I trust will have the attention of my readers.

To Mrs. Austen, Cardinal Manning's venerable surviving sister, I am indebted for a correction in the matter of genealogy, which is the more noteworthy, inasmuch as what I had stated about the Cardinal's mother's family being of Italian extraction (pp. 3, 4, and 179) I had from his own lips. Mrs. Austen, however, sent me word (Sept. 14, 1892) that "his mother's family were of *French* extraction, being *Venours* up to about 1550, when the name was Anglicized into 'Hunter.'

The Manning pedigree is an old Kentish one, and can be seen in the Visitation of that county, printed in the *Archæologia Cantiana*, vol. vi." And two days later she wrote herself:—"I ought to have given you my authority for the statement I sent you. The extract is taken from my great-grandfather's own diary in his own handwriting. The diary consists of two large volumes, which one of his grandsons, Sir Paul Hunter, Bart., (now deceased) condensed into a smaller form. I may add that *I* never saw it till now, and I feel quite sure the Cardinal never saw it." The matter is perhaps of no great importance, but it is also not without interest, and it illustrates the almost proverbial difficulty in securing accuracy in matters genealogical.

My topography of Totteridge also needs correction, as I have confused Copped Hall with Totteridge Park. It was in the latter house that Bunsen lived at a later date, and it is this house that is now a boys' school. St. Edward's Orphanage, of which Manning laid the first stone on his 78th birthday, is within a few yards of it. Copped Hall, the house near the church, in which the Cardinal was born, has never ceased to be a private residence. Bulwer Lytton wrote some of his novels while living here, and it is at present occupied by Mr. Samuel Bagster Boulter, J.P. The monument to Manning's grandfather is not in the church but in the churchyard, and bears the date Nov. 24, 1791.

Manning was presented to the living of Lavington, not by Samuel Wilberforce, but, on the latter's recommendation, by Mrs. John Sargent: and it has been pointed out to me by one who can speak with authority, as having been Manning's contemporary and intimate friend from 1829 to 1851, that I have not sufficiently

emphasized the decidedly **Evangelical** tone of his mind
at this time, and until about 1835. As to minor corrections, the **F. Meyrick** whom **Manning** caught out in
1825 (p. 6) was not the present Secretary of the Anglo-
Continental Church Society. One of Manning's comrades
on the platform in 1872 was **Mr.** George Odger, not
Odgers. The late Father Dalgairns and Mr. **St.** George
Mivart were Catholic members of the Metaphysical
Society (p. 235) in addition to Manning and **Dr. W. G.
Ward,** and the Society itself was, I am told, actually
founded by Lord Tennyson and **Mr. James** Knowles.

On some other **points on which** correspondents have
written to correct me, I may fairly claim that they are
matters of opinion on which **I am entitled** to hold my
own. At any rate I do not think I have exaggerated
the influence which Manning exercised over the temperance and education controversies. And, in the face of
several critics who will have it that what I have termed
his "migration" from the Church of England to the
Church of Rome was really due to a sense that his
powers were being wasted in a remote country parish,
and that his now highly developed Churchmanship left
him without hope of promotion, I retain my judgment
that, although it is strictly impossible to unveil motives,
and although it is likely enough that no great step is
taken without a variety of motives, of some of which
the actor himself is barely conscious, Manning had
ample reasons for deciding on the change on conscientious grounds, without the need for looking round
for less honourable considerations. It may be true that
"from **1851 to 1868** no High Churchman had any
chance of becoming a bishop"; but this was in great
measure due to the fact of Manning's secession and of

other secessions that followed it. Had he remained an
Anglican the distrust of High Churchmen would have
been less ; and who among them was more likely then
to have obtained preferment than the close friend of
Mr. Gladstone ? I am confident that if these weighers
of ignoble motives could place themselves in Manning's
position when the Gorham judgment and the events
which followed it shattered his faith in the Catholicity
of the Church of England, they would need no dismal
anticipations as to their prospects of preferment, but
only his force of character, to compel them to decide
as he did.

To the bibliography appended to the first edition it
should be added that "The Blessed Sacrament the
Centre of Immutable Truth," a Sermon, 1864; "Our
National Vice," *Fortnightly Review*, 1886 ; "Henry VIII.
and the English Monasteries," *Dublin Review*, 1888 ;
and "Leo XIII. on the Condition of Labour," *Dublin
Review*, 1891, have been reprinted in a popular form by
the "Catholic Truth Society," 18, West Square, S.E.
The article last named was accidentally omitted from
the bibliography.

A. W. H.

CONTENTS

CARDINAL MANNING.

CHAPTER I.

EARLY YEARS.

IT was the singular fortune of Cardinal Manning, that, after nearly twenty years of active and honoured service within the Church of England, he should enjoy, in the course of some forty years of no less active and honoured service as a Catholic ecclesiastic, the intimate friendship and the special confidence of two Roman pontiffs so dissimilar in taste and in temper, and to some extent even in policy, as Pius IX. and Leo XIII. It has further been his lot to make a mark on the religious history of his country, greater perhaps than that made by Newman, though he had none of the latter's genius, none of his critical power, none of his poetic sensitiveness, nor that singular magnetic personality which sometimes fascinated and sometimes repelled. Manning's work was done by sheer industry, whether he had in view the revival of a Catholic temper within the Church of England, or the assertion and definition of the prerogatives of the Pope, or the consolidation of Catholicism

B

on a democratic basis; he was not content, probably he was not able, to throw out one pregnant word and then to wait and watch while it bore fruit; he laboured for what he had in view day after day and year after year; and it is the history of this perseverance, rather than any brilliant or epoch-making exploits, that the pages which follow will have to record. And, though the religion in which he was a leader, or, as it may be better expressed, the faith and the polity which he championed, were such as the majority of Englishmen are disposed to reckon as un-English, it still remains true that Manning was never other than a thorough Englishman, English in his limitations as well as in his abilities and in his temperament, and one who looked to his country's welfare rather with the eye of a states-man than with that of an ecclesiastic. Further, although we commonly associate the idea of leadership in religion with progress towards a higher and more spiritual ideal, while Manning as an Anglican took part in a movement that was essentially reactionary, and as a Catholic was urgent for an extension of the reign of dogma,—still he possessed and exercised the qualifications of a leader; and the extraordinary change in the position of the Roman Church in England during the last thirty years may be ascribed, so far as it can be ascribed to the exertions of any one man, to Manning's skilful guidance and unremitting toil. Newman in the decade following 1841 bore the burden and the heat of the day; his intense earnestness, his genius, his satire, and most of all his rare rhetorical power, serving to break down the wall of prejudice that until then had separated almost all that was of any account in English thought and culture from the religion of Sir Thomas More, of Chateaubriand,

and of Pascal; but Newman confessed that he had not the gifts that go to make a leader; and it was rather Manning's task to lead his followers through the breach, and to assist in organizing the new ecclesiastical state; while the work of vindicating for the Church an honourable place as an efficient social reformer was his even more distinctly, both in its initiation and in its progress.

Henry Edward Manning, who was thus to prove an English leader in religion, was born at Copped Hall, Totteridge, Hertfordshire, July 15th, 1808. Although the name of Manning is found in the registers of more than one parish in that county, as it is also found in Norfolk and in the south-eastern counties, there is no reason to suppose that the future Cardinal's family had been resident in Hertfordshire for any long period. The house at Totteridge was bought by his grandfather, William Manning, who was a West India merchant, and had previously resided in Billiter Street in the city of London. His wife was a Miss Ryan. The handsome monument in Totteridge Church, which gives Nov. 23rd, 1791, as the date of his death, bears the arms of the Mannings of Norfolk. His son William was also a West India merchant, who took an active part in public life. He sat in Parliament for some thirty years, representing, in the Tory interest, Plympton Earle, Lymington, Evesham, and Penryn respectively. He was twice married, his first wife being a daughter of Abel Smith, a Nottingham banker, who represented several places in Parliament, and died in 1789, his eldest son having been created the first Lord Carrington two years previously. Mr. Manning's first wife died in the same year as her father; and a few years later the widower married a Miss Mary Hunter, whose family were

said to have come from Italy, where they bore the name
Venatore. Cardinal Manning recollected being shown
by her brother a portrait representing one of her ancestors
in an Oriental dress. The family was also understood
to be in some way related to the Bosanquets, but, so far
as he knew, no records of its history existed anywhere.

William Manning was in the height of his prosperity
when his third and youngest son, Henry Edward, was
born in 1808. The previous year he had contested
Evesham, and had been returned at the head of the
poll.[1] His fortune now for some years steadily increased; he became a Director of the Bank of England,
and was Governor in the years 1812-13. About the
year 1815 he sold the property at Totteridge, and
purchased of Lord Frederick Campbell the beautiful
estate known as Coombe Bank, in the parish of
Sundridge, about three miles from Sevenoaks. Manning's earliest recollections were thus associated with
the charms of English country life. The beauties of
Totteridge were noted by Bunsen, who at a later time
lived in the house in which the future Cardinal had
been born, and wrote there a part of his work on *Egypt's
Place in Universal History*. In one of his letters he
says, "Oh! how thankful I am for this Totteridge!
Could I but describe the groups of fine trees, the turf,
the terrace walks!" Since that time the place has
become a boys' school.[2] But it was chiefly at Coombe

---

[1] Some benefactions to the poor of Totteridge, and a picture
presented by him to the church in 1809, and first placed over the
Communion-table, but subsequently removed to the west end,
also mark this period.

[2] On his 78th birthday, July 15, 1886, Cardinal Manning laid
the foundation stone of a girls' orphanage at Totteridge, within a
few yards of the place of his birth.

Bank that Manning's boyhood was passed; and there he had the companionship of Charles and Christopher Wordsworth, the one a year or two older, the other about his own age, sons of Dr. Christopher Wordsworth, a brother of the poet, who became rector of Sundridge, and simultaneously of St. Mary's, Lambeth, in 1816.[1] With these boyish companions, who were later to become bishops, of St. Andrew's and of Lincoln respectively, the youthful Manning had what is popularly called "a good time." Of the three he seems to have been the most venturesome and mischievous; but a story that he told with some humour of an exploit in which they were all engaged—a raid on the vinery at Coombe Bank—puts the three future prelates pretty much on a level in this respect.[2] His boyhood was distinguished from that of others who have subsequently become known as great ecclesiastics, in that he was a thorough boy, fond of games and of sport; riding, shooting, boating and cricket being his special favourites. As an old man he would still tell, with a gleam of satisfaction in his eye, that he killed a hare with his first shot.

After some preparatory training at a private school he was sent, at the age of fourteen, to Harrow, whither Charles Wordsworth, the second brother, had preceded him, while John and Christopher, the elder and younger brothers, were sent to Winchester. During two out of the four years that he was at Harrow, Manning was in the eleven, and played in three matches against Eton

---

[1] Four years later he was elected Master of Trinity College, Cambridge, a post which he held till 1841, when he was succeeded by Whewell.

[2] *Strand Magazine*, July 1891, p. 56.

and Winchester, in all of which, however, Harrow was
beaten. The full score of one of these matches has
been published in the late Bishop of Lincoln's memoir,
the occasion being one that the latter always recalled
with pleasure. It was not often that the fervour of his
anti-Catholic prejudices allowed him the brief relaxation
of such humorous reminiscences; but he would then
narrate, not without a chuckle of satisfaction, how at the
inter-school match, **played at Lords in 1825,** he had
" caught Manning out."[1]

As little has been recorded of Manning's school life
as of the rest of his early years; whence it may fairly
be concluded that it did not differ much from that of
other boys. He was, however, remarkable, even **in**
these youthful days, for a certain precocious dignity of
address, which earned him the *sobriquet* of "the General,"
and his contemporaries report that he was good-looking,
indolent and popular.[2]

[1] Manning might have retorted that in this same match he caught
out F. Meyrick, afterwards well known for his controversial
writings, and for his connection with the Anglo-Continental
Church Society. But Wordsworth would still have the advantage
in having caught Manning out before he had scored a run. Charles
Wordsworth was captain of the Harrow eleven at this time.

[2] Bishop Oxenden, **one** of Manning's schoolfellows at Harrow,
says of him, "He did not then appear to be a boy of unusual
promise; but he was steady and well-conducted . . . There was,
even **in** those early days, a **little** self-assertion in his character.
On **one** occasion he was invited to dinner at Mr. Cunningham's,
the **vicar** of the parish. On his return at night one of his friends
questioned him as to whom he had met, whether he had enjoyed
his evening, and especially as to what part he had taken in the
general conversation. To these inquiries he answered, that he
had spent the evening pleasantly enough, but that he had said
but little, and indeed had been almost silent, for there were two
or three **superior** persons present; and **he** added, 'You know
that **my motto is,** *Aut Cæsar aut nullus;* **I** therefore held my
tongue and listened.'"

In the spring of 1827 he matriculated at **Balliol** College, Oxford; and from this time his career does **not** lack distinction. It was first in the University Debating Society, afterwards called the Union, that he made a name. Sir Francis Doyle records that he possessed a fine presence, and that his delivery **was** effective. His great natural talents were reinforced by a manner that seemed to imply age and experience, **so that** his maturity increased the ascendancy which he would in any case have asserted. Before sending him to Oxford, his father had planned for him a commercial career; but this was now set aside in favour of the service of the State. It is with reference to Manning's impressive and somewhat imposing manner that Sir F. Doyle tells a story which is at any rate *ben trovato*, and **one** that illustrates what his critical contemporaries have always recognized as a weak spot in his character—a readiness to assume omniscience. There had been, it appears, **some discussion** in Parliament on "the barilla duty." **Stephen** Denison, a young Balliol man, and a devoted admirer of Manning's, had been puzzling himself over this new and strange expression. Accordingly, in all humility he sought out his Pope, and asked for an explanation of the unknown word. "Dear me," replied Manning, "not know what *barilla* means? I will **explain it.** You see in commerce there **are** two methods **of** proceeding. At one time you load your ship with **a particular commodity**, such as tea, wine, or tobacco; **at another time** you select a variety of articles suitable **to the port of** destination. And in the language **of trade we** describe this latter operation *barilla*." Stephen **Denison, thus** carefully instructed, went his way; but in a **week or so** he found out that *barilla* meant **burnt seaweed, or its** equivalent; and his faith in Manning's infallibility was no longer the same.

Bishop Charles Wordsworth has told us that Manning owed his readiness as a speaker and the felicity of his diction to the constant use of his pen, both in analyzing what he read and in other ways. This is, he adds, in accordance with Lord Brougham's advice to Macaulay, and in accordance with the teaching of a still higher authority in oratory—Cicero, who says, *Nulla res tantum ad dicendum proficit quam scriptio.* Doubtless he was careful to train a faculty which was likely to prove of the first importance to him in the career for which at that time he was destined; but it is equally certain that Manning was one of the comparatively few Englishmen who have been born orators. Even in these early days he had a gift of persuasiveness that was due, not to originality of thought nor to critical power, but to a readiness of expression, a way of putting things, that made a crude and commonplace argument seem convincing and conclusive. Several pens have recorded the famous Union debate in November, 1829, on the question whether Shelley were not a greater poet than Byron. Three Cambridge undergraduates came over especially for the occasion to vindicate the cause of Shelley—Arthur Hallam, Lord Houghton (then Richard Monckton Milnes), and Sunderland, whose life was shortly after wrecked by a mysterious brain disease. The speeches of two of them at least were brilliant and effective, and, after Milnes had spoken, there was silence for a time. Then Manning rose, the recognized leader of the Union debates, and spoke extremely well, with great courtesy and dignity, and carried the "house" with him. Yet his argument was only this, that we had all read Byron and had not all read Shelley. If Shelley were a great poet we should all have read him. Hence it is clear he is not a great poet, and therefore not so great a poet as Byron. A jovial supper, at which Gladstone was present, followed this most conclusive argument.[1]

The next term Gladstone succeeded Manning as president of the Union, the latter withdrawing almost entirely from the society of the young men about him, so as to read steadily for the schools. Circumstances had occurred about this time to make his place in the class-lists a matter of the greatest moment. His father had sustained severe losses in business, and was no longer in a position to leave his sons independent of any necessity to work for their livelihood. This change and disappointment had, as his private tutor records, an ennobling effect upon Manning's character. He found himself thrown upon his own resources, and he was transformed into a thoughtful, industrious man, with the result that he obtained the distinction of a first-class in the final examination.

It may well be believed that this success was no small consolation to his father, whose circumstances compelled him to resign, in 1831, his position on the

[1] Another speech of Manning's at the Union, interesting as the earliest indication of his democratic temper, was a protest he made against the discontinuance of two American newspapers. Beginning by asking a simple question as to the fact, he went on to denounce, in a speech of an hour's duration, delivered without note and apparently without preparation, a step so retrograde. He urged that we knew too little and not too much about the United States, that it was in the order of Providence that we should be bound closely with them ; for, if we could not be under the same government, we had at any rate a common blood, a common faith, and common institutions.

Directorate of the Bank of England. Coombe Bank was sold, and he retired to a small house in Upper Gower Street, where he died in 1835, his widow surviving him until 1847. There must be many people yet living who remember them both; but the Cardinal seldom referred to either, and he has put nothing on record that could illustrate their influence on his character and career.

In 1831 Manning was given a place in the Colonial Office, his father's reduced circumstances not leaving him free to share the fortunes of his college friend, Gladstone, and to serve the State, as had originally been proposed, in the House of Commons. It is interesting, although unprofitable, to speculate on what the future of these two men would have been, had Gladstone been permitted by his father to devote himself to the service of the Church, and had Manning been free to follow out his own and his father's ambition as a statesman. There are and have been many who have held that the former as Archbishop of Canterbury, and the latter as Prime Minister, would have occupied posts better suited to their special characters and abilities than those to which they did actually attain. But it is only with the latter that we are concerned.

A passage from a letter which Cardinal Manning wrote to the *Times* in February, 1888, vindicating a proposition he had made for the relief of the unemployed at that time, is important as showing that he had in the period now under consideration taken serious steps to prepare himself for a statesman's career—

"[My critic] asks me who are my 'older and higher teachers in political economy'; and I will gladly tell him; but he forces me to speak of personal matters of

which I should not have written. In the years 1829–
32, when I had other thoughts of the world before me,
I read no little political economy, beginning with
Ricardo. I was intimate with some of the chief
members of the Political Economy Club, and I had
the honour of dining with them and of hearing the
discussions of such men as Archbishop Whately, Mr.
Grote, Mr. Tooke, and others."

It will appear in the sequel that much of the success
of Manning's career as an ecclesiastic may be traced to
this secular side of his training. The education of a
Catholic priest is ordinarily confined to scholastic
philosophy and theology; that of an Anglican clergyman was, until recently, almost exclusively literary.
Manning had the good fortune to have added to these
some knowledge of economic questions. He had been
interested in the wealth of nations and the problems of
poverty; he knew something of the relations between
capital and labour; and the fact that this knowledge
proved to be of no little practical value to him makes
one wonder that it is not ordinarily regarded as an
indispensable part of the training for a clerical career.
Perhaps it may come to be so regarded, now that all
sects and churches agree that social reform is their most
important sphere of work.

The episode of life at the Colonial Office was of only
a few months' duration. Unfriendly critics have suggested that Manning's decision in 1832 to take holy
orders was a consequence of his father's embarrassed
affairs, and that he had in more senses than one a
"living" in view. Doubtless his father's misfortunes
influenced his decision, but not in so crude or sordid a
way, as a comparison of dates will show. The loss of

fortune had preceded by some months the date of Manning's taking his degree. It necessitated his taking a remunerated post in a Government office instead of seeking fame in parliamentary debate; and in that post he would have remained, and have secured at any rate a comfortable maintenance, but for the sobering effect on his character which this early disappointment had produced. Already he had learnt to discriminate between "the Church" and "the world," and to hold the latter in something like contempt.[1] That undercurrent of sadness, which distinguished him in later years, especially after he had experienced the trials of doubt and of responsibility, was already noticeable; and to this must in part at least be traced that sense of a "vocation" to the Christian ministry which brought him back to the quiet gardens of Oxford in the very year of the great Reform Act, when, whether in

---

[1] In a letter to the *Times*, Jan. 20, 1892, Lord Forester has pointed out that the chief agent in Manning's conversion at this time was Miss Bevan, afterwards Mrs. Thomas Mortimer, a sister of his schoolfellow Robert Bevan, the well-known banker, at whose house at Trent Park Manning used often to spend a portion of his holidays :—"After his father's losses, which changed his whole career, when he next came to Trent she perceived how depressed he was ; in their walks together she endeavoured to cheer him, telling him there were higher aims still that he had not thought of. 'What are they?' he asked. She replied, 'The kingdom of heaven ; heavenly ambitions are not closed against you.' He listened, and said in reply, he did not know but that she was right. She suggested reading the Bible together, saying she was sure her brother Robert would join them. This they did during the whole of that vacation, every morning after breakfast. It was her conviction that this was the beginning of Henry Manning's religious life. He always used to speak of her as his spiritual mother." This pious evangelical lady was in later years well known as the author of *Peep of Day*, *Line upon Line*, and other children's books, of which hundreds of thousands of copies have been sold.

hope or in fear, a born politician would surely have
preferred to remain in the stormy atmosphere of
London. It is not necessary to attribute to this
decision anything of the romance of *il gran rifiuto*;
perhaps the prospect of material prosperity *was* on the
whole more hopeful in the Church than in the world;
but it is only fair to insist on the fact that, from the
moment of his decision, religion and piety were everything to Manning. Whether it were Anglican or
Roman, he was for sixty years devoted heart and soul
to the service of "the Church," regarding it as the
divine organization of society on earth, and so as deserving above all things strenuous support and veneration.

Elected a Fellow of Merton College, Oxford, in 1832,
he was ordained the same year, on a title given him by
the Rev. Preb. Stevens,[1] who held two livings in Oxford-
shire and one in Norfolk, and the year following he
was presented to the rectory of Lavington with Graffham,
in Sussex. On Nov. 7th, 1833, he married Caroline,
third daughter and co-heiress of the Rev. J. Sargent,
of Lavington, the ceremony being performed by the
bride's brother-in-law, the Rev. Samuel Wilberforce,
afterwards Bishop of Oxford and of Winchester.[2]
Manning's married life was of brief duration. His
"young and beautiful wife," as one who knew her
has described her, was of a consumptive family, and
it was hardly to be expected that her life would be

---

[1] Some letters that passed between Mr. Stevens and Mr. William
Manning in reference to his son's ordination are still in existence.
Mr. Stevens' only surviving grandchildren have become Catholics
"indirectly through the Cardinal's influence."

[2] It was also Samuel Wilberforce who presented him to the
living, and who performed the ceremony at Mrs. Manning's
funeral.

a long one. She died childless within four years of her, marriage, July 24th, 1837.

A new and lasting sadness was thus added to Manning's life. A second marriage, if such were ever contemplated, was ruled out by his acceptance of ecclesiastical principles, which (however lightly they may be thought of now) are certainly based on the plain language of more than one passage of Scripture, as interpreted by an unvarying tradition preserved throughout orthodox Christendom. Possibly too a few years later a dim presentiment that ultimately he might be seeking admission to a celibate priesthood, may have had some corroborative influence in leading the young widower to decide on a single life.

Meanwhile he had already begun to make an impression as a clergyman with a future before him. Living in the seclusion of a country parish, where he devoted himself systematically to pastoral work, especially among the agricultural labourers, whose deplorable economic condition pained and perplexed him, he took no part actively in the movement that was simultaneously in progress at Oxford; and probably, had he remained in residence as a Fellow of Merton, instead of taking a country living and marrying, he would not have found it easy to co-operate with the Tractarian leaders. He had come up to Oxford in the year that Keble's *Christian Year* was published, and, so far as his churchmanship was taken into account in his undergraduate days, he would have been reckoned a High Churchman of the old school, with an infusion of the philanthropic temper acquired by intercourse with the Evangelicals. To this position he substantially adhered; and in later life he would affirm that he had never been

a Tractarian or a **Ritualist.** At the same **time he**
certainly read the Tracts, as they appeared, **in the**
seclusion of his village rectory, and was not uninfluenced
by them, as will appear shortly, when reference is made
to his earliest publications. But on the whole he may
be said **to** have worked out for himself the position
which he held, as indeed did many **others in** the days
when Tractarianism was " in the air." Students of this
and of similar movements must have observed that
those who are described as the leaders often do no
more than express, more plainly and uncompromisingly
than the rest, thoughts that had already risen, it would
seem independently, in the minds **of the** many **who are**
reckoned the disciples. And, although Manning **in**
later years, with the somewhat exaggerated courtesy **of**
a dedication, described Newman as " the master-builder,"
" to whom I owe a debt of gratitude for intellectual help
and light greater than to any [other] one man of **our**
time," he would never allow that he was actually one
of **his** followers. The two men **were of** such widely
different temperament that, although in their later
life they spoke vaguely of **" a** friendship of some sixty
years' duration," neither at Oxford nor within the
Catholic Church were they **at** all intimate, while
throughout their aims were substantially the same.

The principle which from first to last laid the strongest
hold over Manning's mind was, that **unity is the** prime
necessity of ecclesiastical organization. **There is** much
in his earlier sermons that may be described **as " unction,"**
much **that** is by **no** means **mere pulpit rhetoric,**
but well-reasoned **discourse,** expressed **in terms** that
deserve as well as any to be described **as** genuinely
eloquent; but on the whole it **is to** questions of eccle-

siastical polity that he is mostly drawn. His first published sermon [1] is a good illustration of this; and, though its sentiments may be the commonplaces now of nearly every Anglican pulpit, they can hardly have seemed less than a new revelation to many who heard the sermon nearly sixty years ago :—

"For the first fifteen hundred years of Christian antiquity Christ's earthly Church was one, till apostolical unity of faith and practice withered away in the hollow sameness of Romish ceremonial. And now, for these three hundred years, men have seemed to sicken at the very name of unity, and to contemplate the self-production of sects and divisions within the bosom of the Church with a spurious charity, a cold indifference, and even a misguided satisfaction."

Though almost every statement in these sentences is more or less open to question—and especially that which asserts that the unity of the Church was preserved until the Reformation—the main point is persuasively conveyed, and the method is characteristic. A little later he says :—

" Our commission to witness for Christ hangs on this question, Are the Bishops of our Church the successors, in lineal descent, of the Lord's Apostles ?" And in support of an affirmative reply he dwells on the alleged independence of the ancient British Churches and Bishops, "of whose sees five or six remain to this day." The question of the continuity of the succession at the Reformation is passed over with a bare reference to "the futile objection of the Papists" to the "Nag's

[1] "The English Church, its Succession and Witness for Christ." Preached at Chichester Cathedral, July 7, 1835, at the Visitation of the Archdeacon. Published by request.

Head consecration "; and the sermon, which is full of stately and eloquent passages, is backed up by notes and quotations from the Fathers and the Anglican divines of the seventeenth century.

A subject of more general interest is dealt with in a sermon on " National Education," preached in Chichester Cathedral, May 31st, 1838, at a time when the country was dimly beginning to realize, what it partially carried into effect more than thirty years later, that the efficient education of the people is a national concern.

Admitting that there was a growing feeling in favour of secular education maintained by the State, religious education being left to be carried out independently by the clergy of all denominations at other times and places,—recognizing somewhat superciliously that " a large number of persons who agree in little else, agree that civil rulers are bound to provide education for a people," he goes on to assert in opposition, and in most uncompromising fashion, the right of the Church to educate :—

" There is but one law for all men, whatsoever may be their after-part in the great spectacle of life, in the pomp of courts and parliaments, in crowded cities or in lonely hamlets, high-born or low, lettered or unlettered, ruling or obeying, urging on the advances of science or plying some unheeded craft, for all men, of all ranks, characters and destinies, there is one and only one great idea running through all, the first aim and groundwork of education, the vital element and perfecter of the whole work, and that is the right determination of the will, confirmed by the formation of Christian habits, for God's service here and for salvation hereafter." On the question, then first mooted, whether the Bible should be excluded from public elementary schools, or parts of it read " without note or comment," he is of course equally plain :—" Very much more than the bare unmutilated letter of Scripture must be admitted into the system of education. There must be the full and correct sense, the right and unreserved interpretation." These latter phrases refer, of course, not to the correct interpretation as ascertained by competent scholars and historians, but to the mystical sense imposed by scholastic theologians.

In the latter part of the discourse he takes a statesmanlike, but not less characteristic view of the necessities of the situation. He recognizes the importance of the recent growth of the middle-class, " a new population of millions for whom we have no education." A new body of teachers of a superior class must be provided for them ; Cathedral institutions should be made the rallying-points for a new effort ; and ultimately the Church will be able to cope with the education of the whole nation, " with the Universities for the key-stone of the arch and the parochial schools for the basis." At this time Manning took a leading part in the formation of Diocesan Boards of Education to cooperate with the National Society.

In this same year he addressed to his Bishop, William Otter, who had formerly been Principal of King's College, London, a letter criticizing the principle underlying the recent appointment of an Ecclesiastical Commission. It is full of assertions of the independence of spiritual jurisdiction, the writer's position being that " our Bishop is to us the source of authority and the centre of unity." This authority the Commission appeared in some degree to impugn ; it set at naught the legislative commission of the spiritual power, and so it was "a virtual extinction of the polity of the Church." One of the historical references by which he vindicates a kind of supremacy for the throne of Canterbury is certainly imposing in its show of erudition :—"The violent dismemberment of the province of Canterbury, and the erection of Litchfield into an archbishopric, was effected by the Royal and Papal powers by means of a synod at Calcyth. And the whole proceeding was reversed by a Provincial Council convened by Archbishop Aedelheard at Cloveshoo." The writer of these words had clearly yet much to learn as to the relations held by Pope and King towards the Church in England. He saw, however, clearly enough the position into which the Anglican Church was, as he thought, drifting; though a more accurate historical estimate would have convinced him that it was the position it had for nearly three hundred years occupied :—

"We have once well seen the corruption of the Church in discipline and faith from the supremacy of the Roman Patriarch. We have now another supremacy to beware of. The two swords have passed from the Pope to the King, from the King to the people. The next Patriarch of the English Church will be Parliament, and on its vote will hang our orders, mission, discipline and faith ; and the Pontificate of Parliament is but the modern voluntary principle in disguise." This last phrase accords precisely with the view of those latter-day Liberals who would prefer to disestablishment in England a measure that would render effective the nationalization of the Church which was in principle brought about in the sixteenth century. But Manning of course only recognized this as a danger to be wrestled with at the risk of the loss of all the temporal advantages of establishment :—"Better far to undergo another exile from our hearths and altars, to wear out in patient waiting the long delays of another twelve years' oppression, than to yield for peace or policy one tittle of Apostolical order."

Another publication, important as illustrating Manning's position at this time, is his sermon on "The Rule of Faith," preached at Bishop Otter's Primary Visitation on June 13th, 1838. In it he states clearly the uncompromising attitude that dogmatic theology must hold in the face of intellectual speculation and scientific progress, —a matter in which he was himself from first to last consistent :—

"These are times to try our constancy. Men are possessed by an insatiate lust of ever-progressing discovery. The rapid growth of science has silently insinuated into all its branches of knowledge a disposition, healthful or spurious, to expand. It is assumed that all knowledge is or ought to be ever on the move. The rude mechanical and physical sciences of earlier days have grown up and consolidated themselves into full and harmonious systems, gathering fresh vigour with their growth, accumulating fact on fact, piling induction on induction, building theory on theory, until we are amazed at the gigantic height to which in the last two centuries they have sprung. And, with the advance of science, the intellectual habits of men have also got a new character and a new momentum; they have acquired a keen hunger for discovery, and a loathing of fixed and measured knowledge. Progression and new results are indeed the very life of science ; but the rule of faith is retrospective altogether . . . . God has set up the landmarks of revelation, and no man may remove them." In a footnote this very rigid doctrine is, as far as may be, reconciled with what St. Vincent of Lerins says about *profectus religionis*, the saving clause which tempers his unprogressive teaching about the *quod semper, quod ubique, quod ab omnibus*, and which served Newman as a fruitful theme for his theory of religious development. In another note Manning controverts some strictures of Wiseman's on the sixth Anglican Article, to the effect that it made the doctrine of the Church liable to variations. "This is," he says, "the well-known argument of Bossuet, to which it deeply concerns Protestant communities to find a sufficient reply." But the Church of England, he maintains, has no interest in the matter. She acknowledges only the supreme authority of "a Council truly general, freely assembled." Speaking of the Articles generally he anticipates to some extent the view maintained in Tract XC., which was published three years later, though his phrase is wordy and ambiguous:—"The Articles are not new theological determinations . . . . but depositions of evidence exhibiting interpretations that have obtained from the beginning."

To this sermon on the "Rule of Faith" was added an elaborate Appendix of nearly 150 pages, in which the *via media* of Anglicanism is stoutly and learnedly defended, with many quotations from the Fathers and the seventeenth-century English divines. Both the Roman and the Protestant theories, Manning maintains, oppose universal tradition, and introduce new doctrines. To illustrate the dangers of the former position he quotes (through Newman's *Lectures on the Prophetical Office of the Church*, published the previous year) the words of Cornelius Mussus, Bishop of Bitonto, who acted a conspicuous part at the Council of Trent: "I for my part, to speak candidly, would rather credit one Pope in matters touching the faith, than a thousand Augustines, Jeromes or Gregories."[1] Manning concludes by showing that the principle of submission to "antiquity" has great moral advantages, and is "a safeguard against a controversial temper."

Writing to Sir Charles Anderson from Brighstone Rectory, December 7, 1838, Samuel Wilberforce said, "Henry Manning is gone to Rome for the winter. The Bishop of London [Blomfield] wickedly says he thought he had been there ever since publishing his last volume of sermons." It thus appears that so early as this, more than twelve years before he actually seceded from the Church of England, the Romeward tendency of Manning's theology had been detected by at least one discerning eye. Samuel Wilberforce, who was however never much of a theologian, was also of opinion that some of his brother-in-law's statements in the "Rule of Faith," as to the need of tradition to interpret Scripture, tended "to lead men to undervalue God's Word, and to regard the Romish view of tradition without suspicion and dread . . . . I could not therefore," he adds, "have written as he has done; but when I have talked with him, I have found it difficult to fix him to any meaning beyond what all Churchmen hold."[2] This likeness to Mr. Pliable has been more

[1] In the third edition of these Lectures, published in 1877, Newman pointed out that this declaration of Mussus is no more than a deduction from the doctrine of papal infallibility.—*Via Media*, vol. i., p. 82.

[2] *Life of Samuel Wilberforce*, by Canon A. R. Ashwell and R. G. Wilberforce; 2nd ed., 1883, vol. i., p. 213.

often recognized in Manning's critic than in Manning
himself; but, however that may be, it may be taken
as certain that the logical outcome of his ecclesiasticism
was not apparent to the preacher of the "Rule of
Faith," either in 1838 or for many years later. No
one can read Manning's Anglican writings and doubt
the substantial soundness of his confidence in the
Anglican position, until it was so rudely shaken in
1850, by events which will be chronicled in due course.
A letter which Manning addressed to Bishop Otter in
1840 deserves a passing mention. Some alienation of
Cathedral revenues was to be effected by a bill introduced to carry out the fourth Report of the Ecclesiastical Commissioners, which dealt chiefly with the
suppression of prebendal stalls. Some of his clergy
had petitioned the Bishop to retain the dignities even
when the revenues were gone. In support of·this view
Manning wrote "On the Preservation of Unendowed
Canonries," urging the importance of securing "a chosen
body of presbyters round about the Bishop's throne.
To the idea of a Prebendary," he added, "a prebend is
of course essential; but the name of Canon may be
henceforward adopted to express the office of the unendowed, non-residentiary members, who are nevertheless
under the rule of the Cathedral Church." Many years
later, when this suggestion was carried into effect by
his old playmate, Christopher Wordsworth, Bishop of
Lincoln, no one, probably, except it were the Bishop,
remembered whence it first came. Perhaps the result
has been hardly more than to detract somewhat from
the ideas of dignity and affluence which used, in the
Church of England, to be associated with the title of
Canon.

Bishop Otter died in this year, 1840, and was succeeded by Philip Nicholas Shuttleworth, Warden of New College, Oxford, who only held the see two years. Archdeacon Webber resigned his office soon after the accession of the new Bishop; and in January, 1841, to the post thus vacated, Shuttleworth appointed Manning, an event which the *Christian Remembrancer* hailed as " a blessing to the whole Church."

CHAPTER II.

THE office of an Archdeacon, to which Manning was thus appointed before he had attained his thirty-third year, is commonly more suggestive of dignity than of work. An Archdeacon's duties have been accounted so light as to be incapable of further definition beyond being "archidiaconal functions." But the Rector of Lavington took a more serious view of his new position; and, having defined it as "an office to which belongs chiefly the care and cognizance of the exterior system and administration of the Church," he went on to make it a practical reality. Not content with the somewhat misnamed "Visitations," at which the order is inverted and the clergy and their churchwardens present themselves before their Archdeacon and are duly "charged" by him, he superadded to this more formal and general exercise of his jurisdiction, particular official visits to each parish within his district; and in 1842 he was able to report that he had already in this way gone over one half of it, and hoped to have completed the task by July, 1843.

The new Archdeacon took a leading part in the

formation of the "Colonial Bishoprics Fund" in April, 1841, at the Jubilee Meeting of which, in 1891, Mr. Gladstone made a notable speech, in the course of which he said :—

"I am possibly the only one of all those here present who was also present at the important meeting held in the month of April, 1841. I am certainly the only man—I will not say the only man living, but the only person living and also available for this purpose—who took part in the proceedings of that memorable occasion. . . . But there was a remarkable speech made on that day, which sent a thrill of exaltation through the whole assembly in Willis's Rooms, delivered by a man of eminence, of known devotion to his work in his own sense, whose whole mind and whose whole heart were then given to the service of the Church of England. He was then known as Archdeacon Manning. Archdeacon Manning, in a most striking and a most powerful speech, delineated the condition of the English Church of the Anglo-Saxon race of our colonial empire. He pointed out upon how vast, how gigantic a scale we were then occupying the waste places of the earth, and multiplying millions of human beings who trod the face of it ; and then he pointed to the scanty evidence which up to that time had been given of any care which had been taken by the Church of England for the propagation of the Gospel in those vast countries. He contrasted the meagreness and feebleness of our spiritual efforts with the wonderful, undying, untiring energies of the commercial powers, and the spirit of emigration, which were even then achieving such vast results in the world. He contrasted, I say, the one spectacle with the other. He said the Church of England has now to make a choice between the temporal and the spiritual. She has to determine whether she will be the beast of burden, or whether she will be the evangelist of the world. That was a noble appeal, a noble challenge. The force of it was felt. It was taken up and duly answered."

In another part of his speech the Archdeacon had given a lamentable account of the condition in which, upon his recent tour through the Continent, he had found members of the Church of England placed with regard to their religious wants. It was of course the period when the Anglican Church was only just beginning to arouse herself from her lethargy; and prominent among the awakeners was Manning. About this time Bishop Phillpotts, the famous "Henry of Exeter," is reported to have said, "There are three men to whom the country has mainly to look in the coming years— Manning in the Church, Gladstone in the State, and Hope [afterwards Mr. Hope-Scott, Q.C.] in the Law"; and Manning's colleague, Archdeacon Hare, an Evangelical of liberal views, also confessed, "Manning is a truly wise and holy man—zealous, devoted, self-sacrificing and gentle."

In illustration of this latter testimony a passage may be quoted from a sermon on the "Moral Design of the Apostolic Ministry," preached in Chichester Cathedral on Trinity Sunday, 1841, at Bishop Shuttleworth's first ordination. After insisting on the importance of holiness in the clergy, and on the possibility of its attainment by all, unlike "the endowments of intellectual power, the acquisitions of learning and critical knowledge in the spiritual sciences," he proceeded,—"The lowliest and unlikeliest of Christ's

servants gain by holiness an incredible dominion over
the most stubborn and inveterate minds. . . . It is
precisely those characters which the world counts
weakest that gain the most absolute mastery. It is
by gentleness and a yielding temper, by conceding all
indifferent points, by endurance of undeserved contempt, by refusing to be offended, by asking reconciliation when others would exact apology, that the sternest
spirits of the world are absolutely broken into a willing
and glad obedience to the lowliest servants of Christ."

A month later Manning gave his first formal Charge
to the clergy and churchwardens of his archdeaconry.
After defining, as noted above, what he took to be the
nature of his office, he referred briefly to the condition
of Christianity on the Continent:—"It is not more
certain that the Reformation was a gracious and searching work, wrought by the purifying hand of God, than
that the history of Western Europe after the Reformation exhibits an appalling process of declension. . . .
If the rationalistic infidelity of Germany may be traced
to the Lutheran bodies, the sensual infidelity of France
may be traced to the communion of the Gallican
Church." Turning then to the Church of England he
said :—" No Church in the last three hundred years has
borne what she has met and overcome. She has been
slain by the secular arm, nerved and guided by foreign
enmity, and crushed by a lawless rebellion, kindled in
domestic schisms ; she has been pampered by the wily
protection of civil rulers, till her own internal energies
were well-nigh deadened, and lured by the ease and
the gain of a luxurious commercial people. Of all
the chilling and isolating spells of the world, none are
more deadly to the Christian life than politics and

trading; they are the foster-fathers of self-will and self-interest; and these lie at the root of our modern English character."

At this time Convocation was only formally assembled, and did not deliberate or pronounce judgment. In this his first Charge Manning admitted that this loss of the power of canonical legislation was a grave one, and he even regretted that the Church of England was thus disabled from the former "correction of moral offences by penalties and penance. . . . She preserves in all its integrity the apostolical deposit of the faith and polity, ... but by the suspension of her living administrative power of legislation and correction it is not to be denied that she is at a disadvantage in the task she has to fulfil as the teacher and guide of the people." The Convocations of Canterbury and York were revived in 1852 and 1856 respectively; but hardly with such important consequences as the grave language here used about their suppression would seem to have anticipated.

In December, 1841, Manning preached a sermon at St. Peter's, Brighton, before the Bishop and clergy of the diocese, which was afterwards published under the title of "The Mind of Christ, the Perfection and Bond of the Church." In it he refers to one aspect of the unity of the Church, foreshadowing some of the contents of his treatise bearing that title, which was published the following year. Perhaps he somewhat exaggerates the unity which obtained among the earlier Christians :—

"As all national diversities were lost in the one Catholic Church, so were all oppositions of personal character merged in the one pattern of life. . . . How

different soever men were before their conversion, by
the traditions of nations and home, by cast of mind or
habits of life, as Justin and Ambrose, Vincentius and
Augustin, soldiers, statesmen, pleaders, rhetoricians,
philosophers, all were assimilated by one dominant
spiritual energy, likening them to one universal type.
. . . This may be taken as the key of the unity of the
Church in its first stages of probation." Subsequent
divisions of the Church and within the Church are the
result of " the antagonist powers of the individual will
having prevailed against the mind that was in Christ.
. . . . From this source in all Christendom arise the
manifold streams of schism, each cutting for itself a
deeper channel of separation ; particular traditions of
isolated churches and of individual teachers; false
schemes of doctrine thrown out by individual minds;
heresies with the names of men upon them; schisms
for a vestment or a ritual order; false notions of the
Christian character and of its perfect idea ; lower types
of sanctity, and a lower tone of devotion, even within
the body of the Church; caprice, affectation, love of
deviating from common rules, the singularity of prejudiced or fanciful or self-contemplative minds; in a word
the dominion of the subjective character of men over
their views of the objective truth and a mind of Christ."

In this year Manning was appointed Select Preacher
by the University of Oxford, and a volume of sermons
delivered in St. Mary's was published in 1844. He
did not reprint in this volume the anti-papal sermon
which so offended Newman. The story of it cannot be
better told than it has been told by Mr. Kegan Paul :—
" While the commemoration of the Gunpowder Plot
was still a scandal to the English Liturgy, Archdeacon

Manning preached before the University of Oxford a violent tirade against Popery with a vehemence unusual in an English and still more in a University pulpit. He declared it to be impossible that the Pope should ever again have jurisdiction in the realm of England; and his indignant declaration profoundly distressed many of those who, though not aware that they might themselves be drawn into closer relations with the Roman Church, yet desired to 'speak gently of our sister's fall.' Newman was then in retirement at Littlemore, preparing for the end which was shortly coming—his own reception into Catholicism. Archdeacon Manning walked out to Littlemore to call upon him; but the report of the disastrous sermon had already preceded the preacher. The door was opened by one of those young men, then members of the quasi-monastic community, who had to convey to the Archdeacon the unpleasant communication that Newman declined to see him. So anxious was the young man to cover the slight, and to minimize its effect, that he walked away from the door with the Archdeacon, bare-headed as he was, and had covered half the way to Oxford before he turned back, unaware, as was his companion, of his unprotected state under a November sky. So strangely do we change in these changing times, that it is hard to realize that the perplexed novice was James Anthony Froude."[1]

It is hardly necessary to make any extracts from the University discourses, or from the four volumes of Sermons published between 1842 and 1850, as they are well known and readily accessible, which is not the case

---

[1] *The Century*, vol. xxvi. (1883), p. 129.

with those occasional publications from which quotations have been made. It is however worth noting that, unlike Newman, Manning made no attempt to give a special character to his University sermons. Instead of dealing with fundamental principles of faith, or attacking the rationalism that was beginning to make its voice heard in such men as Sterling and Arnold,[1] Manning adhered steadily to that method of preaching in which he was doubtless at his best,—practical, didactic, and—to use a word which should not be allowed to become obsolete—*affective*. It is this last characteristic that gives to his writings the value that they have.

A special interest attaches to the Charge delivered in July, 1842, as it is a landmark in the progress of the Church "restoration" movement, then only just beginning, which has since literally transformed the face of the country. As it has sometimes been said that Manning knew nothing of the fascination of this great artistic revival—for such, with whatever defects, it undoubtedly was—and that, had he been associated with it and with the revival of ritual and mysticism which accompanied it, he would never have left the Church of England, it is well to show from his own words that he was an active and successful pioneer in the movement, and did himself not a little to infuse into it that enthusiasm which is even yet hardly spent. Addressing the clergy and churchwardens of his archdeaconry he said :—

[1] In June, 1839, S. Wilberforce wrote to R. Chenevix Trench, "I thought there was a certain *brusquerie* about Sterling's manner, which took off from the pleasure of a first meeting. But many things spoke of substantial kindness. I hope he has misconveyed himself to H. E. Manning ; for Manning identifies him in some very painful points with the rationalism of Germany." —*Life*, vol. i., p. 153.

"A love to the very stones of his parish church is rooted deeply in the heart of every genuine Englishman. . . . The churchwardens of Sussex cling with no little attachment to our old plain and weather-stained churches. Their very antiquity is a token of sacredness, and in the thick rubble walls, the unsculptured windows, and the heavy timber-work, especially in the churches of the Weald, there is something that claims of us a reverential and filial treatment. . . . I can turn my thoughts to no part of this archdeaconry without seeing churches either restored or rebuilt. I believe the time will come when it will be thought incredible that the furniture of the church, such as bells and chalices and the lining of fonts, should ever have been sold; that lead roofs should have been stripped, transepts and aisles pulled down, and bartered away to meet the cost of penurious repairs; that mullioned windows should have been filled in with wood, or stopped up with bricks to save mending the quarries with glass; that monuments, galleries and pews, put up to gratify private feelings (the chief causes of the mutilation of churches), should ever have been permitted in the freehold of God. Not only are the aisles and passages of the church choked by pews, but I have seen screens of beautiful carved work cut to pieces, wrought capitals and bases of columns hacked and broken, shafts of the finest stone, the piers of arches and the very arches themselves altogether cut away to make room for the backs and corners of private pews. All these things have been, but are now matters of bygone history; too certain, alas! because too freshly done. One day they will be rejected as incredible, or believed only as the act of some few mutilators of things sacred to God.

D

The work of restoration now on foot will not settle down into inactivity when the arrears of decay are overtaken and the more glaring irregularities corrected. We are on our way to recover the true theory and practice of divine worship, and to recognize the symbolical order of our churches and the emphatic meaning of architecture, and the relation of all that is costly, beautiful and majestic in forms and harmonies with the worship of Almighty God."

Some further condemnation of the pew system is enforced by a declaration that no pew shall henceforth be erected within the archdeaconry unless a faculty have been first obtained for it.

Other points referred to in this Charge are the establishment of a weekly "offertory,"—a point that was made much of by the earlier High Churchmen,[1]—the project for founding a Colonial episcopate, and national education. Confidence in the Church of England was expressed in conclusion as follows:—

"It is not the token of a declining Church to be restoring her altars, multiplying her clergy, and educating a new order of teachers; to be falling back again on her original basis, and gathering into her fold whole congregations of her separated children. . . . It is not the token of a divided Church to be banded in self-denial and self-sacrifice, to act with one common purpose for the extension of one and the same com-

[1] The *Christian Remembrancer*, commenting on this part of Manning's Charge, said (June, 1843), "St. Paul's must be the missionary station for the conversion of London, and the Church must be seen to be the real 'Society for the Propagation of the Gospel,' and the real 'Guardian of the Poor.' A uniform compliance with the Archdeacon's recommendations respecting the Offertory would ultimately lead to these results."

munion. There is no gainsaying these notes of unity.
. . . Be our diversities of opinion manifold more and
greater than they are, they do not amount to a
division."

The treatise on "The Unity of the Church," the most
considerable work that Manning published as an
Anglican, appeared a few weeks after the delivery of
this Charge. Mr. Gladstone, to whom it was "affec-
tionately inscribed," wrote of it in October, 1891,
"Cardinal Manning's book on the 'Unity of the
Church' was shown in proof to James Hope (Scott),
a very close friend, and he said to me, 'That is going
to be a great book.' I have read it over within the
last six weeks, and think the Archdeacon's a valuable
work which the Cardinal would not find it easy to
answer; though here and there it is thin in texture and
a little glib."[1] There is however not much in it that
the Cardinal would feel called upon to reply to, as by
far the greater part of the treatise is taken up with a
positive exposition of the history and moral importance
of the doctrine of Catholic unity, illustrated by copious
extracts from Scripture and the Fathers. Only within
twenty pages of the end of the book does the writer
refer to "the suspension of communion between the
Roman and English Churches," and what he says on
that is simply a repetition of Bramhall's *Just Vindica-
tion of the Church of England* :—

"If any man will look down along the line of early
English history, he will see a standing contest between

---

[1] Manning himself in a letter to Dr. Wordsworth (the father),
dated Jan. 31, 1842, had modestly anticipated a part of this
criticism :—" I fear my book on Unity will be both dry and thin ;
so do not expect anything."

the rulers of this land and the Bishops of Rome. The
Crown and Church of England, with a steady opposition,
resisted the entrance and encroachment of the secular-
ized ecclesiastical power of the Pope in England. The
last rejection of it was no more than a successful effort
after many a failure in struggles of the like kind.
And it was an act taken by men who were sound.
according to the Roman doctrines, on all other points.
Questions of faith had hardly as yet arisen in the
Church of England when it released its apostolical
powers from the oppression of a foreign and uncanonical
jurisdiction. The corrections in doctrine and usage
which were afterwards made were neither the causes
of the beginning nor of the continuance of the division,
It was believed that the state of the Anglican Church
would have been for the most part confirmed by the
see of Rome on the submission of the Queen."

How the Archdeacon could have been satisfied with
so very superficial and inadequate a treatment of the
question on which depended all the cogency of his
arguments, so far as the Church in which he was a
dignitary was concerned, it is not easy to understand.
We must suppose that, either he was unconscious of
the gravity of the controversy between "Rome and
England," and was so confident of the strength of the
Anglican position that any bare statement in justification
of it seemed to him to suffice, or else, as is more probable,
that he realized to some extent the precariousness of
his position, and shrank from seriously tackling its
difficulties, thinking it wiser, with Newman, to fall
back on the language of Anglican seventeenth-century
divines, and to affect to be satisfied with what satisfied
them. In any case, to confuse Henry's breach with Rome

with Elizabeth's establishment of Anglicanism five-
and-twenty years later, and to be content with some
gossip recorded by Camden as to the Pope's readiness
substantially to accept that establishment,—this certainly deserves to be censured as " glib." For the rest,
the author no doubt may claim the credit of having
called the attention of men, who had acquired the
habit of appealing confidently and continually to the
authority of " the Church," to the fact that its unity
is, as St. Augustine says, "among those things that
are chiefly necessary to be inculcated with much of
awe "; and the grave and dignified tone of the treatise
as a whole is a proof that he at any rate realized its
importance, and was not likely to remain permanently
satisfied with an evasion of the conclusion towards
which his arguments tended. The book, however, never
attained the position that James Hope had anticipated.
A second edition was indeed called for ; but, since the
date that its author sought to realize his dream of
Church unity within the communion of Rome, it has
ceased to be read.[1]

It was however not as an author and controversialist,
but as an administrator, a devoted parish priest, and,
most of all, as a pulpit orator, that the Archdeacon
made his mark ; and his sweet and persuasive eloquence
was much in request when it was a question of stimu-
lating Christian charity. As a specimen of his pathetic

---

[1] On its first appearance the *Christian Remembrancer* (Sept.
1842) welcomed Manning's *Treatise on the Unity of the Church*
as " a most heartening book, written with that implicit confidence
in the strength of our position as a Church, which, more than any
work we have ever read, will tend to settle the young and un-
settled." In the issue for Jan. 1843, the work was reviewed at
greater length.

appeals, some passages may be given from a sermon
preached at St. George-in-the-Fields, in behalf of the
Magdalen Hospital, in May, 1844:—

"None are to be pitied more; none are more sinned
against. Shame, fear and horror bar their return.
The drop has fallen; behind them is a gulf they cannot
pass. . . . God alone is witness of the groanings which
are breathed unknown, and the burning tears which are
shed in the very depths of impurity. What harrowing
recollections of faces dearly loved, last seen in anguish,
of the fresh years of early childhood, and the hopes and
joys and fair prospects of an innocent and gentle life all
seared and blasted, come back upon them in the hours
of unholy revel, to be their mockery and torment. No
eye but His can read the visions of home and happy
days which rise upon their desolate hearts in the tumult
and darkness of these crowded streets, and the agoniz-
ing dreams of a blessedness no longer theirs, by which
their broken sleep is haunted. None other but He can
know what unutterable agony goes up by day and by
night from the loathsome chambers and pestilential
dens in which these homeless, hopeless, decaying
mortals hide themselves in misery to die. And what
a death is the death of a harlot! When the baffled
heart wanders in dreams of sickness to die in the home
of its birth, and wakes up from the happiness of deli-
rium to madden itself again in the sights and sounds
which harass its miserable death-bed; when the eye
strains itself in vain for the vision of a mother's pitying
face, and the ear is sick with listening for the coming of
brother, husband, child, whose footfall shall never be
heard again. Then comes death, and after death the
judgment, and the great white throne on which He

sitteth from whose face both heaven and earth shall
flee away.   Lamb of God, that takest away the sin of
the world, have mercy upon them and upon us in that
day."

For his Charge delivered in 1845 the Archdeacon
wrote, but apparently did not utter, since the passage
is placed within brackets, some remarks on the dignity
of the office of parish clerk, which it is difficult to read
without a smile when one recollects what kind of men
those functionaries were, and how for the most part
they were hustled out of their high estate by the subsequent progress of the ritualistic movement in which
they were ill-prepared to take a part :—

"It is greatly to be lamented that an office of so
much sacredness should have fallen into so low esteem.
Next to the clergyman, no one bears a charge of more
public example or one more nearly related to the
highest blessings than the clerk who is appointed to
take part in the services of parochial worship.   The
very name is a witness that he is the Lord's servant.
It has come to pass in the smaller, that is, in most
parishes that the clerk has sunk into the sexton.   But
it is manifest that in the Book of Common Prayer,
when the clerk or clerks are spoken of, an order of men
in every way higher and more nearly approaching to
the quality of the clergy is intended."   As an illustration of his meaning the Archdeacon referred in a note
to the reply which Sir Thomas More made to the Duke
of Norfolk when the latter had remonstrated with the
Lord Chancellor, on finding him in the church at
Chelsea wearing the choir habit and taking part in the
recitation of the Office.

Of much greater importance however, as being the

first definite pronouncement indicative of the humane and most attractive side of Manning's character, are his sympathetic references to the condition of the agricultural labourers, the precariousness of their means of support, and the unrelieved weariness of their lives. Of them as a class he says, " They are still a noble-hearted race, whose sincerity, simplicity and patience we should buy cheap at the cost of our refinements." But the disadvantages under which they laboured were enormous. Even their friendly societies or benefit clubs, intended as a support in sickness or old age, worked for harm as much as for good. They were mismanaged and were mostly bankrupt; while seven-eighths of them held their meetings in public-houses, and so opened a door of temptation, which was even more sadly noticeable in the riot and excess of their annual feasts. The Archdeacon showed himself to be no mere high and dry ecclesiastic when he went on to say :—" We have a people straitened by poverty—worn down by toil they labour from the rising to the setting of the sun;[1] and the human spirit will faint or break at last. It is to this unrelenting round of labour that the sourness, so unnatural to our English poor, but now too often seen, is to be ascribed. There is something in humanity which pines for a season of brighter and fresher thoughts, and becomes sharp and bitter if it be not satisfied. . . . Time must be redeemed for the poor man. The world is too hard upon him, and makes him pay too heavy a toll out of his short life. . . . Little is needed to make their holiday. The green fields, and tools idle for a day, the church bells, an active game,

[1] The sun, by the way, gives an "eight hours day " only from Dec. 4 to Jan. 8,

simple fare, the sport of their children, the kindly presence and patient ear of superiors, is enough to make a village festival."

But the ecclesiastical anxieties of the Archdeacon, anxieties not unnatural at a time when Newman's secession was known to be only a question of weeks or months, were bound to find expression somewhere in his Charge. So, towards the end, he referred to conflicts occurring in the Roman Catholic Church on the Continent, to a Protestantizing movement in certain districts of France, and to the "late schism" of the "New Catholics" in Germany, a secession led by a priest named Ronge, who had been scandalized by the exhibition of the Holy Coat at Treves in 1844. Of the Church of England he added with enthusiasm :—"We need no controversial learning to tell us that ours is a living branch." Perhaps a discerning critic might have thought that the Archdeacon did "protest too much."

In his Charge the next year (1846) Manning recurred to a subject he had before only referred to in passing— the measures that the civil power was taking for a reform of the Ecclesiastical Courts—a matter in which, as a born ecclesiastical statesman, he felt most keenly. In this Charge, and on this subject especially, his tone is pessimistic. He anticipated that a law of divorce would be passed by Parliament in spite of the opposition of the Church, and that a Court of laymen would ultimately override that spiritual jurisdiction which he believed the Church of England to have inherited. The spectre of rationalism also confronted him. The French infidelity of the last century was, he admitted, "little more than the working out or even the bare reproduction of the deism of Chubb, Toland, Tindal,

and other free-thinkers of our own"; but he apprehended more danger from the introduction into
England of the rationalism of Germany; and he
quoted Rose's *Protestantism in Germany* to show how
inevitably the latter developed into the former. George
Eliot's translation of Strauss's *Life of Jesus* had within
a few weeks been issued from the press—"a work I will
not here describe." More to the purpose was an
account of the state of higher education in the country,
and the expression of an opinion that Oxford at any
rate, if she did not bestir herself, was likely to be left
in the lurch :—"While the popular instinct has taken
so strong a course in the direction of professional and
abstract science, our Universities, and especially one of
them, have become comparatively unscientific. . . . We
cannot but entertain great and reasonable fear that
the day may come when our Universities may lose the
intellectual supremacy of the people." What however
mainly impressed him was the need for "a distinct
and adequate training for the priesthood of the next
generation." The establishment of diocesan seminaries
was advocated; and doubtless to this advocacy was due
in great measure the foundation, some years later, of
the college at Cuddesden, by Samuel Wilberforce, who
had been made Bishop of Oxford in 1845, and who was
long one of Manning's most intimate friends.[1] The
project also is interesting as the earliest expression of a
policy perseveringly insisted on by the Archbishop of
Westminster, from 1865 onwards, as a dutiful carrying

---

[1] The newly-established *Guardian* was enthusiastic in praise of
this project :—"The powerful and opportune testimony which
the recent Charge of Archdeacon Manning gives, as to the great
wants of our Church in the department of clerical education,
cannot fail to excite deep and general attention."—Sept. 16, 1846.

out of the recommendations of the Council of Trent. Of course the effect of the seminary system is to make of the clergy who are passed through it something of a caste; and this Manning has not been alone in regarding as " necessary for these times," which are undoubtedly too liberal and rationalistic in their temper to permit the growth of a professional clergy in the open air.

One other matter is referred to in this somewhat gloomy Charge, and that is the condition of the convict population in the Australian penal settlements. Attention had been called to this by a Catholic priest who had had several years of most trying ministration in those parts, the Rev. William Bernard Ullathorne, who was consecrated Bishop in this year 1846, and was destined himself to consecrate Manning some years later. The Archdeacon spoke of the condition of this population as " a phenomenon of carnal and spiritual wickedness, such as, I believe, the earth has never seen before. . . . It is a subject so intensely awful that I hardly know how either to touch it or to pass it by." There was however nothing to be done save by way of regret, for the system was already condemned and abandoned; though of course its evils could not be brought to an end in a moment by the stroke of an official pen.

Ill-health was obviously in some measure responsible for the sombre tone of this address. The Archdeacon had been overworked through a too ready compliance with the invitations of his admirers, who called upon him to preach on every possible occasion; and he was also worried and anxious about many things, so that a considerable period of relaxation was decided upon.

No Charge was delivered in 1847; but in the spring of
that year Manning published a short devotional "Letter
to a Friend," entitled, "What one Work of Mercy can I
do this Lent?" in which he refers to the horrors of the
Irish famine, and points to the inadequacy of the wages
received in England by agricultural labourers. It is
the extremes of poverty and wealth that really keep
classes apart. In many households there is "monstrous
and wicked waste," while elsewhere thousands of our
fellow-citizens are "dying on sea-weed." In this way
"we are indeed a divided people."

In the autumn of this year Manning was in Rome,
and saw Newman "wearing the Oratorian habit and
dead to the world." Of their interview nothing further
has been recorded; but as the two had never been
intimate, and were always kept apart by their very
different temperaments, there may have been nothing
else to record.[1] In the May following he was presented
to the youthful Pope Pius IX., with whom he was afterwards so intimate. With what some will account
diabolical astuteness, though it would be fairer and
truer to call it evidence of tact and good breeding, the
Pope talked only of the good works of the English
Evangelicals and Quakers, and especially of Mrs. Fry;
adding, it is said, "When men do good works, God
gives grace. I pray daily for England."

Home again in July, 1848, Manning delivered a long
and elaborate Charge, dealing mainly with the appointment of Dr. Hampden to the see of Hereford, which
had been made during his absence. Newman and his

---

[1] Newman reached England on Christmas Eve, 1847, and did
not visit Rome again until 1879, when he went to be created
Cardinal.

followers had been much disturbed when Hampden was made Regius Professor of Divinity at Oxford, some years earlier, because certain passages in his Bampton Lectures were accounted heretical.[1] It was natural therefore that his elevation to the episcopal bench should occasion, as indeed it did, a more serious flutter; but Manning dealt with the matter in a way to minimize its importance. His object was, he explained, not to defend the new Bishop and his teaching, but to vindicate the Church of England from participation in the affair. This he thought himself able to do mainly on technical and legal grounds. " The Church, as such, has never passed judgment on the theology of Dr. Hampden. . . . The University of Oxford, in 1836, did not pronounce his doctrine to be heretical . . . but only declared it had no confidence in him in respect of doctrine. . . . Dr. Hampden has up to this moment never been condemned by any tribunal of the Church." More interesting than this Charge is the address that was presented to him after its delivery by sundry of the clergy of the archdeaconry. The cordial tone in which it is written, and some of the expressions it contains, show how high a value was placed on Manning's presence and counsel :—" We welcome your return among us after so long a period of absence . . . . and we pray that we may not by a like cause [of ill-health] be again separated, especially in these anxious times,

---

[1] In point of fact Hampden had never dreamed of being heretical ; but, being an easy-going man, he had employed to help him in the preparation of his Bampton Lectures that very interesting and able man, Blanco White, who was just then lapsing from Anglicanism into more liberal views. Hampden was as much annoyed as any one else to find that heresy, which he had not the wit to detect, had been put into his mouth.

from one whom we have ever found so ready to direct, counsel and encourage us amid the difficulties which at times attend upon the fulfilment of our offices."

It is perhaps worth recording, though it is hardly more than a matter of local interest, that on Aug. 17th in this year Manning took part in the ceremony of laying the foundation-stone of the new church of St. Peter-the-Great, Chichester, and that his name appears on the leaden plate which covers an opening in the stone.

But a grave practical matter was to occupy Manning's attention for the next year or so, and was to prove the last in which he would take any active part as Arch-deacon. This was the reopening of the education question on the point of the " management clauses." Manning took the leading part as champion of the Church in this controversy, and spoke on it at length at a meeting of clergy at Chichester in December, 1848, and again at a great meeting of the National Society held in London in June, 1849; and he devoted to it the major portion of his last Charge the month following. It is convenient to notice the last first, as it contains a useful *resumé* of the history of the education movement from the Churchman's point of view, and is in fact a document of some importance to the student of that movement:—

" I had hoped that the contest of ten years past had ended in an honourable and lasting agreement. . . . From 1811 to 1839 the Church laboured to promote the education of the people, chiefly by its own strength alone. In 1833 Parliament made grants for education; but the assistance received from public money was small. In the years 1838 and 1839 an attempt was made to introduce a system of education the effect of which would have been twofold,—first to separate secular from religious instruction, and next to separate education from the Church. From this disastrous scheme the country was preserved by the clergy and laity of the Church, supported by the sound sense and religious conscience of the people of England. The result of this contest was an agreement concluded in the year 1840, embodied in Minutes, and published by order of Council."

This agreement was to the effect that grants of public money should be made as before, in proportion to local efforts, and that the schools so assisted should be open to the " simple inspection " of officials appointed by the Crown, with the concurrence of the Church expressed through the Archbishops of the two provinces. These inspectors were however to interfere in no way with the management of the schools.

Under this system, the Archdeacon maintained truly enough, " the Church has not been inactive. . . . Every diocese has been organized so as to unite the clergy and laity under their Bishop in the work of promoting education. The Diocesan Boards, united with the National Society as their centre, form a system co-extensive with the whole population." But in 1846 the Secretary of the National Society observed that the Secretary of the Committee of Council on Education was recommending to the local promoters of schools certain formulas or clauses of management, and that these were commonly inserted in the trust-deeds of new schools; and upon this a controversial correspondence arose. Certainly these management clauses were all favourable enough to the Church of England. The clergyman in each parish was to be the religious instructor, with the

Bishop as sole judge of all appeals relating to that instruction. The ordinary management of the school was to be in the hands of a Committee, but they must all belong to the Church of England. So close a monopoly—not inconsistent, it must be admitted, with the idea of an Established Church—would have satisfied, one would have thought, the most exacting ecclesiastics; but " the thin end of the wedge " was detected in this mild interference of the State in the freedom of school management; and, at the meeting above referred to, over which the Archbishop of Canterbury (Sumner) presided, twelve other bishops and nearly as many peers being also present,—a meeting that was extremely lively and lasted eight hours—Denison (afterwards Archdeacon) withdrew his motion in favour of Manning's amendments, who proposed that the State grants should be altogether rejected, rather than that the principle of State management should be conceded. The latter showed considerable rhetorical *finesse* in winning Denison, who was four years his senior and never a very tractable man, round to his side :—[1]

[1] Archdeacon Denison, apparently forgetting what actually occurred at this time, and that the compromise was proposed by himself and not by Manning, wrote in July, 1891, " Manning was the agent in the hands of S. Oxford and E. Sarum in leading the National Society to the delay and compromise of its position in 1849, which issued in the sacrifice of the 'Church School'; and not long after he left England for Rome." Denison, inimitable as a dinner-table *raconteur*, and unrivalled as a platform orator, whence he could play on his audience—emotional indeed but often enough hostile—as on a musical instrument, moving them to tears or to laughter at his will, was distinctly ineffective in other departments of life; and his sneer at Manning, evoked solely by the fact that the latter took a step which he himself, in the opinion of many who have known him well, needed only the clear-headedness to have taken also, is quite unsupported by any contemporary record of what actually occurred.

"It has been thrown out, forsooth, as a reason why we should concur in the management clauses proposed to us by the Committee of the Privy Council, that if we do not we may lose the bounty of the State. Where am I standing? To whom am I listening, and who utters it? My dear and revered friend, whose soul would abhor so low a notion as that the Church of Christ should accept as bounty that which the civil power gives us as its duty and for its own benefit? Oh! my lord, the thought was further from his gracious heart than from mine; and when I heard him saying that there was at least a danger lest we should pervert the assistance and co-operation of the State, he reminded me—and the thought operated as a solace to the fear—of a period when a million, or a million and a half of money was granted by the State for the building of churches. I would ask you, what three works has the Church of England attempted in its own strength, in which it has been so signally prosperous, as in the works of multiplying its churches, of extending its missions, and of educating its people? And I would ask, during what period has the Church of England so succeeded, as since the day when the grants of Parliament were diminished or withdrawn? Shall we forget that in fifteen years no less than 1500 churches have been erected; that during the last nine years thirteen bishop-rics have been planted in our colonial possessions? And during the same period, what has the Church done in regard to education? To pass over sixteen training schools, from which 2,000 teachers have issued, there are in communion with the Church of England 17,000 schools, of which 7,000 have been added during the last ten years. . . . Shall we then, through any

E

consideration of the public money, not only compromise
a principle, but even come to an agreement which
would have the effect of destroying the harmony, and
therefore of perilling the unity of our common mother?"

The speech, from which the above are extracts, was
received with much enthusiasm; and after some delay
Manning's amendments were carried, to the effect that
"no terms of co-operation with the State can be satisfactory which shall not allow to the clergy and laity full
freedom to constitute schools upon such principles and
models as are both sanctioned and recommended by the
order and the practice of the Church of England."

Mr. Gladstone, Mr. Beresford-Hope and Dr. Christopher
Wordsworth were among those who took part in this
meeting; and of the clergy present the names may be
noted of Henry Wilberforce, Bathurst and Maskell, who
afterwards joined the Catholic Church. The considerations which induced Archdeacon Manning to take the
same step within two years of this date must next be
passed under review.

CHAPTER III.

THERE are reasons for preferring the term that heads this chapter to the word "conversion," more commonly used, to express secession from the Church of England and submission to the authority of Rome. For one thing, "conversion" implies a change for the better, and so is not complimentary to the communion left behind; while "perversion," besides being a barbarous term in such a connection, is offensive not only to the communion joined, but to the person who, with the best intentions, makes the change in question. So far as Manning's "conversion" is concerned, in any just and intelligible sense, that took place more than twenty years before the Gorham decision, when, in the last year of his undergraduate life, he became, under the influence of family misfortune, a serious, thoughtful, earnest, industrious man, such as he remained thenceforward to the end. There was no change of mind or of heart when he became a Catholic in 1851. He had already been materially, though not formally, a Catholic for years; and that in good faith, so far as his position within the Church of England was concerned. There are indeed indications that now and again he was conscious that his environment was not altogether in harmony with his ideas, much as one may suppose that a cold wind in August evokes temporarily in the swallow the instinct for migration to southern climes; but the time was not come to take any definite and irrevocable step, until events had made it clear that he must arise and depart, since in the Anglican Church it was impossible that he should permanently find rest.

The position occupied by Archdeacon Manning at the opening of the year 1850 was in some respects unique. He was informally the leader of the party which was carrying on the work inaugurated by the Tractarians, and, as such, he was trusted and consulted by an important and increasing number of the clergy. There were many who felt something like an enthusiastic admiration for him, and anticipated great things for the Church of England when he should have become a Bishop, a promotion that was indeed inevitable, and that speedily, had he remained an Anglican. "His practical services, no less than his well-timed occasional works, have for some time marked him out as a man whom the Church needs in her highest offices, and who cannot be allowed to rest even in the honourable post which he now adorns."[1] This is only one of many such testimonies from the High Church side that might be quoted. But it was not only from men of his own party that he won admiration. He displayed as leader such tact and considerateness towards those who held other views, he stated his case invariably with such gentleness and modesty, that he disarmed opposition

[1] *Christian Remembrancer*, Jan. 1843.

without himself yielding an inch. Archdeacon Hare,
of Lewes, has already been quoted; but those words
might be explained as the complimentary language of
one diocesan official towards another. The same account
cannot be given of a generous testimony borne in a
Charge delivered a few months after Manning had made
his submission to Rome, in which he was spoken of as
"one whom we have long been accustomed to honour,
to reverence, to love; one who for the last ten years
has taken a leading part in every measure adopted for
the good of the diocese; one to whose eloquence we
have so often listened with delight, sanctified by the
holy purpose that eloquence was ever used to promote;
one, the clearness of whose spiritual vision it seemed
like presumption to distrust, and the purity of whose
heart, the sanctity of whose motives, no man knowing
him can question." The Church of England, he added,
in Manning's secession, "mourns over the loss of one
of the holiest of her sons." Such words, spoken at such
a time, are an honour no less to the speaker than to his
subject; and they contrast favourably with the sneers
and innuendoes about "restless ambition," and the like,
which would fall from the lips of Oxford High Church
Professors at a later date with reference to the step by
which Manning, to whom the road to Lambeth, with all
its high dignity and affluence, was open, expressed his
readiness rather to be accounted a fool for Christ's sake,
and to occupy in preference a post that in those days
was little else than a pillory for the objects of scorn,
distrust and hatred.

In July, 1843, Archdeacon Manning had thus borne
testimony to the growth of spiritual life and power in
the Church of England :—

"The Church of England is making herself known and felt as a spiritual kingdom in all parts of the earth; and there must needs be at home some intense life and energetic power that can throw out its influence through so remote a sphere. . . . I am firmly persuaded that the last three centuries have opened a new era, so to speak, in the history of Christendom; and that the basis of doctrine and discipline which has been vindicated by this branch of the Church Catholic is destined to be the basis of unity to the Church of the next ages. . . . The first condition of our usefulness at this day is this,—a steadfast and thorough faith in the life and truth of the Church of England; and that, not as a successful controversial dogma, but as a consciousness which is inseparable from our spiritual life. . . . There are many advantages in her favour, such as few branches of the Catholic body have ever possessed, and perhaps none at this day so fully retain."

Seven years later the faith in the Church of England of the writer of these words had been so rudely shaken that it was only a question of a few months, more or less, how long he could remain in her service. What resulted in so momentous a decision may seem but a trifling occurrence, inadequate to the occasion; but a straw will show the direction of the current, and a legal decision acquiesced in by the Anglican Episcopate was really enough to make it clear that the actual Church of England was different altogether from that ideal Church which Manning believed himself to have been serving, and that for the realization of his ideal he must look elsewhere. The incidents which led to that decision belong to a chapter of Church history remembered now only by a few, and must be briefly recapitulated.

The **Rev. George Cornelius Gorham, a** Calvinist theologian, **but** better **known** as an antiquary and **a** botanist, who was **born in** 1787 and died in 1857, had **been** educated under Quaker influences. In 1811, **when** he sought ordination in the Church of England, Dampier, Bishop **of** Ely, was disposed to reject him **on account of the** unsoundness of his **views** on baptismal regeneration, but he ultimately gave way. In 1846 he was presented by Lord Lyndhurst to the living of St. Just in Penwith, Cornwall, and **was** duly insti-**tuted** by Henry Phillpotts, Bishop **of** Exeter. The year following, the Lord Chancellor **presented him** to the considerably less valuable living **of** Brampford Speke, near Exeter, the object of **the** change **being that** he might have facilities for **educating his** children, and also have somewhat less onerous duties **in his declining** years. Meanwhile, **in** connection with the appointment of **a** curate at St. **Just,** the Bishop had learned **some-**thing about Gorham's views, and declined to institute him unless, after examination, he should **be** satisfied. This examination extended over four days in December, 1847, and three days in March, **1848**; and in the end the Bishop persisted in his refusal. Gorham, who in his own special theological line was an able and well-**read** controversialist, held **that** divine grace was not of necessity given either at baptism **or at** conversion, but might be given before baptism, in **baptism, or at** a later period—a view that was **not held** precisely by **Low** Churchmen any **more** than by **High Churchmen.** The Lord Chancellor **insisted on his presentation, and in** August, 1849, Sir **Herbert** Jenner Fust, in the Court of Arches, decided in favour of **the** Bishop's refusal. This decision was reversed, March **8, 1850, on** appeal to

the Judicial Committee of the Privy Council, of which
body Sumner, Archbishop of Canterbury, Musgrave,
Archbishop of York, Blomfield, Bishop of London, and
six laymen were members on this occasion.[1] The
Bishop of Exeter, who was very indignant at the part
Sumner had played, endeavoured to prevent the Court
of Arches from giving effect to the decision of the Privy
Council by appeals to the Court of Queen's Bench, the
Court of Common Pleas, and the Court of Exchequer
successively. These were refused, one after the other,
in April, May and June, 1850; so that in the month
last named it was clear that the decision of the Privy
Council was final, irreversible and effective.

In the present day, when men of every shade of
unorthodoxy are instituted to livings without question
or protest, it is not easy to realize the storm of indignation which this practical assertion of the Royal
Supremacy occasioned. More than fifty works were
published treating of the affair, and excited meetings of
clergy and High Church laymen were held, at which
strongly-worded resolutions were passed amidst much
enthusiasm. We are only concerned with the part
taken by Manning at this time, a part that it was all
the more difficult to play since the excitement over the
Gorham controversy was closely followed by the national
indignation aroused by the " Papal Aggression."

His first step, on the announcement of the decision
of the Judicial Committee in March, was to assist in
drafting the subjoined resolutions, to which twelve
signatures besides his own were appended, being those
of men who might fairly be accounted representative:—

---

[1] The judgment itself was delivered by Lord Langdale, Master
of the Rolls.

1. That whatever at the present time be the force of the sentence delivered on appeal in the case of Gorham *v.* the Bishop of Exeter, the Church of England will eventually be bound by the said sentence, unless it shall openly and expressly reject the erroneous doctrine sanctioned thereby.

2. That the remission of original sin to all infants in and by the grace of baptism is an essential part of the article "One Baptism for the remission of sins."

3. That—to omit other questions raised by the said sentence—such sentence, while it does not deny the liberty of holding that article in the sense heretofore received, does equally sanction the assertion that original sin is a bar to the right reception of baptism, and is not remitted, except when God bestows regeneration beforehand by an act of prevenient grace (whereof Holy Scripture and the Church are wholly silent), thereby rendering the benefits of Holy Baptism altogether uncertain and precarious.

4. That to admit the lawfulness of holding an exposition of an article of the Creed contradictory of the essential meaning of that article, is, in truth and in fact, to abandon that article.

5. That, inasmuch as the faith is one and rests upon one principle of authority, the conscious, deliberate and wilful abandonment of the essential meaning of an article of the Creed destroys the divine foundation upon which alone the entire faith is propounded by the Church.

6. That any portion of the Church which does so abandon the essential meaning of an article, forfeits, not only the Catholic doctrine in that article, but also the office and authority to witness and teach as a member of the universal Church.

7. That by such conscious, wilful and deliberate act such portion of the Church becomes formally separated from the Catholic body, and can no longer assure to its members the grace of the sacraments and the remission of sins.

8. That all measures consistent with the present legal position of the Church ought to be taken without delay, to obtain an authoritative declaration by the Church of the doctrine of Holy Baptism, impugned by the recent sentence; as, for instance, by praying licence for the Church in Convocation to give legal effect to the decisions of the collective Episcopate on this and all other matters purely spiritual.

9. That, failing such measures, all efforts must be made to obtain from the said Episcopate, acting only in its spiritual character, a re-affirmation of the doctrine of Holy Baptism, impugned by the said sentence.

H. E. MANNING, M.A., Archdeacon of Chichester.

ROBERT I. WILBERFORCE, M.A., Archdeacon of the East Riding.

THOMAS THORP, B.D., Archdeacon of Bristol.

W. H. MILL, D.D., Regius Professor of Hebrew, Cambridge.

E. B. PUSEY, D.D., Regius Professor of Hebrew, Oxford.

JOHN KEBLE, M.A., Vicar of Hursley.

W. DODSWORTH, M.A., Perpetual Curate of Ch. Ch., St. Pancras.

W. J. E. BENNETT, M.A., Perpetual Curate of St. Paul's, Knightsbridge.

HY. W. WILBERFORCE, M.A., Vicar of East Farleigh.

JOHN G. TALBOT, M.A., Barrister-at-Law.

RICHARD CAVENDISH, M.A.

Edward Badeley, M.A., Barrister-at-Law.
James R. Hope, D.C.L., Barrister-at-Law.

On March 19, 1850, a few days after the appearance
of the above manifesto, Manning presided in the Cathedral Library at Chichester at a meeting of the clergy
of his archdeaconry, of whom more than a hundred,
including the Dean (Chandler), were present. The
meeting was " to consider what steps it might be necessary to take in order to secure to the Church of
England a proper Court of Appeal in all matters purely
spiritual." The Archdeacon made a very long and
elaborate speech, from which the following passage is
worth quoting, as it serves to explain the conciliatory
line he had taken two years earlier in the Hampden
controversy :—

"The Church is not a succession of books or a succession of formularies, but a living body ; and its fidelity
to the Divine Head consists in its fidelity to the faith
which He has committed to its trust, and to those laws
of sanctity which He has impressed on it. ' The ordain-
ing of fit men is the type of the spiritual body. Its
vitality could not be more directly aimed at than in the
point of fitness for the Apostolic office. It is not more
necessary that the Church should be the ultimate judge
as to truth of doctrine than that it should be the
ultimate judge as to the fitness of those whom it ordains
to preach that doctrine. To invest any other authority
than the Church with the absolute selection of the
persons of its pastors would be as extravagant as to
invest the State with the ultimate decisions of faith.
In one word, the civil power can no more judge with
reference to the fitness of a man for the episcopate than
it can frame doctrinal definitions.' I have read these

words to you rather than speak them, because I have
once before trespassed on you with the same. I did so
in a case which occurred two years past, being then
convinced that the violations of discipline which took
place in the consecration to the see of Hereford carried
with them any extent of violation of the doctrine and
discipline of the Church. I so deeply felt that case,
that if the English Church could have been convicted
of either consecrating a heretic, or of giving up to the
State the power of finally determining the fitness of
men for the pastoral office, it would have been a be-
trayal of her divine trust. I tried to deny both these
accusations; and in denying them I confess I strained
every plea to the utmost, feeling the necessity of the
case to be so vital. I fell under censure for so doing,
which censure I bore in silence, believing and fearing
that the time would come, and perhaps before long,
when an opportunity might be taken—for I would never
make it—of expressing to you why I did so. I felt that
if those two accusations could not be denied, the Church
of England would be put in a position not defensible.
I bore therefore in silence no very measured censure.
I am glad now to be able to say that in so speaking I
did not defend Dr. Hampden but the Church of England.
It appeared to me in that case the securities for both
the doctrine and discipline of the Church were at stake,
and that the power of the State had in effect succeeded
in overruling the highest office of the Church. The
same is the result of the present case. . . . [According
to this decision] the State possesses a jurisdiction
co-extensive with every Church Court, and superior
to it; so that every question that is conceivable as
to doctrine or discipline may be brought before the

Judicial Committee of the Privy Council for final determination."

Later in his speech, referring to the constitution of the proposed purely Ecclesiastical Court, which the meeting had been summoned to advocate, he said :—

"The only form in which the Episcopate can exercise its proper authority, and impress the episcopal character on its decisions, is when it acts according to the law and order of the Church. Therefore, although the State should appoint the whole body of the Bishops taken numerically to sit as a Court, if they sit as Commissioners appointed by the State and not as a Synod convened by the authority of the Church, their decision would be the decision of Commissioners, and not of an Episcopal Synod. What appears to me to be requisite in this case is, such an Appellate Court as shall carry with it the authority of the Church, determining its own sphere. I will go into no particulars as to whom it shall consist of, but only that it shall include the whole Episcopate. . . Let us enter on this discussion with the calmness and gravity suitable to it. It cannot be without its weight; but its weight will be measured by our moderation. If we were to-day to part after a discussion which should tend to excite a conflict of feeling, I believe we should part the worse and not the better. Why should we ? Let us discuss this question in which we are all concerned in a spirit of love and concession. The question is new and difficult. It is the first time we touch it. . . Let us act so as to ensure a perpetuity of truth to those for whom we are trustees. We must not live for the day, but we must remember that at that day when all ages are summed up in one moment, no one will be held to a stricter account as trustees for the future than those who have received the office of pastors of Christ."

At the close of the meeting, which separated without being able to agree to any recommendations as to a new Ecclesiastical Court, Manning said :—

"We have never met in this room on an occasion of greater importance. We have met here before now to discuss the suppression of bishoprics in Ireland, the diminution of the fulness and efficiency of Cathedrals, and the subject of education, which trenches so closely on the faith itself. But I know of no one subject that has ever touched the faith and office of the Church so deeply and to the quick as this question now before us. Holding that belief I should feel I had simply betrayed a trust if I were to allow this occasion to pass without giving expression to my conviction. It has always been my desire to take such a line as would not commit the Church to any unnecessary collision with the civil power. The union of Church and State is an act of God's Providence, and ought by all lawful means, and to the last, to be maintained. At the same time I am bound to say that everything I have seen convinces me that the civil State of England is gradually settling down into religious indifference; and the Church is lashed to the civil State by so many bands that it behoves us to see whither we are being drawn. In all matters purely temporal I trust that her Majesty the Queen has no more loyal subjects than ourselves. In all questions of mixed jurisdiction I think we should strain to the utmost and submit, rather than sustain a breach with the civil power. But, in matters which touch the faith and discipline of the Church of Christ, 'Jerusalem which is above is free, which is the mother of us all.'"

But although the meeting could agree to no suggestion for a new final Court of Appeal, the Archdeacon and a majority of the clergymen present signed the following address to the Bishop of Chichester :—

" We, the Archdeacon and clergy of the Archdeaconry of Chichester, desire to lay before your Lordship, as our Bishop, the deep anxiety awakened in us by the decision lately given in the case of Gorham *v.* the Bishop of Exeter.

" Believing, as a fundamental article of the Catholic faith, that all infants baptized, according to the institution of Christ, with water, in the Name of the Father and of the Son and of the Holy Ghost, are regenerate by the Holy Spirit, we are convinced that the Church cannot, without betraying her highest trust, permit that doctrine to be denied.

" We therefore urgently pray that your Lordship will take such steps as shall seem most effectual for the declaration and maintenance of the doctrine of Holy Baptism, and for relieving those who feel grieved in conscience by the legal sanction given by the late sentence to the denial of that article of faith.

" *March* 19, 1850."

As might have been expected, during these anxious times Manning withdrew in great measure from the part he had been accustomed to take in Church consecrations, and the like, and he delivered no Charge as Archdeacon in 1850. But there was one special work in which he was interested—that of St. Barnabas', Pimlico; and to this he remained faithful so long as his conscience allowed him. He had preached at St. Paul's, Knightsbridge, on June 11th, 1849, the occasion being the dedication anniversary of St. Barnabas' College, or clergy-house, the church itself being not yet completed. No Bishop was willing to take any part in the proceedings, and at the luncheon which followed, Manning had to return thanks to the toast of their Lordships, humorously remarking that it was new to him to find that an Archdeacon was a Bishop's mouth as well as his eye. The year following he preached twice in the new church, one of the sermons, entitled " Self-Sacrifice," appearing in the volume that commemorates the consecration.[1]

Early in July was printed Manning's letter to his Bishop, entitled "The Appellate Jurisdiction of the Crown in Matters Spiritual," in which he lays down calmly and clearly the conclusions to which he had been "irresistibly compelled" by the appeal and judgment in the Gorham case. A good deal of the letter is occupied by an historical justification of the position that "there is no supremacy in ecclesiastical matters inherent in the civil power or prince, but either such power as all princes, Christian or heathen, alike possess, or such as has been received by delegation from the Church itself"; and later he deals with the apology that some Churchmen had put forward to the effect that the Privy Councillors did not profess to decide whether the doctrine put before them was true or false, but only whether it was the doctrine of the Church of England. In the end his conclusion was, that "there never has

[1] "Sermons preached at St. Barnabas', Pimlico, in the octave of the consecration, 1850." Other preachers on this occasion were Sewell, Paget, Pusey, Keble, Henry Wilberforce, Neale, F. H. Bennett, Gresley, Eden, Upton Richards, W. H. Mill, and Charles E. Kennaway; the last of whom, it is interesting to note, in view of later developments of the High Church movement, preached on " the Socialism of the Early Church."

existed, and does not exist, in any society recognized as or claiming to be a portion of the visible Church, such an appellate jurisdiction as that lately exercised by the Crown over the Church of England. . . . There cannot be brought from any period of our history, Saxon, Norman or English, any precedent or shadow of precedent to show that the power to judge in appeal on a question such as this was ever possessed by our princes as a part of their 'ancient jurisdiction.' . . . All this is too deeply humbling for me to do more than recite such a fact, which is bringing down shame where I have ever striven only to pay honour." As regards the special point of doctrine, on which the Judicial Committee had ruled that the Church of England was indifferent, he added:—" I hardly know of any doctrine more vital to the spiritual life, more fundamental to the visible Church, more intimately related to the revealed character of God and to the moral probation of man, than the regeneration of baptism. . . . No doctrine is more manifestly universal in its reception in all ages of the Church, both before the division of the East and West, when its united voice gave unerring witness to the faith, and since that division, in all members of the visible Church unto this day. If there be therefore such a thing as material heresy, it is the doctrine which has now received the sanction of the law. . . . I do not see how the Church of England can permit two contrary doctrines on Baptism to be propounded to her people without abdicating the divine authority to teach as sent from God; and a body which teaches under the authority of human interpretation descends to the level of a human society."

The tone of the letter is throughout reserved and

F

gentle. There is not from first to last any threat of
action on the part of the writer, should his views not
prevail. It is a clear and moderate statement of the
case, showing no little familiarity with ecclesiastical
law, but none of the violent language of remonstrance,
protest, and even of menace that is commonly found in
such documents. Probably however the writer of an
article in the *Guardian* [1] was right in his criticism when
he said, "We confess some doubt whether the most
effective case for the Church of England as against the
prerogative lawyers lies in the considerations to which
Archdeacon Manning has mainly devoted himself.
Arguments founded on definitions of the abstract functions of the Church, and still more on the application
of canon law to the *status* of an existing Church, long
separated from the Roman See, which is the main
fountain of that law, are like arguments from pure
mathematics when applied to the actual phenomena of
motion." Manning had appealed to Cæsar, if one may
so describe the royal ecclesiastic who has his throne in
Rome, and so to Cæsar he was bound to go. To other
words of the Archdeacon the writer went on to appeal
in vain, for these words were not *ad rem* in the controversy that was to hand :—"Meanwhile, while our
discipline is paralyzed, our people disquieted, our prospects uncertain, we will endeavour to find consolation
in thoughts which Archdeacon Manning has expressed
nobly, though with a different purpose : 'The doctrine
of the Church of England is not only in its written
formularies, but the oral teaching of its twenty-eight
Bishops, its fifteen thousand clergy, its many more
thousand school-teachers, its two or three millions of

[1] July 17, 1850.

MIGRATION.

ing and perpetual sense which is taught at our altars
and from house to house all the year round.'" The
writer in the *Guardian* refers to this as "a picture of
living strength and unanimity"; but even in those
days of comparative unity within the Church, this
was not the $\pi o\hat{v}$ $\sigma\tau\hat{\omega}$ for which the Archdeacon was
seeking.

On July 23rd, 1850, a great meeting was held in
St. Martin's Hall, Longacre, London, to protest against
the decision of the Privy Council in the Gorham case.[1]
Mr. J. F. Hubbard presided; and the Bishop of Bath
and Wells (Hon. Richard Bagot, translated from Oxford
in 1845), Archdeacons Wilberforce, Manning, Thorp
and Bartholomew, Keble and Pusey, Neale, Denison,
W. J. E. Bennett, H. Wilberforce, R. Liddell, Beresford-
Hope, and many others were present. Denison was
one of the principal speakers, and aroused the enthusiasm
of the audience by the boldness of his language and
the vehemence with which he urged the necessity for
decisive action, if the position of the Church of England
was not to be permanently discredited. Manning spoke
at the close, proposing a vote of thanks to the chairman.
He did not add much to the discussion of the main
question—indeed there was little to be added—but he
made some very sensible remarks on what should be
the estimate of the value of the meeting in case the
Church as such should take no action to dissociate

[1] A sketch of this meeting appears in the *Illustrated London
News* for July 27, 1850. The hall, which had recently been
built as a high-class music hall for Mr. John Hullah, later
became the Queen's Theatre. It was afterwards transformed
into the University Co-operative Stores, and is now a gymnasium
of the Young Men's Christian Association.

herself from the decision of the Judicial Committee. "It appears to me," he said, "that there are two dangers we may run the risk of falling into,—the one of under-rating the crisis, the other of over-rating the meeting. I say of under-rating the crisis, and for this reason. It has often been said that first thoughts and third thoughts are generally alike, and also generally correct, while second thoughts—those little arguments and pleadings by which crafty and able men mislead—are the most perilous. I think this is so. We are told that the judgment of the Privy Council does not touch doctrine, and that the claim of the civil power to appoint judges is not for the purpose of interfering with matters of doctrine, but merely for the purpose of dealing with benefices, emoluments, and civil questions in connection with the Church. These are the second thoughts—the intermediate, crafty arguments by which honest men are misled and wise men are troubled. The only thing for us to do is to meet the difficulty in its full length and breadth. . . . I would urge every member of the Church, layman or priest, not to be misled by any artifice or skill or authority, so far as to be induced to look upon what has happened as of light importance. . . . If this meeting pass over with no other result than the excitement of our present feeling, then it will do infinitely more harm than good. It would do more harm than good if, after such an exhibition of zeal and earnestness, a man should go home and think he had done a great act, and that no more was necessary to be done. May this be averted."

Any hope that Manning and others might have entertained as to the possibility of the two Archbishops revoking in their spiritual character the sentence that they had joined in pronouncing as Privy Councillors was crushed before this month of July was ended by the replies made by Sumner to the committee of the "Metropolitan Church Union." He declined to receive an address which, he said, assumed that he was in a position "to reverse the sentence of the legitimate court"; and in answer to a remonstrance he added, "Nothing that I find in the law of God gives me reason to believe that I should be acting in conformity with His will if I refused Mr. Gorham admission to the cure of souls on the ground of his hesitating to affirm the spiritual regeneration of every baptized child." One further effort was however made, if not to clear the Church of England from the reproach that its doctrines were subject to revision by the civil power, at any rate to relieve the consciences of those who felt themselves compromised by the recent judgment in appeal; and the following Declaration touching the Royal Supremacy was put into circulation, and received numerous signatures during the autumn :—

"Whereas it is required of every person admitted to the order of deacon or priest, and likewise of persons admitted to ecclesiastical offices or academical degrees, to make oath that they abjure, and to subscribe to the three articles of Canon xxxvi., one whereof touches the Royal Supremacy :

"And whereas it is now made evident by the late appeal and sentence in the case of Gorham v. the Bishop of Exeter, and by the judgment of all the courts of common law, that the Royal Supremacy, as defined and established by statute law, invests the Crown with a

power of hearing and deciding in appeal all matters,
however purely spiritual, of discipline and doctrine:

"And whereas to give such power to the Crown is at
variance with the divine office of the Universal Church,
as prescribed by the law of Christ:

"And whereas we, the undersigned clergy and laity
of the Church of England, at the time of making the
said oath and subscription, did not understand the
Royal Supremacy in the sense now ascribed to it by
the Courts of Law, nor have until this present time so
understood it, neither have believed that such authority
was claimed on behalf of our Sovereign:

"Now we do hereby declare:—

"1. That we have hitherto acknowledged, and do
now acknowledge the supremacy of the Crown in ecclesiastical matters to be a supreme civil power over all
persons and causes in temporal things, and over the
temporal accidents of spiritual things.

"2. That we do not, and in conscience cannot acknowledge in the Crown the power recently exercised to hear
and judge in appeal the internal state or merits of
spiritual questions touching doctrine or discipline, the
custody of which is committed to the Church alone by
the law of Christ.

"We therefore, for the sake of our consciences, hereby
publicly declare that we acknowledge the Royal Supremacy in the sense above stated, and in no other.

"HENRY EDWARD MANNING, Archdeacon of Chichester.

"ROBERT ISAAC WILBERFORCE, Archdeacon of the
East Riding.

"WILLIAM HODGE MILL, D.D., Regius Professor of
Hebrew, Cambridge."

The possibility of Manning's secession from the Church of England was however now recognized by those who best knew his mind, and especially by Mr. Gladstone and by the Wilberforces, three of whom were sooner or later to take the same step, leaving only the Bishop of Oxford behind. Mr. Gladstone was not insensible to the inconsistency of the decision of the Privy Council with the principles of sound churchmanship; but he was naturally of a cautious temperament, and slow to move; and the friendship he had formed some five years earlier with Dr. Döllinger had disposed him to take a more favourable view of the Anglican as compared with the Roman Church, on historical rather than on strictly dogmatic grounds. With the modern Roman devotional system moreover he had no sympathy, and probably could never have acclimatized himself to it; whereas Manning, judging from some letters recently published in Bishop Charles Wordsworth's autobiography, had for some time past felt a considerable attraction towards it.[1] Mr. Gladstone was of opinion that if,

[1] Thus, in Jan. 1842, he wrote to Dr. Christopher Wordsworth (the father) : " You represent the mind of the English Church before the storm and confusion of modern theologies broke in upon it. . . Our young men have to work out by investigation what they ought to have inherited from the living Church. . . Our oral traditions are shallow and ambiguous ; and our only hope is to withdraw into the seventeenth century."
To Charles Wordsworth he wrote in Feb. 1842 : " I mean to write a book which to our priesthood shall be what Morinus is to the foreign. I mean a dogmatic scholastic work." And in Feb. 1845, "I exceedingly desire to read systematically and exactly some of the Fathers and Schoolmen. Every day makes me feel more my want of deep and thorough study in early life. And I feel continually more conscious that there must be a science of the Saints, based upon infallible truths, and capable of a full and methodical statement. Our popular theology is a perfect chaos. . . We hardly know what is capable of statement

immediately after the decision of the Privy Council, a majority of the Bishops had openly in combination declared that they would uphold the doctrine of the Church on baptism, even though such a declaration would not have been precisely a corporate act, yet it would have sufficed to retain, not only Manning but many others who, like him, were longing for some authoritative declaration. But this seems doubtful, judging from a letter which Samuel Wilberforce, who was Manning's guest at Lavington, wrote to Gladstone under date Sept. 14, 1850 :—" My stay here has let me see much of Manning. Never has he been so affectionate, so open, so fully trusting with me. We have been together through all his difficulties. But, alas! it has left on my mind the full conviction that he *is* lost to us. It is, as you say, the broad ground of historical enquiry where our paths part. He seems to me to have followed singly exactly the course which the Roman Church has followed as a body. He has gone back into those early times, when what afterwards became their corruptions were only the germ-buds of Catholic usages ; he has fully accustomed his mind to them, until a system which wants them seems to him incomplete and uncatholic, and one which has them is the wiser and holier and more Catholic for having them ; until he can excuse to a great degree their practical corruptions, and justify altogether their doctrinal rightness. All this has been

and what is not ; we have no scientific exposition of doctrine, ethics and practical wisdom. I am not wishing for a merely intellectual system. I believe what is called the science of the Saints to be eminently productive of sanctity and devotion, as we see in the life of St. Thomas Aquinas. And such work as this, together with active charity, is to you and to me our home and our all."

stirred up and rendered practical in his mind by our own troubles; but the result of all leaves me very hopeless of the issue. Few can understand what his and my brother's present state are to me. I believe you can; the broken sleep, the heavy waking before the sorrow has shaped itself with returning consciousness into a definite form; the vast and spreading dimensions of the fear for others which it excites; the clouding over of all the future."

To this letter, so admirable in its tone—and thus contrasting sharply with later letters from the same hand, wherein Manning's "subtleties" and "denunciations" were bitterly referred to, as accounting for other secessions from the Church of England—Mr. Gladstone replied to the effect that from his own personal knowledge he had concluded that even before the Gorham judgment the Archdeacon's mind had become imbued with Roman Catholic ideas. He had not before that date ceased to believe in the authority and mission of the Church of England, but he had recognized behind that Church the presence of a communion more august, more venerable, more commanding. He had dwelt for near upon ten years on the vital importance of the unity of the Church. Of the three centuries of the Church of England's separate life, the seventeenth was the only one in which he could find a congenial refuge; and the more he scrutinized the doctrine of the Jacobite divines, the more he saw it was based on political expediency, without foundation in the Reformation period, and that it crumbled to nothing on the accession of William III. The demonstration that a civil court could, without remedy, decide for the Church of England a point of doctrine, could hardly fail to shake an allegiance which such considerations had already effectively undermined.

Manning however remained in residence at Lavington till nearly the end of the year, and was present in the autumn at a gathering at St. Nicholas College, Shoreham, and also attended the Bishop's Charge at Chichester. The agitation against the "Papal Aggression" at this time placed him in an awkward position. The Bull establishing a Diocesan Hierarchy to supersede the former Vicars Apostolic was dated Sept. 24th, 1850, and Cardinal Wiseman's famous letter, dated "out of the Flaminian Gate," was written on Oct. 6th. Lord John Russell's "Durham Letter" appeared a month later; and thenceforward the country was in a blaze, some six or seven thousand indignation meetings being held before the close of the year. Manning, as Archdeacon, had perforce to preside at such a meeting of the clergy of his archdeaconry, held in the library of Chichester Cathedral on Nov. 27.[1] According to the report of the proceedings, he began by explaining with calmness and gentleness the reasons that had induced him to accede to the request to call his clergy together, and he went on to state, with touching sincerity and

[1] On Nov. 23 he had written to James Hope-Scott:—"Your last letter was a help to me, for I began to feel as if every man had gone to his own house and left the matter. . . Events have driven me to a decision. This anti-Popery cry has seized my brethren, and they asked me to be convened. I must either resign at once, or convene them ministerially, and express my dissent, the reasons of which would involve my resignation. I went to the Bishop and said this, and tendered my resignation. He was very kind, and wished me to take time; but I have written and made it final." The Bishop in fact hoped against hope much longer, and did not appoint a successor to Manning until April, 1851.

candour, the difference of opinion on the question now
before them which separated him from his brethren.
He reminded them that it was seventeen years since he
had first attended with them a meeting in that room,
and that this was probably the last occasion on which
they would see him there. After such an opening the
meeting was held in comparative calm, without personal
allusions or manifestations of angry feelings; and the
Archdeacon responded to a vote of thanks for his
conduct in the chair proposed by the Dean.

A fortnight later the *Guardian* announced that he
had resigned his living and his archdeaconry and was
about to travel abroad, a denial being given to the
"painful rumours" about his impending secession.
He travelled however at this time only as far as St.
Barnabas', Pimlico, the mission church of the poor
inhabitants of "a remote corner of the fashionable
parish of St. George, Hanover Square," which had
been dear to him from its foundation. There were
"surplice-riots" in and about the church at this time,
and Manning offered to address the rioters in the
street; but he was dissuaded from attempting it, as it
seemed likely he might sustain some serious injury,
the mob being "composed of some of the worst
characters about Westminster, Chelsea and Pimlico."
It was noted also at this time that he was out of
health—a consequence doubtless of the anxieties that
had been pressing upon him—and a period of rest and
recollection was still necessary before he found himself
able to take the step that was in fact inevitable ever
since it had become clear that an authoritative repudiation of the Gorham decision by the Church of England,
as such, was not to be looked for. During this time

he took no ministerial part in the Anglican Church services, though the *Guardian* recorded that he was a communicant at St. Paul's, Knightsbridge, in January, 1851. It was a time of transition; and some correspondence with the Rev. T. W. Allies, Rector of Launton, Bucks,—whose book, *The Church of England cleared from the Charge of Schism*, 2nd edition, published at Oxford in 1848, still remains the ablest document on that side—as also some letters to James Hope-Scott, illustrate in an interesting way the gradual progress of his convictions. In June, 1850, while admitting that the book just mentioned was, to his mind, "ample ground for doubting any contrary conclusion without more evidence," he confessed that he felt with its author the need for a re-examination of the subject, on which he hoped to enter "with a single intention to obey the truth and will of God with all my heart." He regretted that a life which had been "active to excess" had left him little time for reading; and "the mistrust of his own conclusions and opinions made him the readier to accept those of his friend, who had far outgone him in real study." When therefore Mr. Allies, promptly deciding on his duty after the Gorham decision, was received into the Catholic Church by Newman early in September, 1850, and published a small book, *The See of St. Peter, the Rock of the Church, the Source of Jurisdiction and the Centre of Unity*, in defence of the step he had taken, it was natural that Manning should reply, on receipt of a copy from its author, "I have read it once, and shall read it again closely, and with the examination you would desire. It is very able, and demands a full treatment by any one who will answer it. Let me have your prayers, that I may know and do the will of God in all things." To Hope-Scott, with whom he felt the fullest sympathy all through this anxious time, he wrote in November, " I should be glad if we might keep together; and whatever must be done, do it with a calmness and deliberateness which shall give testimony that it shall not be done in lightness "; and in December, " I feel with you that the argument is complete. For a long time I nevertheless felt a fear lest I should be doing an act morally wrong. This fear has passed away, because the Church of England has revealed itself [in the agitation against the newly-established Catholic hierarchy] in a way to make me fear more on the other side. It remains therefore as an act of the will. But this, I suppose, it must be. And in making it I am helped by the fact that to remain, under our changed or revealed circumstances, would also be an act of the will, and that, not in con-formity with, but in opposition to, intellectual real conviction ; and the intellect is God's gift, and our instrument in attaining knowledge of His will. . . . It would be to me a very great happiness if we could act together, and our names go together in the first pub-lication of the fact. . . . I entirely feel what you say of the alternative. It is either Rome, or license of thought and will."

A few days short of four months after the date of this letter, on April 6th, the 5th Sunday in Lent (Passion Sunday), 1851, Manning and Hope set out from 14, Queen Street, Mayfair, the residence of the latter, for the neighbouring church of the Jesuits in Farm Street Mews, and were there received into the Catholic Church by Father Brownbill, S.J. To men with their minds so long and so fully made up it was but the coming

into harbour after much labour and anxiety on a stormy
sea. Writing to Hope at a later time Manning said,
"I feel as if I had no desire unfulfilled, but to persevere
in what God has given me for His Son's sake. . . . How
blessed an end! As the soul said to Dante: *E da
martirio venni a questa pace.* . . . You do not need
that I should say how sensibly I remember all your
sympathy, which was the only human help in the time
when we two went together through the trial, which to
be known must be endured. . . . We made no mistake
in our long reckoning, though we feared it up to the
last opening of Father B.'s door." To the *Times*, which
announced a year later that Manning's return to the
Church of England was expected, he wrote, under date
May 31, 1852,—"I have found in the Catholic Church
all that I sought, and more than, while without its pale,
I had even been able to conceive." Such a man had
doubtless now found his true home.

The episodes connected with Manning's migration
from the Anglican to the Roman Church have been
given in detail, at the risk of tediousness, because on
the judgment which we form on his action in this
matter depends our judgment on his moral integrity;
and, if this latter is unfavourable, he fails at once to
command our respect as an English leader in religion.
Apart from greatness as an administrator, which belongs
to a lower plane than moral or intellectual eminence,
no one would claim a foremost place for Manning,
except it be for courage, honesty and singleness of aim.
It is important therefore to show, as far as may be,
from his own words and actions, that these qualities
did not desert him at this crisis of his life. It is a
grave matter for any man to change his religion, graver

for an office-holder in a Church, and gravest of all for
the recognized leader of an active and successful school.
Englishmen have seldom condoned submission to the
Church of Rome. In the case of Newman they came
to do so, but it was partly because they doubted whether
his submission was complete, and whether his heart
was not really at Oxford and in the Church of England
all the while. But about Manning's submission there
could be no such doubt; and it is certain that it has
been less generally condoned. The question may be
considered apart from the truth of Catholicism and
the merits, or otherwise, of the system. Would he have
been morally justified in remaining in the Church of
England? This again may be considered apart from
the case of others who at the same time held opinions
much the same as his, and did so remain. In matters
ecclesiastical and theological—and, one may now add,
theosophical—there are no limits to the diversities of
opinion to which men, apparently well-informed and not
unintelligent, may come, and that, it would seem, quite
honestly. This must be accepted as a first principle by
any one who would judge fairly from outside. But, on
the other hand, when a man has expressed himself
frankly, fully and frequently, as Manning had done, on
the position which he occupied, and has confessed, not
less frankly, that events have occurred inconsistent with
that position, we are able to judge whether or no he has
acted honourably in abandoning it or in holding to it.
And in this case the conclusion seems clear, that if the
Archdeacon of Chichester had elected to remain such
in 1850, and had risen thence to the Anglican Primacy
of all England, we might have had a very successful
Archbishop of Canterbury, but a man who could not have

been accounted great, since his own conscience would ever have condemned him as wanting in moral courage.

It was doubtless a difficult step to take, infinitely more difficult then than now, when the external aspects of Catholicism have ceased to offend any one, and Catholics themselves are recognized as good citizens, no less respectable than their Protestant fellow-country-men. A special difficulty was also raised, as has been noted, by the contemporary no-popery agitation, fierce, suspicious and unreasonable; and this incidentally placed another stumbling-block in the way of possible converts to Catholicism, as it disclosed a want of unity among the English Catholics themselves. Sundry Catholics, especially in the north, attended meetings to protest against the "Papal Aggression," and supported the resolutions proposed. Lord Beaumont, a Catholic peer, declared that the Pope's "ill-advised measure" gave to Catholics "the alternative of breaking with Rome or of violating their allegiance to the constitution of these realms"; and the Duke of Norfolk wrote to him expressing his entire concurrence in this view, adding his belief that "Ultramontane opinions are totally incompatible with allegiance to our Sovereign and with our constitution." Manning had long been a better Catholic than these men, and was better able to distinguish between the spheres of temporal and of spiritual authority. Nor was he the less Catholic-minded for never having dabbled in Catholic ceremonial. Copes, chasubles and stoles, and even the "eastward position," were unknown in the Church of England in his day. Daily service, weekly communion, the surplice in the pulpit, and the retention in the church until the conclusion of the prayer for the Church Militant of those who did not intend ultimately to "stay,"—these were the distinctive marks of the High Churchmen of half a century ago,—innocent enough and authorized by the rubrics, but nevertheless provoking suspicion and even arousing riotous opposition. It was from the headship of a movement strong and growing, one that was, as we have since seen, going forth conquering and to conquer, that Manning withdrew, because he saw that, while it appealed to history, it was not historically sound. And to become a Catholic in those days was socially to die, as far as the great world of England was concerned. In academic, literary, political and other cultured circles he was to be known no more for a season, and was to be mentioned, if at all, in sad whispers, as if dead or mentally deranged; but it mattered little to him, as he believed he had found that ideal which for more than twenty years he had desired to serve.[1]

[1] Manning's present successor at Lavington, the Rev. Rowley Lascelles, in reply to inquiries as to whether any memories of their former Rector still existed among his old parishioners, wrote:— "The tradition among the old people here is that Manning and Samuel Wilberforce were fellow-pupils at Lavington Rectory, and fell in love with the Rector's daughters. One old man, now dead, said to me, pointing to the setting sun, glowing large and red through the mists, 'Ah, sir! that is just what the Archdeacon was so fond of. He used often to admire it, as he stood, over the hill there : "Don't it look beautiful, John, sinking to rest when his work is done. That is how you and I will sink to rest when our work is done, if—"' the old man's memory seems to have failed him just at this point—'"*if we has luck!*"' One old woman now living in the parish (Jan. 1892) was converted by Manning from Roman Catholicism. In later years he made a journey to Graffham in the hope—a vain hope, as it turned out—of changing her opinions once more."

CHAPTER IV.

ROME AND BAYSWATER.

THE distinguished convert was welcomed by the *Tablet* in language not unworthy of the occasion :—

"Whilst congratulating the Catholic Church on the general conversions,[1] we must not omit to mention in particular the great importance of one of them. The name of Manning has always stood next after that illustrious triumvirate, one of whom, the greatest, has long since brought all the treasures of his learning to the service of our holy Mother. In some respects we may even say that Mr. Manning has commanded a yet greater influence than Dr. Pusey or Mr. Keble. Whilst Dr. Pusey has been the idolized guide of a very small party of very sincere and blindly-devoted followers, whom he has influenced by the charm of a particular sort of spirituality, purely subjective, hostile to reasoning, deeply tinged by individual heresy, Mr. Manning has really attempted to work the English Establishment on

---

[1] Among a considerable number of Anglicans who also made their submission to Rome at this time, the most noteworthy case was that of four clergymen and several lay-helpers attached to the church of St. Saviour's, Leeds.

Catholic principles, in a high and important official
position. We see in what he did all that a great ecclesiastical functionary in that Establishment could do.
His singular capacity for business and knowledge of the
world gave him advantages which no other chief of the
Tractarian movement enjoyed for carrying out Catholic
principles, as far as they could be carried out in the
Established Church. None of the three other leaders
approached him for possessing at once the complete
confidence of the Catholicizing party and the high
respect of the opposite faction. If any man therefore
could have restored unity and rebuilt that house of sand,
he could have done it. *Si Pergama dextrâ*, &c. But
even Manning, with all his great position, as Archdeacon
of Chichester, his important connexion, as brother-in-law
to the Bishop of Oxford [to Mrs. Samuel Wilberforce],
his prudence, his eloquence, his remarkable aptitude for
and acquaintance with affairs, his forbearance, his
patience and his holiness, has at last felt that he could
do nothing,—that the Church of England is Protestant,
and Protestant it will remain, that it is not the Church
of Augustine and Anselm, but of Cranmer and Burnet,
that if men wish to be Catholics they must have re-
course to the Chair of Peter, to the Roman unity. There
alone shines all the fulness of truth.

  " But whilst we thus congratulate our readers on this
important accession of one of the leading minds of the
Anglican Establishment, we shall hardly have done our
duty as journalists or as Catholics if we did not say
something on the great, the heroic sacrifices this man
has made for the sake of Catholic truth. He has given
up all that is most dear to that lofty ambition which
forms the peculiar temptation of minds of the noblest

mould. A position exactly suited to his talents, of widely-extended influence and a splendid future, the favour of great men, and the almost certainty (had he preferred it to his conscience) of ultimately carrying out his views as Bishop, the devoted adherence of troops of friends, an abode as fair as any of those we see scattered over England and occupied by her ministers—fortunate in this world's goods! an abode amid calm streams and green woody hills, with that ancient village church, in its present state almost the creation of his genius and cultivated taste—all this, and far more, Mr. Manning has given up with a great heart, generous and liberal to Almighty God, who has been so liberal of graces to him, counting all as nothing so that he may fight for the Holy Catholic Church, now that he has seen her star in the distance. He has not, like others, pointed out the way to Bethlehem, and then refused to go thither himself."

It is evidence of a certain continuity of which Manning was conscious in his clerical career, that he never for one moment hesitated, as Newman had done, about serving the Catholic Church as a priest; and it is evidence of a considerateness on the part of Cardinal Wiseman— rare in the circumstances, though in Manning's case these were doubtless exceptional—that he threw no obstacles in the way, but conferred on the neophyte the

[1] Manning himself never published any defence of the step he had taken. Some years later he wrote :—" I have never thought it necessary to publish the reasons of my submission to the Church of God. I felt that those who knew me knew my reasons, for they had followed my words and acts, and that they who did not know me would not care to know. I felt, too, that the best expositor of a man's conduct is his life, and that in a few years and in the way of duty I should naturally and unconsciously make clear and intelligible to all who care to know the motives of faith which governed me in that time of public and private trial."

tonsure a week after he had been received into the Church—thus at once constituting him a Catholic ecclesiastic—and, dispensing with the "interstices," proceeded rapidly with the minor and the sacred orders, so that he was admitted to the priesthood on the Saturday in Whitsun Week, 1851, before he had been ten weeks a Catholic, and said his first mass in the church in Farm Street on Monday, June 16, having been previously instructed in the ceremonies by Father Faber, of the Oratory. The assistant priest on the occasion was the eloquent French Jesuit, Ravignan; and a large congregation was present, and, according to custom, kissed the new priest's hands at the conclusion of the ceremony. The rapidity of his promotion was, however, viewed by some with dissatisfaction, perhaps because of anxieties caused by the extravagances of some of the recent converts: and the correspondent of the *Tablet* concluded his account of the proceedings with the caustic remark, "I hear that it is Mr. Manning's intention to visit Rome in the autumn, *for the purpose of commencing his theological studies*." Fourteen years later, when he had been appointed Archbishop of Westminster, the same journal, describing Manning's previous career, used language more courteous :—"Ordained priest by the late Cardinal Wiseman very shortly after his conversion . . . he did not remain in England, but went at once to Rome, to continue at the centre of all theological learning the course of study which had been his favourite pursuit, even before his conversion." There was however something more than mere jealousy in the earlier criticism. However well read in theology a man may be, however familiar with the Fathers, the Schoolmen, the Jesuits and later writers, it is certain that, unless his

studies have been pursued within the Catholic Church,
there will be wanting something which an infinitely less
lettered seminary-student, or a newly-ordained "religious," will securely possess. And Manning, though fairly
well read, was never, either as an Anglican or a Catholic,
a profound theologian. Nevertheless, in his case there
was no occasion for misgiving. His theological temper
at any rate had been for years as nearly Catholic as is
compatible with a materially non-Catholic position ; and
as a priest he could be trusted to utter nothing for
which he had not the fullest authority ; while he was
eager to make good at the fountain-head of theology
those deficiencies of which he was conscious. Advised
however, for health's sake, not to proceed to Rome till
the autumn, he was employed during the summer in
assisting the invalid priest of the Kensington district
who died at this time. By Christmas he was settled
in Rome, with his nephew, the Rev. W. H. Anderdon,
and he was soon a familiar sight in *tricorne* and *fer-
raiuolo*, in the neighbourhood of the Church of the
Minerva and the Collegio Romano, where he attended
the lectures of the Jesuits Perrone and Passaglia.[1]

[1] Newman also attended their lectures, 1846-47. Perrone
(born in 1794) took refuge in England during the Roman revolution, 1848-50. He was appointed Rector of the Collegio Romano
in 1853 ; and in that year he published a treatise on Protestantism
and the rule of faith—one of some sixty works that he wrote—in
the preparation of which he made use of information obtained
from his distinguished pupils, and during his residence in England.
Passaglia (born in 1802) wrote a learned treatise on the immaculate
conception, which may be said to have rendered possible the
definition of that doctrine by Pius IX. in 1854. In 1861 he
declared himself against the temporal power as understood by the
Pope ; and he was thenceforward excommunicate, though he
never abandoned any Catholic doctrine, and indeed put forth a
reply to Renan's *Vie de Jésus* in 1863.

He was resident at this time, and generally when in
Rome until 1854, at the *Accademia dei Nobili Eccle-
siastici*, which he had been recommended to enter by
Pius IX., who received him in Rome with much
satisfaction, recalling an interview they had had four
years earlier, under very different circumstances.[1] This
college, which is situated near to the Church of the
Minerva, is designed mainly for the ecclesiastical education of young men of good family and of recognized
ability, likely to find their home in the Roman Curia,
and it is often described as " a nursery of Cardinals."
Special instruction in diplomacy is given to promising
pupils, the traditions of Rome in this branch of learning
being here jealously guarded. Many of the students
are men of some experience in the priesthood, and the
régime of the college is therefore unlike that of an
ordinary seminary, and corresponds more with the
freedom of a college at Oxford or Cambridge. A pecu-
liarity in Manning's position at this time was the special
interest taken in him by Pope Pius IX. He was for
three years a student at the Accademia, in obedience to
the Pope's wishes, and " during that time,"—to quote
Manning's own words after the Pope's death in 1878,—
" he used to admit me with great frequency to speak
with him. Every step I took was taken with his sanction, and to him and to his guidance I owe the chief

---

[1] During later visits to Rome—in all Manning made about five-
and-twenty—he usually resided at the English College, otherwise
known as "the venerable College of St. Thomas *de Urbe.*" Of
this he wrote in 1875 : " Though not an *alumnus*, I am a true,
loyal and old friend. I have from time to time lived within its
walls so long as to amount to years. Every part of it is as familiar
to me as if it had been my home. Its memories and traditions
are sacred to all Catholics."

decisions and acts of my later life. He permitted to me a freedom of speech, and he used towards me an openness, which made the relation in which he allowed me to stand to him intimate and filial in no common measure." Perhaps this was, in spite of painful separations and misunderstandings, the happiest period of Manning's life. Material advantages were doubtless greater while he was at Lavington; and in later years he obtained a full measure of the esteem which in this country at least is not denied to a man who occupies worthily a public position of dignity and influence. But in the former case he was not free from the haunting anxieties of doubt—this may perhaps be recognized in his portrait painted by Richmond in 1844—while in the latter, the responsibilities of his office could not fail to weigh gravely on him. At any rate, a newly-acquired liveliness of manner made some old friends, who remained in the Anglican communion, shake their heads and talk sadly about the "moral deterioration" which they detected in him; the truth being, in his and in similar cases, that the atmosphere of Rome, with its ecclesiastical cocksureness, being precisely the climate for which he was by temperament designed, a sense of security combined with the delight of realizing past dreams in the devotional system of Rome, inexhaustible in its tender sentiment and fascinating in its wealth of historic lore, aroused in him a "joy in believing" which he had not known before; and this brushed away that earlier anxious mode of treatment of things religious, which is indeed a characteristic of Protestant divines, and not an unpleasing one to those who appreciate how truly these things are "past finding out."

About a year after his own reception into the Church,

Manning's brother Charles, with his family of four
children, took the same step—an event which afforded
him the greatest satisfaction ; [1] and a few days after his
return to England, at the end of May, 1852, he himself
"received" Mr. Edward Badeley, Q.C., the ecclesiastical
lawyer, who had pleaded the Bishop of Exeter's cause
before the Privy Council two years before ; and from
this time onwards Manning was exceptionally active in
this particular matter, so that in 1865, when he was
appointed Archbishop, it was said that he had admitted
more converts into the Church than any other priest in
England. He was the guest of James Hope during the
summer of 1852, said mass daily at Farm Street, and
preached almost every Sunday at various churches on
behalf of some charitable object. In the spring of 1853
he first spoke publicly in a church in Rome, opening a
course of instructions in English at S. Andrea delle
Fratte, the church that was at one time famous for a
vision which converted a Jew named Ratisbonne.[2] The
summers of 1853 and of 1854 were also passed in
England, the latter period being marked by a sermon
preached at the Oratory in London on the feast of
St. Philip Neri, and by the important conversion of
Robert Isaac Wilberforce, Archdeacon of the East
Riding. Manning visited him at Burton Agnes, shortly

---

[1] This is another point in which Manning's influence contrasts
with that of Newman, who was never followed into the Catholic
Church by any relation, distant or near.

[2] Another sermon in Rome worth noting was preached January
7th, 1854, on the occasion of the consecration of Abbot Burder, in
the church of St. Gregory on the Cœlian, which was afterwards
Manning's titular church as Cardinal, being selected doubtless
because it was from the monastery connected with it that St.
Augustine of Canterbury and his companions were despatched
for the conversion of England in 596.

before he actually seceded from the Anglican Church,
a circumstance which gave occasion for Bishop Samuel
Wilberforce to write some indignant sentences about his
having gone there "trying to land his prey." But in
point of fact the Archdeacon had made up his mind
some time previously, and was only waiting to complete
the formalities of his resignation. He was certainly
a very distinguished convert, far the ablest of the
Wilberforce brothers, and a theologian whose works
on the Incarnation and the Holy Eucharist are still
read with admiration in the Church of England;
though his later and not less able work on the
" Principles of Church Authority," in which he explains
his submission to the Roman Church, is neglected.
His life as a Catholic was of brief duration, and was
almost tragic in its sudden close. As being un-
married he was free to enter the priesthood, and he
became a student, as Manning had been, at the Accademia. It was practically settled that he was to assist
Manning in the contemplated work in Bayswater, but
dis aliter visum. The mode of life at the Accademia
did not suit him, and in January, 1857, he went out to
Albano, accompanied by Manning, for change of air,
and there died of gastric fever, on Tuesday, February 4th.
He was a deacon, and was to have been ordained priest
in a few weeks.

Meanwhile, during the summers of 1855 and 1856,
Manning's activity never flagged; and, besides the usual
record of his sermons, two of which were preached in
the churches of religious orders in London—the Passionists at Highgate, and the Redemptorists at Clapham—he
was appointed by Cardinal Wiseman diocesan inspector
of schools in August, 1856. In the autumn of this year

it was understood that he was to have charge of a new
mission called " St. Helen's, Westbourne Grove," where
he was to be assisted by Robert Isaac Wilberforce, as
noted above, by C. H. Laprimaudaye, who had once
been his curate-in-charge of the parish of Graffham, and
by his nephews, W. Manning and W. Roberts ; [1] but the
character the community was to take remained as yet
undecided.

Manning's own mind on the subject was, however,
already pretty well made up ; and in December, 1856,
travelling to Rome with his nephew William Manning,
he halted a few days at Milan, and was the guest of the
community there known as the " Oblates of St. Charles."
This society, founded by the famous Archbishop of
Milan in the sixteenth century, is not precisely a religious order, but corresponds very closely with the
institute of the Oratory, being an association of secular
priests who live together in community, voluntarily
submitting to a common rule of life, but taking no vow
of poverty, and being free to quit the society at their
own request. In one important matter, however, it
differs from the Oratory, and it is this characteristic
which doubtless attracted Manning, whose line was
always to co-operate with and to strengthen the Bishop,
as the source of unity and authority within the diocese.
The Oratorians are directly subject, through their
Superior, to the Pope, and are only subject to the Bishop
of the diocese in which they live in having to obtain
faculties, etc., from him ; and this is barely more than a
matter of form. The Oblates of St. Charles, on the
other hand, are, by their constitution, at the beck and

[1] A nephew of Cardinal Wiseman's, named Burke, was also
mentioned.

call of their Bishop, and are thus of the greatest service to him in countries, like England, where priests are comparatively few, and where there is consequently a difficulty in finding men suitable to undertake the spiritual direction of religious communities of women, or men who can at a moment's notice supply vacancies caused by death or ill-health. Manning's visit to Milan satisfied him as to the utility of this institute for the diocese of Westminster; and, shortly after his arrival in Rome a few days before Christmas, he submitted to the Pope a rule modified slightly from that of Milan, which was without hesitation approved. During this visit to Rome Manning stayed at the Minerva Hotel, so as to be near his old friends at the Accademia, and especially Wilberforce, whose death-bed he was to attend. Four days after that event Manning preached in the church of San Carlo in Corso the first of a course of three sermons in English. His subject was that devotion to the Blessed Virgin is a necessary consequence of a real belief in the Incarnation, and "he was listened to for over an hour with breathless attention. The sermon was rather controversial than practical; and closeness of reasoning," the correspondent of the *Tablet* goes on to say, "is not perhaps the most striking feature in Manning's style of eloquence; but there are great difficulties in preaching a Catholic sermon to a Protestant congregation; and the Catholics were comparatively few." The third of this course, on the authority of the Church in the interpretation of Scripture, was reckoned "the most brilliant and effective of the three."

Shortly after Manning's return to England it was announced that the Pope, who had conferred on him

the degree of D.D. at the close of his course of study at
the Accademia in 1854, had appointed him Provost of
Westminster, the patronage falling to him because the
former occupant of the post, Dr. Whitty, had resigned *in
curiâ*, in order to become a Jesuit. This post corresponds
with a Deanery in the Anglican Church, though lacking
the comfortable residence, the ample income and the
otium cum dignitate that are associated with the latter.
At this time began to be noticeable among the more
old-fashioned Catholics, laymen as well as priests, some
alarm and jealousy as to the rapid advancement of the
active convert who was doing so much to infuse a
specially Roman flavour into the hitherto rather sleepy
Catholicism of England. The same men, some of
them, had experienced a similar fear on the establishment of the hierarchy six years previously. They did
not carry their opposition farther than the murmurs of
private conversation; in a sense they were really proud
of the man whom they feared; but it was new in
England to hear so much about the prerogatives of the
Pope and the sanctity of his temporal power; and a
revival of anti-Catholic agitation, perhaps even of persecution, was dreaded. Meanwhile Manning was more
active than ever, often preaching two sermons at
different churches on the same Sunday, and receiving
numerous converts.[1] On the night of Whitsunday,
1857, he took up his residence with his community in
the house of the Oblates of St. Charles at Bayswater,
and the new church was opened on July 2nd.

A mere record of sermons preached is however no

[1] Among converts received in the autumn of 1857 was Henry
Nutcombe Oxenham, curate of St. Thomas', Oxford, who was
destined later to be a thorn in Manning's side.

test of the work done by a Catholic priest, though in Manning's case it is a remarkable record, even in point of numbers, and also means more than an equal number in other cases, which might be a mere repetition of well-worn commonplaces and pious platitudes. The work of a priest in a community, such as that of which Manning was now the Superior, is a daily one, and begins early and often ends late. His morning meditation, followed by mass and thanksgiving, would occupy from an hour to an hour and a half before breakfast. In addition to this, the rapid recitation of the " office " contained in the Breviary occupies at least another hour. Then there is correspondence and the business of the community to attend to, as well as theological study, which, with other reading, would occupy the whole morning; but these duties are sure to be interrupted, and that more than once, either by the confessional bell, or by a summons to see some one in an "instruction-room," who may be an anxious inquirer, a plausible beggar, or a hardened time-waster, probably of the female sex, whose desire to discuss trivialities with Father A. or B. is inexhaustible, and, without some rudeness, irrepressible. The afternoon would be devoted to visiting among the poor, or to giving catechetical instruction in the public schools; after which would follow the special devotions of the community in the private chapel of the house; and an evening, designed like the morning for study, or for the preparation of sermons, would be even more persistently disturbed, and attendance in the confessional might be prolonged, certainly on a Saturday, to a late hour. After this there would probably remain some " office " to recite; and now and again the wearied priest would

have his rest broken **by a summons—never to be neg**-
lected—to convey the last sacraments to some **dying,
or supposed** to be dying, person. Such, with the
additional burden of the duties of Superior, presiding
at the weekly meetings of the community in chapter,
was Manning's daily life in London for the eight
years during which his home was **in Bayswater,**
strenuous and earnest, with the only relaxation **of**
periodical visits to Rome, where he made a prolonged stay in the spring and early summer of 1860.
At this time the Pope showed **him** a fresh mark of
favour—perhaps a special reward for the lectures on
the Temporal Power delivered **at Bayswater in Feb**-
ruary this year—by conferring **on** him the dignities **of**
Protonotary Apostolic and Domestic Prelate to his Holiness.[1] Manning thus became "Monsignor" **or "Right**
Rev.," and acquired the privilege of "pontificating," **or
of** using the insignia of **a Bishop,** on solemn occasions
approved by the diocesan; a luxury in which he in-
dulged once or twice. These titles, however, and ritual
peculiarities were comparatively novelties in England,
and were not altogether acceptable **to the** older generation of priests, over sundry of whom, **as** Provost of the
Canons of Westminster, Manning had at times to preside.
In 1860, moreover, **the temporal power of** the **Pope
was seriously threatened, as indeed it had been many**
times **before;** but it was **new to the British public to**
find that a number of **the Queen's subjects regarded
the** Pope's cause as their **own. The successes of Gari**-
baldi in Sicily and Naples **had given general satisfaction**

---

[1] In March this year the Pope excommunicated, without naming,
the invaders and usurpers of sundry provinces in the Pontifical
States.

in England, as did also, even in a greater degree, the
southern progress of the Piedmontese army; and when
the latter took Spoleto by assault, and the capture
involved the defeat of some three hundred Irish volun-
teers under a Major O'Reilly, it was natural that some
uneasiness and irritation should be felt in England,
which was not allayed when a month later a Requiem,
at which Manning preached, was sung at St. Patrick's,
Soho, "for the souls of the Pope's defenders."

There was nothing specially eventful in Manning's
life as Superior of the Oblates of St. Charles and Provost
of Westminster; but other occasions of some interest
that may be noted are: a discourse before the Accademia
in Rome in April, 1863, his subject being "Rome," at
which he was enthusiastically received;[1] a sermon
preached at the laying of the foundation-stone of the
Dominican Church, Haverstock Hill, in August the
same year, the ceremony being performed by Père A.
V. Jandel, General of the Order; an appeal made at
the English College in Rome, in January, 1864, on
behalf of the proposed new church of St. Thomas of
Canterbury in Rome, for which object he also preached
a sermon at S. Carlo in Corso, which was printed;
another sermon in Rome at Santa Maria in Monte,
in March the same year, on the "Essays and Reviews"
decision; and speeches made as chairman of meetings
at which steps were taken, in the one case to secure

---

[1] There was nevertheless among a section of the Roman pre-
lacy some dislike entertained for Manning, perhaps occasioned by
jealousy of his intimacy with the Pope. By these men he was
nicknamed *Monsignor Ignorante*, partly on account of his not
being a deeply-read theologian, but more because of a certain
unreadiness, which he never got over, to perform his part accurately
in the less ordinary ceremonial of great Church "functions."

better provision in Reformatory schools for Catholic
children, and in the other, to establish on a more
permanent footing the collection of "Peter's Pence" in
England,—both of them objects which lay very near
his heart.[1]

In January, 1865, he was again in Rome, and walked
on February 2nd in the Pope's Candlemas procession
at St. Peter's. On returning to his room he found a
telegram to the effect that Cardinal Wiseman was
dying. He at once set out for London, and was in
time to be present at and console his Archbishop's last
hours—indeed he said mass in his chamber some
mornings before the end came.

In conjunction with Mgr. William Thompson he found
himself appointed Wiseman's literary executor, and the
two took some pains to make it known that other
memoirs and biographical sketches of the late Cardinal
that had been advertised would not be authentic, as the
documents necessary for an adequate biography were in
their possession. They also invited the assistance of the
late Cardinal's friends and correspondents in furnishing

[1] An anecdote told of Manning at this period of his life is
perhaps worth recording. He had been commissioned by Cardinal
Wiseman to enquire into the truth of certain serious allegations
made against a priest of the diocese. Arrived at the house, he
was shown into the parlour; and in a few minutes the priest
appeared with a stole in his hand which he gave to Manning,
saying, "Please, father, hear my confession"; and in a moment
he was on his knees beginning it. "Not yet," said Manning,
perceiving the trick and rising. When he had completed the
enquiry, and had read over to the priest the notes of the evidence
he had taken, he expressed his willingness to hear him; but the
other's zeal had by this time evaporated. Of course a confession
of his delinquency, made *in foro conscientiæ*, would have prevented
Manning from using the knowledge thus obtained, and so his
mission would have failed. It is said that the priest had foiled a
previous enquiry by this ingenious *ruse*.

them with copies of his letters or other writings, and in giving information as to marked events in his life. But nothing came of the project. All that the literary executors actually published was an incomplete lecture on Shakespeare. Perhaps it was inevitable that the career of a great ecclesiastic, like that of a great statesman, should not be related with full detail until his own generation has passed away.

The jubilee, or twenty-fifth anniversary of Wiseman's consecration as Bishop, was to have been celebrated on June 8th, 1865; but the day was destined to witness the consecration of his successor. A set of gold altar-plate was being made in Rome to be presented to him on the occasion; but at a meeting at the Stafford Club a month after his death it was agreed that, the testimonial now having become a memorial, the form the latter should take should be a Cathedral church and establishment for the diocese of Westminster. At a subsequent meeting Manning expressed his approval of the scheme and subscribed £1,000 towards it. But in his speech he showed clearly that he would have preferred it to have taken another form, and that, while he would encourage the building of the Cathedral, he would not let another and a more important matter be forgotten. "My first thought," he said, "was that we could not give the late Cardinal a more beautiful memorial than some institution for the benefit of the 20,000 poor neglected Catholic children of London. But afterwards it seemed to me that this work of building a Cathedral might be done straightway, while the virtues of the Cardinal are fresh in our minds. So I will go in heartily for this work; but I will also keep the case of these 20,000 children before my mind."

The event showed that he thought more highly of the less pretentious memorial. The sum of £16,000 was however subscribed in the room, and arrangements were made for the collection of subscriptions on the Continent and in America. But the story of the slow progress of the Westminster Cathedral scheme belongs to a later period.

Nothing authoritative was ever published explaining the circumstances under which Manning was selected to succeed Wiseman, nor indeed would any such statement have been regular. But it was generally understood that the Chapter of Westminster, of which Canon O'Neale had been elected Vicar-Capitular during the vacancy, submitted to the Pope three names as *dignus*, *dignior* and *dignissimus*, and that Manning's name was not among the three, and that none of the three was approved. But it was explained later, in excuse of what would otherwise have seemed the arbitrary conduct of the Pope, that Dr. Grant, of Southwark, and Dr. Clifford, of Clifton, had both sent to Rome a decided expression of their unwillingness to accept the post, and that the Pope, being thus left with only one name, that of Dr. Errington, was deprived of his customary power of selection, and so put them all aside. However that may be, it may be taken as certain that the Pope would have insisted on the appointment of Manning. Grant was a saintly man, undoubtedly, but he had little or no knowledge of affairs; Clifford was well connected with the Catholic aristocracy, and was accounted a learned man, but he was not an ardent Papist—using the term as equivalent to the popular sense of the ambiguous "Ultramontane." And, as to Errington, strong man as he certainly was in some directions, it is not easy to see

how the Canons could have recommended him without
some impertinence. He had been Bishop of Plymouth,
1851—1855, and it is true he was created titular
Archbishop of Trebizond on resigning his see in the
year last named, in order to become coadjutor to
Cardinal Wiseman, *cum jure successionis*. But in 1862,
the Pope, either because he misliked Errington's influence over Wiseman, or because he had already resolved
on Manning's advancement, "relieved" him of this
appointment, on Errington's refusal to resign, and he
remained in retirement until September, 1865, when he
took charge for a time of the Catholic missions in the
Isle of Man, and later lived in seclusion at Prior Park.
Of the wisdom of Manning's appointment there could,
from the Pope's point of view, be no sort of doubt; or,
if there had been any, it was dispelled by the contemptuous language with which the *Times* greeted the
announcement:—"The Pope has seldom given a clearer
proof of his fallibility. . . A Clifford would be welcomed
by thoroughbred Catholics as a legitimate and heredi-
tary ruler; a Manning is no more than an aspiring
refugee from a hostile camp." Doubtless, in days when
the distinction between "old Catholics" and "converts"
was much more marked in England than it has been
now for many years past, there was among the former
some disappointment in not having an Archbishop
chosen from their own body; but their sentiments were
much exaggerated in the language of one or two self-
constituted spokesmen, personally hostile to Manning;
and, whatever discontent there may have been, it was
lost in the general chorus of approval. The *Tablet*
welcomed the new Archbishop with dignified reserve:

"The Metropolitan see of Westminster is no longer

vacant. . . The nomination was made **by the Holy Father** on April 30th, after many prayers had been said, and many **masses** offered up, **to obtain the Divine** assistance in the momentous choice. . . . We are sufficiently familiar with the Catholic press to be aware that the appointment of a new Bishop is generally considered as affording a Catholic editor an opportunity of reassuring the Holy See by a decided expression **of** editorial approbation, and of comforting the flock by the announcement, upon editorial authority, that a **better choice** could not possibly have been made. But **we** have never attained to this sublime view **of our** editorial mission, **and have** always held to the old Catholic and Conservative doctrine, that **when a ruler or a** superior is appointed by a competent authority, he is to be accepted and reverenced within the sphere of his commission as one whose claims are founded on **a** right divine. It happens, indeed, that the new Archbishop is known as a holy priest, zealous and devout, endowed with more than ordinary power both to **convince** the reason **and to move the** will of men. And it is right that Protestants as well as Catholics should appreciate and recognize these qualifications. But for **us** Catholics, who believe that the prayers of the successor of St. Peter, and of the faithful, are powerful to obtain light and inspiration for the government of the Church and the **appointment of its rulers, the highest** recommendation to our allegiance that a canonically instituted Bishop can bring is that he is an Apostle who comes because he **has been sent to us by** God. **And our Protestant** readers must not be surprised if the appointment of a Catholic Archbishop is not deemed by a Catholic layman **a** fit occasion for offering to the new dignitary such complimentary congratulations, and such flattering testimonies, as a newly-made Minister or Chancellor properly expects and receives from his colleagues at the Bar or in Parliament. Such language would ill accord with the circumstances or with the spirit in which the new Archbishop undertakes the heavy burden laid upon him, and enters on the thorny path which he is called to tread. Truly an arduous task, a difficult situation, in trying times! The burden of the first Archbishop of Westminster was not light; that of his successor will be heavier still."

The *Tablet's* correspondent wrote from Rome in a more enthusiastic strain :—" *Habemus Pontificem !* All who feel with and for the Church are rejoiced beyond measure at the decision. On merely human grounds there is everything to assure us that we shall have a great and holy priest to rule over us, and one who can grapple, as few men could, with the great evils of the time: who may live to see and act in a period when the Church will stand face to face in England with infidelity rather than heresy, and whose familiarity with every phase of uncatholic intellect and teaching, from his long and earnest struggle against rationalism in the Anglican Church, gives him an advantage in dealing with it we might look in vain for elsewhere." And, a few days later :—" The feeling of satisfaction at his appointment, in France and among all Continental Catholics, is as great as that of the great majority of Englishmen. Even the *Italie* approves the choice, and cannot find an exception to take to the Pope's line of action in this case."

Manning was consecrated at St. Mary's, Moorfields, at that time the Pro-cathedral and the most spacious church in London, by William Bernard Ullathorne, O. S. B., Bishop of Birmingham, on June 8th, 1865, the day on which Wiseman was to have received congratulations on his episcopal jubilee. Newman was present on the occasion, an interested but not altogether a sympathetic spectator ; for, though the recent publication of his *Apologia* had gone far to set him right in the general opinion of the country, and had evoked numerous addresses expressing admiration and confidence from Catholics almost everywhere—including one from the priests of the diocese of Westminster—the divergence in sentiment between him and Manning had been growing for some four or five years, and was to grow wider still.

In September Manning left for Rome, and received the *pallium* from the Pope on Michaelmas Day. Returning to London he was enthroned at Moorfields on Nov. 6th. Replying to an address from the clergy on the occasion he said :—" We are not strangers to each other. In these last fourteen years and more it has been my happiness to live and labour among you. There is not a mission in London in which your invitation has not given me, year after year, a share in your work. There is hardly a mission in the diocese the details of which I have not learned from yourselves." Seldom has a Bishop begun to rule a diocese more fully equipped already with knowledge of its wants, or with a mind more fully made up as to his own duties in regard to them.

CHAPTER V.

ARCHBISHOP OF WESTMINSTER.

THE versatile Hebrew who at one time controlled the destinies of the British Empire, and for whom Catholicism had much of the attractiveness that it had for Thackeray, made in *Lothair* something of a portrait of Archbishop Manning under the title of " Cardinal Grandison." But he drew a far more real likeness of him in the " Nigel Penruddock " of the later chapters of *Endymion* :—

" Nigel Penruddock had obtained great celebrity as a preacher, while his extreme doctrines and practices had alike amazed, fascinated and alarmed a large portion of the public. For some time he had withdrawn from the popular gaze; but his individuality was too strong to be easily forgotten, even if occasional paragraphs as to his views and conduct were not sufficient to sustain and even stimulate curiosity. . . . He was changed. Instead of that anxious and moody look which formerly marred the refined beauty of his countenance, his glance was calm and yet radiant. He was thinner, it might almost be said emaciated, which seemed to add height to his tall figure. . . . Instead of avoiding society, as was his wont in old days, the Archbishop sought it. And there was nothing exclusive in his social habits; all classes and all creeds, all conditions and orders of men, were alike interesting to him; they were part of the mighty community with all whose pursuits and passions and interests and occupations he seemed to sympathize, but respecting which he had only one object—to bring them back once more to that imperial fold from which in an hour of darkness and distraction they had miserably wandered. . . . So the Archbishop was seen everywhere, even at fashionable assemblies. He was a frequent guest at banquets which he never tasted, for he was a smiling ascetic; and, though he seemed to be preaching or celebrating high mass in every part of the metropolis, organizing schools, establishing convents and building cathedrals, he could find time to move philanthropic resolutions at middle-class meetings, attend learned associations, and even occasionally send a paper to the Royal Society."

Apart from a certain tawdriness, characteristic of all Lord Beaconsfield's conceptions of the Church and of society, the above may be taken as a very fair account of what Manning was during the first twenty years of his career as Archbishop, so far at least as that career could be watched by the outside world.[1] But the real

---

[1] As to the title "Archbishop of Westminster," which was, strictly speaking, illegal until the repeal of the Ecclesiastical Titles Act in 1871, it may be worth noting that Manning, in July, 1867, gave evidence before a Parliamentary Committee as to the inconveniences resulting from the Act, and that in February, 1870, while absent in Rome for the Council, he was prosecuted by a Mr. W. Cobbett for using the title. Judgment however was given against the plaintiff, as he had not obtained the consent of the Attorney-General, which was a necessary preliminary, in accordance with the terms of the Act.

arduousness of his task was not so easily gauged. His
predecessor, Cardinal Wiseman, had held the reins
loosely. The Catholic clergy in this country some
thirty or more years ago were, speaking generally, able
men, many of whom, having been educated on the
Continent, had a somewhat wider horizon than their
successors of to-day. But they had much less of the
ecclesiastical spirit.[1] The traditions of an earlier day
had not yet completely died out, when a priest was
reckoned an alien in the land, was usually dressed as a
layman, and consoled his solitary evenings with a glass
or two of whiskey, or with a rubber of whist at the house
of perhaps the only educated member of his flock.
Moreover, the priests educated in France had decided
Gallican leanings; and, if they had suspected Wiseman
of Ultramontanism, what were they to think of the very
advanced views of his successor?

Manning's ideas of Church government had something of the military element about them. A priest
should be prepared to move at the bidding of his
superior and with brief notice from one end of the
diocese to the other. Under the constitution established in England with the Diocesan Hierarchy in 1850,
only the Bishops are permanently settled as parish
priests; the others, not excluding the more dignified
"missionary rectors," are removable *ad nutum episcopi*.
Wiseman had availed himself of this power but

[1] So late as the early years of this century the four Catholic
bishops there were then in England would meet in lay attire at
some out-of-the-way country inn, and there discuss and decide
details of Church government over churchwarden pipes and a pot
of beer,—adjuncts of a secret meeting of Catholics that were
regularly provided in the back parlour when mass was to be said,
so as to conceal the real cause of the assembly.

sparingly. In his amiable desire to give as little trouble as possible, it was only under external pressure that he would order a priest to quit his post and to begin a new work elsewhere. Manning, on the other hand, believed in the bracing effects of a change of air; and when a priest was congratulating himself on the work he had accomplished and the popularity he had achieved, say in Kensington, he would find himself one morning under orders to begin a new and difficult work in the east of London. Naturally, although obedience is the first rule of a Catholic priest, this system did not always work without friction; and there were from time to time rumours of covert resistance to the new Archbishop's rule; indeed in one case it was said that an elderly priest flatly refused to quit the presbytery in which he had made his comfortable nest; and, after remaining in it for some years contumacious and excommunicate, died there, penitent and submissive only at the last moment, the work of reconciliation having been effected by the Archbishop himself, who more than once came to plead with his rebellious subject.

Another difficulty that the new Archbishop had to contend with was the persistent hostility of the press. There had of course been a tremendous outburst against Wiseman in 1850-51, but it died away in no long time; and it became rather the fashion to speak kindly of the benevolent old gentleman who seemed so anxious to disarm prejudice, and who really was never so happy as when lecturing to a young men's institute on botany or some other branch of science that did not in those days conflict at any rate markedly with theology. But Manning had espoused with his whole heart two causes which were the objects of the British public's implacable

hostility,—the Temporal Power and the Pope's infallibility; and, as he was instant in season and out of
season in writing, lecturing and preaching on the former,
which was menaced and in effect destroyed during the
first five or six years of his episcopate, he supplied
ample materials for the pens of reporters, sometimes
hostile but more often ill-informed on the subject, and
through them for able editors, who showed up the
dangerous tendencies of the Archbishop's Ultramontanism with untiring zeal. Perhaps the only exception
in the London secular press was to be found in the
Spectator, which treated both these burning questions
with fairness, respect and intelligence.

There was however another aspect of the Archbishop's work, to which he devoted himself with no less
intensity than to the upholding of Papal privileges,—
the work of reclaiming and retaining within the Church
the children of the Catholic poor; and for this he could
not fail to win admiration from all to whom it became
known; though its full extent is hardly known even yet.
Manning was not blind to the importance of winning
wealthy and aristocratic converts to Catholicism; he
had indeed special aptitude for such an undertaking;
but his experience as a priest at Bayswater had taught
him that, while eloquent Monsignori might compass sea
and land to make one such proselyte, a dozen or more
poor children would be lost to the Church through the
indifference or poverty of their parents, and especially by
their transference to workhouse or other public schools
in which Protestantism alone was taught. He had
proposed, before his consecration to the episcopate,
that provision for these children, whose number he
estimated at 20,000, should be the form taken by the

Wiseman memorial; and, although he was at the time over-ruled in favour of a worthy cathedral for Westminster, he never worked for the latter scheme with one quarter of the zeal that he worked for the former, in advocacy of which he addressed public meetings and preached, not only in London, but throughout England, at all the great centres of population, with the result that—to take his own diocese only—there were in the year 1890 (by which time his activity in this direction had of necessity succumbed to the infirmities of age), exclusive of the public elementary schools which will be referred to later, some fifteen Reformatory, Industrial and Poor-Law schools, certified by Government, mostly in the outskirts of London, in addition to about an equal number of Homes and Orphanages, not under public inspection. The mere statement of the fact, however, is insufficient to convey any impression of the long and arduous struggle that was necessary before these results could be obtained.[1] The main outcome of his exertions was that the children of any Catholic family in the diocese of Westminster,

---

[1] The main difficulty lay in the unwillingness of Boards of Guardians—composed often enough of ignorant and prejudiced men—to make the legal transfer of Catholic children. An argument that carried weight was the saving of expense. It was pointed out that in consequence of the economical management of the Catholic institutions, the Richmond Board of Guardians saved eleven shillings per week on every child transferred. Oddly enough, the last Board to be convinced was that of St. George's, Hanover Square, which was only persuaded to act after the Cardinal, in a Pastoral issued in the spring of 1886, had expressed himself thus:—"The Guardians of St. George's continue their stubborn refusal to transfer our poor children to schools of their own religion. This Board is the richest and represents the highest and most educated parish in London. It now stands alone in the metropolitan district for this unjust and ignoble oppression of the poor."

driven to the workhouse by poverty, were sure of receiving board and education (such as it is in Poor-Law schools) in a distinctively Catholic establishment.[1]

Manning also worked hard and successfully to obtain the privileges of their religion for Catholic prisoners. The Prison Ministers Act of 1863 empowered the authorities to appoint and pay a Catholic chaplain where his services were required; but, speaking at the Birmingham Catholic Reunion in Jan. 1867, Manning pointed out that, out of thirty-five prisons to which the Act was applicable, in at least twenty-five it had not yet been carried into effect. There was no denying the justice of his criticism, nor the moderation with which he made it; and in due time there was little or no cause left for complaint.

Work of this kind was infinitely more to his taste than the collection of funds for a Westminster Cathedral; though this object was not altogether neglected. In 1867 he laid the foundation-stone of a church in Kensington, which has been subsequently known as the "Pro-Cathedral"; but he referred at the time to the larger scheme "for which he had neither money nor land." A year later it was announced that a site of three acres in extent for the Cathedral and the Archbishop's residence had been secured in Westminster, at a cost of £36,500, and that Mr. Clutton (Manning's nephew) and Mr. Gilbert Blount were to be the architects of the two buildings respectively. The necessity

---

[1] In October, 1883, the *Tablet* pointed out that the number of children in industrial and reformatory schools, and cared for as Catholics, had risen from 400 in 1866 to 2700 in 1883; while the number of Catholic children in parochial schools had risen from 11,342 to 24,423 in the same period.

for using a part of the site **for a residence was obviated**
when, in June, 1872, **by** a real **slice of good luck,**
Manning was able to purchase, at a reasonable price,
and without trenching **on** the funds that had been
accumulating meanwhile for the Cathedral, a building
erected six years previously and known as the "Guards'
Institute." This afforded all the accommodation required, and it was not without a certain appropriate
dignity. The Archbishop resided there from March,
1873, during, therefore, the whole of the period when
he was so much before the public eye; and the building **will** thus be always associated with his name and
his striking personality. As to the Cathedral, plans of a
building of a foreign Gothic type were exhibited at the
Archbishop's annual reception in May, 1873, and since
that date adorned, **if** they did adorn, the walls **of his
room.** But in 1874, at a meeting of the Westminster
Diocesan Education Fund, he formally disclaimed any
intention to go further with the work :—" I remember
the very first act I had to do, after the burden I bear
was laid upon me—and even before I had received
consecration to enable me to bear it—was to preside
over a public meeting in order to declare that the work
which a number of the friends of my lamented and
great predecessor had determined to accomplish—I
mean **the** building of a Cathedral to his memory—was
a work that I would take up, and would, to the utmost
of my power, promote. But in saying so I said at
once, ' When the work of the poor children in London
is accomplished, and **not** till then. I will never **pile**
stone upon stone until souls have been built up in the
spiritual Church, which is the true Cathedral of Westminster.' The Jews have a wise proverb, full of

charity:—'Even the building of the Temple must be suspended that the children may be taught.' I have acted in that spirit. I passed my word that I would do my utmost for the building of that Cathedral. I have done my work, and I have laid my first stone; that is, by the kind and generous help of friends, who nobly and with great self-denial assisted me, I have been able to buy the land, and to render the building of the Cathedral possible. . . . I shall be content to leave the happiness of laying the first stone to my successor, if I can see the work of the poor children of London accomplished." Nevertheless in 1884 the original site was disposed of in part payment for a much finer one, which cost £55,000, and has since remained for the most part a desolate and unprofitable wilderness. It must not be supposed, however, that Manning was indifferent to the need of building churches. He expressed himself indeed as rather in favour of more numerous buildings of a somewhat temporary character, each served by two or three priests, in preference to a single monumental structure in a conspicuous site, such as might impress on all men the growth and vitality of Catholicism in London— there is none such in the most central and most frequented thoroughfares; but a number of spacious and dignified churches were erected under his rule; while others, due mainly to the energy of religious communities, such as the new church of the Oratory at Brompton, that of the Dominicans at Haverstock Hill, and that of the Passionists at Highgate, are also to some extent commemorative of the enthusiasm which he did so much to inspire and to direct.

A work that he had much at heart was the erection and endowment of an adequate Diocesan Seminary, such as should enable him to carry out the decrees of the Council of Trent on the training of the clergy. In April, 1869, it was announced that an old convent of Benedictine nuns at Hammersmith was to be transformed into a seminary, so that the *alumni* might be within easy distance of the new church at Kensington, which was to serve as Pro-Cathedral, instead of being trained at St. Edmund's College, Ware, and other places. Seven years later this building proved insufficient, and the Archbishop appealed for funds to enable him to build a new one. "It is a primary duty to provide for the rising priesthood of the diocese a seminary in which they may learn the simplicity and even the hardness of a priest's life, without exposing themselves to needless privations. Too much comfort unfits a youth for a priest's life, and too little discourages those who as yet have not the support of the pastoral care, which makes all things tolerable. . . The care of the seminary ought to take precedence of all other works; for a well-formed priesthood will multiply everything, churches, convents, schools. . . This then is the next work, which, after ten years of experience and careful thought, I am convinced is the most urgently needed for the future welfare of the diocese. It is also the last work to which I can hope to lay my hand. If I can leave this behind me, I shall feel that the work of my life is done." And in a sermon in which he pressed this appeal, he added, "I feel confident that my people, my flock, will not fail me in this last effort. We have done many works together hitherto. I may say that not one appeal I have ever made has fallen to the ground. I no sooner made known the need of the diocese than some three or four persons immediately put into my hands an

I

amount which warranted my going on. I do not call upon my poor to help me in this. They have enough to do with the education of their children." The amount required was estimated at £15,000, and of this sum £10,000 was raised in a month. The first stone of St. Thomas' Seminary was therefore laid on the feast of the Translation of St. Thomas of Canterbury, July 7th, this same year (1876). Five years later it was stated that £32,000 had been spent on the work, but that a chapel was still required, for which an appeal was made. In 1884 it was announced that the whole had been completed at a cost of near upon £38,000. These figures are an apt illustration (one among many) of the generosity of Catholics in supporting their religion, a generosity that is all the more striking when it is remembered that Catholicism in England possesses little or nothing in the way of endowments, and that the great majority of its adherents are poor. In a sermon preached at Moorfields in April, 1873, Manning expressed himself as not dissatisfied with this poverty of the Church. "It is," he said, "a great security for its energy and its purity; and I rejoice that in England, the richest of all nations, the Catholic Church is poor. Without the establishment which might prove a bondage, and without the endowment which might prove a burden, the Church is doing her work vigorously, and the faith is becoming more widespread than ever."[1]

[1] An interesting illustration of the zeal of English Catholics in maintaining the dignity of their hierarchy, and of the economics of a Church that is bound to maintain that dignity without the advantages of establishment and endowment, is to be found in the presentation of the sum of £6,500 to Manning from the English Catholic laity on his elevation to the Cardinalate, and in

The Archbishop was bound to do what in him lay,
not merely for the training of the clergy of his diocese,
but for the higher education of the lay Catholics of

---

the following reply which he made to the Duke of Norfolk in
acknowledgment:—"My dear Lord Duke, I do not know in what
way I can better convey my thanks . . . than by way of a private
letter. The private and delicate way in which this valuable and, as
I will show, timely expression of your kindness has been conceived
and made, seems to prescribe to me the same way of thanking
you. And first, I thank you that what you have so kindly done
has been done, not by public appeal, but by a private letter.
Any publicity would have caused me no little pain. Some two
or three years ago, in a circular letter, I told you that I have no
shame in begging for the spiritual need of the diocese, or for the
Cathedral, but that I could not beg for anything which seemed to
confer a personal benefit on myself. I hope there was no pride
in this ; if there be, I hope it may be forgiven. But in the work
of true friendship which you have now fulfilled towards me, I
say at once that anything beyond a private communication, elicit-
ing with equal privacy an unconstrained spontaneous offering of
free will, would have caused me great regret. Knowing that
when others have been called to the office I now bear, their flocks
and friends have united to relieve them of the very heavy charges
which were thereby imposed on them, I did not doubt but that
I also might be relieved of those first and sudden expenses. But
it did not enter into my thoughts that you would extend your
considerate care to the increased charges to which I may be
exposed. This your kind and generous foresight has done ; but
I do not think that any of you were fully aware of the importance
of the service you were rendering to me and to the Metropolitan
see of Westminster. Your delicate kindness justifies me in saying
what has hitherto been known to very few.
  "The old London Vicariate possessed a Mensal Fund sufficient
for the needs of the Bishop. On the erection of the Archbishopric
of Westminster many new and heavy charges were thrown upon
my predecessor. For these, his private means, and the annual
provision attaching to him as Cardinal, with the Mensal Fund,
sufficed. When I was called upon to fill his place the provision
as Cardinal ceased ; the Mensal Fund was divided with the diocese
of Southwark ; the charges, public and private, upon the Archbishop remained undivided ; and, if I had not possessed a very
narrow income of my own, the Mensal Fund would not have
sufficed by some hundreds every year. With the little I possessed,
the see has never failed, year by year, to meet its expenses. But

England; and in this matter it must be confessed that
he achieved no success. Such results as he obtained
did no more than negative certain evils which in his
judgment were greater than the absence of any University education at all. This was the question on
which he and Newman differed markedly, and differed
to the end. After his withdrawal from the Catholic
University of Ireland, Newman established at Edgbaston
a boys' school for the upper classes. When it had run
its course a few years he began to cast about for some
provision for the subsequent University training of such
of his pupils as might be fitted for it. Of foreign
Catholic Universities, such as that of Louvain, he knew
but little and cared but little for what he knew, while
towards the Irish University he had left he still felt
some soreness. But there was his own beloved Oxford,
at which, thanks to the removal of tests, Catholics could
now matriculate and obtain at any rate a bachelor's
degree. Why should he not establish a branch of the
Oratory in Oxford, reside there himself, and keep his

---

without my private means—and they have yearly become less in
the work of the diocese, to which they will be altogether left—
the income of the see would not have sufficed. Your generous
kindness has, for the first time in the ten years I have held the
see, placed it in a condition to meet its inevitable annual costs.
My successor will be in some measure where my predecessor
was. The see will once more possess a Mensal Fund equal to the
charges from which the Archbishop cannot in any way exempt
himself. The public and permanent benefit rendered to the
diocese will, I hope, add to the satisfaction which I know you
feel, in doing me this private and personal act of friendship.

"Of what you have so generously brought to me, so much as will
defray the present and future costs of receiving the office laid
upon me will be set aside. The rest will be invested as a permanent endowment of the Metropolitan see of Westminster, and
as a record, which will remain in the archives, of your generous
kindness to myself."

boys from Edgbaston still under his own eye as undergraduates? Accordingly, early in 1867, a plot of land
in Oxford, the site of the old workhouse, near Worcester
College, was purchased, a circular was issued by Newman announcing the project, and a number of Catholic
noblemen and gentlemen made to this circular a joint
and formal reply, indicative of approval and support.
But the great Oratorian had reckoned without his Archbishop. Although he was never himself in any intelligible sense a " Liberal Catholic," he and his community
had acquired some such reputation, and fears were entertained whether he might not be gathering round him
the nucleus of a school of minimizing Catholics, such as
has from time to time arisen in France and elsewhere.
And thus, while Newman himself repudiated any idea
of establishing a Catholic College in Oxford, he found,
to his dismay and indignation, that even the founding
of a branch house of the Oratory at Oxford would only
be approved at Rome on the condition of his not residing
there. He had met Manning face to face two years
before this, on the occasion of the latter's consecration;
he was not willing so to meet him again until he could
do so as a brother Cardinal some fourteen years later.
But, though his own pet project was thus foiled, he
throughout declined to co-operate with Manning and the
other English bishops in discouraging the matriculation
of Catholic youths at Oxford. Many of his own pupils
went there from time to time; and, as lately as 1884, he
made use of a visit of a Catholic graduate to Rome, to
attempt to obtain from the Pope the permission which
he had before assumed. But again the Archbishop prevailed; and in Feb., 1885, he received from the Cardinal
Prefect of Propaganda a letter declaring that the mind

of the Holy See was unchanged on this matter since
the instructions given to the Bishops in 1867; and in
the following May he issued a Pastoral[1] dealing with the

[1] "The Office of the Church in the Higher Education of
Catholics," a Pastoral Letter, 1885. Cardinal Wiseman's name
having been mentioned as of one who had taken a more liberal
view on this Oxford question, Manning referred to him as follows :—"There was no one who ever manifested so large and
generous a sympathy with the conversions that issued from
Oxford. . . His learned and powerful writings in defence of the
Catholic faith were studiously directed, both in matter and in
manner, without sacrifice of jot or tittle of the truth, to attract
and conciliate the members of the Anglican communion and the
writers of the Oxford movement. His zeal for their conversion
and his joy at their coming was so generous and so great as to be
turned to his reproach. It was the dream of his life to break
down the wall of separation between Catholics and those that are
without, and to throw open wide the gates of the heavenly city,
that all might enter. If ever therefore there was any one who,
if it had been possible to sanction it, would have rejoiced over an
association of prayer for the reunion of Christendom, and the
return of Catholic youth to the Universities which Catholic
England had erected, it would have been our late Cardinal. But
two things forbade him in any way to accept these invitations :
his unerring Catholic instinct, and his keen intuition of the im-
possibility of combining fidelity to the divine tradition of the
faith with the intellectual deviations and contradictions of modern
England. His decision therefore on both these questions was
prompt and final. I shall not, I hope, appear to make any undue
claims for myself if I say that, in pursuing the same course,
under the guidance of his memory, I have had to resist even more
powerful influences, which he could never know, as well as solicit-
ations and affectionate memories, in which he could have no part.
If therefore in these two questions it were lawful to follow the
promptings of old affection, I should be among the first to do so ;
but the highest authority upon earth confirms the unchanging
conviction of my reason and of my faith." A further reason for
not allowing Catholics to matriculate at Oxford and Cambridge
was the injury that would probably be incurred by the Catholic
colleges at Ushaw and Stonyhurst. It may be worth adding
that, although Manning's explicit statement must be taken as
decisive, there certainly has been widely prevalent among Catholics an impression that Wiseman had anticipated a college or a
hall at Oxford being specially set apart for Catholics, and that he
was prepared to welcome such a proposal.

whole question at length, a document which should be read by those who would know his mind on the subject. Of course he was not ignorant of the many advantages, social and intellectual, that Catholic young men would secure by residence at Oxford, and perhaps by passing through the University course of studies. He himself hardly loved Oxford less than Newman, though, as he once expressed it, "the love that is above all other love made me an outcast among my mother's children." But, as a Catholic first, he would be no party to a possible weakening of the faith of any single Catholic youth, such as might result from following a course of study in history, philosophy or science laid down and taught by men who themselves did not hold the faith. Catholic control of Catholic education is a not unintelligible principle; and fidelity to it induced Manning to sympathize, though he had no occasion actively to co-operate, with the hostility of the Irish Catholic Hierarchy to Mr. Gladstone's Irish University Bill of 1873.

This purely destructive action was not accompanied by anything constructive that achieved success. At one time Manning had hoped to obtain for St. Mary's College, Oscott, an University charter, with power to confer degrees; but the most ambitious scheme, approved by the Fourth Provincial Synod of Westminster, was to raise £25,000 to found a "College of Higher Studies" at Kensington, which, if successful, would ultimately, it was hoped, be recognized as a Catholic University. It was opened in October, 1874, with seventeen students, and with Monsignor Capel as Rector. But debt, mismanagement and misfortunes encumbered and soon ruined the institution, which was formally closed in 1878. Its Rector, who had been much before the public as a popular preacher and writer, and, as the successful proselytizer of Lord Bute, had obtained such renown that he figured, under a thinly-disguised name, in one of Lord Beaconsfield's novels, resigned at the unanimous request of the Bishops, and disquieting rumours were afloat about him. Some grave charge, it was said, had been brought against him, a charge which, it was also said, he traced to a violation of the seal of the confessional. He appealed to Rome, and laid his case before the Cardinals individually, and there were rumours again that he was to have been reinstated with all his privileges in the diocese of Westminster, had not the Archbishop declared that in that case he would resign his see. Whatever may have been the truth in this matter— and the truth will never be known, for the Catholic Church is successful beyond everything in hushing up scandals—the Kensington scheme was certainly a disastrous failure, and, as such, holds an exceptional place among Manning's many undertakings.

A difficulty which cropped up from time to time during the first fifteen years of Manning's episcopate was the relation between the ordinary jurisdiction of the Bishops and the special privileges of the Religious Orders. It is a difficulty that has existed throughout Christendom from mediæval times, and that may be expected to last as long as the Church does. It is from time to time especially acute in the case of the Jesuits, a numerous and united body, of higher average ability than the clergy at large, and marked by a very decided *esprit de corps.* And undoubtedly there is among the Jesuits a disposition to disparage the ordinary government of the Church by Bishops, as being an old-fashioned arrangement, ill-suited to modern requirements. Bishops themselves are of course treated with the utmost respect, as being very necessary to discharge certain functions, and especially to continue the succession; but for purposes of administration a more elastic method than the diocesan and parochial is thought to be better fitted for the present day. This being so, a Bishop who does not, as some do, resolve to exclude the Jesuits from his diocese, finds himself under the necessity of binding them to regard a certain district as alone under their jurisdiction, else he may find his own parochial clergy complaining that the very means by which to live are taken from them through the superior attractiveness of "the Society." This is the whole explanation of the feud that was occasionally hinted at as existing between the Archbishop and the Jesuits. True, he felt the difficulty rather keenly, and regarded as something like a traitor to his own authority any priest who from being a secular became a son of St. Ignatius Loyola; and it was remarked that two of his own clergy who took this step were never afterwards permitted to preach in the Westminster diocese;[1] but beyond this the difference did not go.[2] And what is true of the Jesuits is true, *mutatis mutandis*, of the other Religious Orders. The difficulties that arose from time to time between the Bishops and the Regulars had nothing whatever to do with the peculiar privileges of the various Orders in regard to their own internal affairs; they were due to

[1] One of these was his own nephew, Father Anderdon.
[2] He has been heard too to express the opinion that the Jesuit missions to England in the sixteenth and seventeenth centuries did as much harm as good to the cause of the restoration of Catholicism in England; and the zeal with which he took up the beatification of sundry secular priests was not uninfluenced by some jealousy of the corresponding work which the Jesuits had undertaken in honour of their own English martyrs.

certain doubts about jurisdiction in connection with the
"cure of souls." A Constitution to meet these difficulties had been issued by Benedict XIV. in 1753 ; but
there had been no subsequent legislation, and the regu-
lation in question was ill-adapted to the new state of
affairs. In the years 1879 and 1880 Manning was
often referred to in the secular press as meditating
some arbitrary suppression of the rights of the Religious
Orders. In point of fact, not he alone but all the
English Bishops had appealed to Rome for guidance in
the matter, and a Commission of Cardinals had been
appointed to investigate and advise upon it. The
results of their deliberations were embodied in a Bull,
Romanos Pontifices, dated May 8th, 1881, which, for a
time at any rate, has set the vexed question at rest.
Doubtless Manning, as an apt ecclesiastical legislator
and administrator, pressed the matter for settlement,
and obtained pretty much the solution that he desired ;
but to treat the matter as if there were ill-will on his
side, or a danger of a schism on the other, is altogether
to mistake the issue.

Manning's political opinions will be referred to later
on ; but it may here conveniently be noted that, as
Archbishop, he was very jealous of politics masquerad-
ing as religion, and that he consistently treated the
former as subordinate to the latter. In 1888 he forbade
the celebration at the Church of the Carmelites in
Kensington of a solemn mass of requiem on occasion of
the centenary of the death of the Pretender, Prince
Charles Edward ; and within a few months of his death
he prohibited Catholics from joining, under pain of
excommunication, an association that had been started
by some feather-brained young men for the restoration

of the **Stuart** dynasty. In **1878** he had hesitated to allow **a** similar celebration on **the death of Victor** Emmanuel, and only permitted it when **he had learned** from the promoters that the occasion would not be used as a demonstration hostile to the temporal power of the Pope. On the other hand, when the Prince Imperial of France came to an untimely end, Manning, treating the event as a specially severe domestic bereavement, took himself an active part in the religious celebrations that **were** arranged ; and was severely rated by Mr. C. Kegan **Paul** for the sermon that he preached on the occasion.[1]

[1] " The language in which he allowed himself to speak of the son of the perjured usurper of France, stricken down as a filibuster in a war with which he had nothing to do, was a profound grief to many who deeply admired his Eminence. Making all allowance for the feelings excited by **a** mother's sorrow, and the death of a prince, so-called, who chanced to be a Catholic, it was distressing **to** hear so powerful a voice lamenting the extinction of **a dynasty** which not all the sacred oil of Rheims could have made **other than** accursed, and from whose right hand the **blood of the** slaughters of the 2nd of December could never have been washed. And indeed it is this coquetting with tyrants, in spite of the **up**surging from time to time of nobler and better feelings ; it is **this** retrogression to the side of all that is base and foul in government, which, far more than dogmas—of which nearly all can be accepted metaphysically and transcendentally—keeps at a distance those who might be attracted by the great history or the soothing promises of the Church which Cardinal Manning has adopted."—*The Century*, vol. xxvi. (1883), p. 130. But all this invective is wide of the mark. The Napoleonic dynasty was **not** extinguished by the death of the Prince Imperial, and so there could be no lamentation over its extinction. There **was** only sympathy aroused by the death of an amiable young man, " the only son of his **mother, and she** was a widow." And **as** to the rest **of the charge, it is** true no doubt that Catholicism has many historical memories that link it with a monarchical government and with other **features** of the *ancien régime*. But it should be remembered that **the last** quarrel with Catholicism that Newman and others **had was that it** allied itself with the Revolution. The Church, in fact, recognizes and uses all established governments, but is strictly bound to no particular form.

As an ardent believer in the Church's right to legislate, and as a lover of all that is dignified and orderly
in the Church's system of government, Manning took
a real delight in the Diocesan and Provincial Synods
that were assembled, or that he himself called together
from time to time, and especially in the great Œcumenical
Council of the Vatican, of which a separate and special
account will be given below. At the first Provincial
Synod of Westminster, held at Oscott under the presidency of Cardinal Wiseman in July, 1852, Manning,
though he had barely been ordained a priest twelve
months, was invited to preach.[1] At the second and
third Synods, also held at Oscott in 1855 and 1859
respectively, Manning was present as " theologian," and
may be presumed to have had a hand in the preparation
of the decrees, one of which (made in the third Synod)
had to do with the establishment of diocesan seminaries.
But the one Provincial Synod over which Manning presided (the fourth, that held at St. Edmund's College,
Ware, in 1873) is naturally the most deserving of study,
as indicating his mind on a number of the *minutiæ* of
ecclesiastical order. Not that the decrees can be allotted
a place in a bibliography among his works, for they are
strictly anonymous, and indeed are not published until
they have been confirmed at Rome, perhaps a year after
they have been submitted. Still they are undoubtedly
characteristic of the Archbishop, and a number of disciplinary regulations on Church music, " acatholic " Universities, mixed marriages, the order of a priest's
household, and other smaller matters, may be studied

---

[1] It was before this Synod that Newman preached his memorable sermon, " The Second Spring," which Thackeray, it was said,
could repeat throughout by heart.

with interest and edification.[1] A Synod itself, a singular combination of stern business in private with impressive pageantry in public, is deserving of notice as the historical original of modern methods of Parliamentary government; though the divergent tendencies of the two, towards autocracy and democracy respectively, have in process of time produced very marked differences.

It had been the custom for all the clergy at a diocesan Synod to receive communion from their Bishop's hand, and this was done at Manning's first Synod in 1865 ; but it was afterwards discontinued, as involving many inconveniences. Another practice which the Arch- bishop prohibited in his diocese was the public midnight mass at Christmas, which has not been celebrated in London since 1867. It was found that the occasion attracted public-house loungers, and others whose condition was equally dubious; and, to avoid scandalous scenes, the prohibition was considered necessary. In the matter too of Church music Manning enforced regulations that savoured rather of discipline than of art. So far as he admired music at all, he admired Gregorian music, and anyway he was positive that only that music was consonant with the ecclesiastical spirit. " It will," he once said, " suffice for me till I go to the grave." He ultimately effected a great change in this matter; but it had to be done very gradually, as many interests were involved, and musical people are not the least touchy of mankind. When he became Arch- bishop the music in some of the principal churches was

---

[1] See *Decreta Quatuor Conciliorum Provincialium Westmonas- teriensium*, 1852—1873. Burns and Oates (1885). The volume contains a number of other ecclesiastical documents, including the *Syllabus* and the Vatican decrees.

of a florid kind, the choir including women, on occasions even famous singers from the opera, with an orchestral accompaniment. In the smaller churches it was not less pretentious, but was often enough execrably performed. In some places the choir and orchestra together cost several hundreds a year; but this was supposed to be recouped by the congregations attracted, who paid fixed prices for their seats. The performers moreover were regularly advertised in the public press. All this was extremely distasteful to Manning, who in 1868 addressed a letter to Canon Oakeley, stating his decided preference for male choirs. Four years later the rule was made absolute, not without much indignation and murmuring on the part of those concerned. But the Archbishop's " mild persistence " could not fail to win the day; and his own solemn requiem at the Oratory in January, 1892, sung throughout by priests to the ancient plain chant, varied occasionally by passages harmonized in the strict Church style, was a kind of triumph for him in this department of Church discipline.[1]

Although he was not on other than friendly terms with sundry distinguished Catholic actors and actresses —and it is astonishing how large a proportion of those whose business it is to amuse the public are Catholics— he never relaxed in any degree the prohibition which

[1] It is a matter of minor importance, but one not without interest, that Manning substituted throughout his diocese—and the example is being followed throughout the province—the use of the Italian form of vestments and the Italian pronunciation of Latin, for the Gothic or French styles that had before been used. Gothic vestments had been introduced not many years before, under the influence of the elder Pugin. The Jesuits and some of the orders that have been long established in England retain the old-fashioned pronunciation of Latin.

prevents the clergy from being present at public dramatic performances. By a decree of one of the Provincial Synods a priest violating this rule is *ipso facto* suspended, and can only be relieved from the sentence by his own Bishop.[1] It is easy to criticise this prohibition, and to point out that it is an inheritance from a period when the stage was ordinarily offensive to modest ears, whereas it is now only offensive, in certain cases, to modest eyes. Of course there are playwrights and theatrical managers with whose productions it could be only for the benefit of the clergy and of their flocks to be brought into contact. But legislation in such a matter as this is of necessity a clumsy weapon; and, if the Bishops hold that, without legislation, their clergy would not resist the temptation to attend performances of a questionable kind, there remains no alternative but to make the prohibition inclusive.

In the matter of prohibiting the reading of objectionable books, the Archbishop, perhaps perforce, used a policy more liberal and more in accordance with the ideas of those who hold that there springs eternally within the human breast a fount of morality better fitted to guide men and women in the right way than any grandmotherly legislation. "We are told that an *index expurgatorius* is impossible in such a country as this. In countries where the unity of the faith still exists it may be possible to restrain the evil; but in

---

[1] The prohibition does not extend of course to the admirable dramatic performances which are so common as to be almost the rule in Catholic schools and convents. Nor is an English priest bound by the decree referred to when he is outside the Province of Westminster. The writer is not unacquainted with one who availed himself of this liberty to witness a performance of *Die Meistersinger von Nürnberg* at Munich in the summer of 1883.

such a land as this, where liberty of thought and speech, oral and written, have run to the extreme of licence, it is no longer possible. Who can pull up the weeds in a wilderness? A man may weed a garden, but a desert must be left to its rankness. Nevertheless, the *index expurgatorius* may be transcribed upon the delicate and enlightened conscience of those who love purity and truth." [1]

No account of Manning's life as Archbishop would give an adequate idea of his inexhaustible zeal and energy, that did not include some notice of his "holidays" in the North. For twenty years, from 1865 to 1884, almost without a break, it was his regular summer recreation to visit the northern dioceses of his Province, and to preach, to lecture, to hold receptions and to take part in ecclesiastical functions, with the freshness of a man who had nothing to do all the rest of the year. In 1885 his forces had begun to flag, and it was observed that he contented himself with addressing, for the most part, audiences of children only, as this involved less mental strain. In 1886 he did no more than visit Manchester; and in 1887 these "holidays" came to an end. There can be no doubt but that he thoroughly enjoyed these expeditions, which brought him into contact, in some parts of Lancashire, "God's county," and of Durham especially, with the robust Catholicism of the North, which has never lost the traditions of the Middle Ages. A passage from the *Tablet* [2] aptly illustrates these archiepiscopal visitations

---

[1] *Ecclesiastical Sermons*, vol. ii., p. 219. The decisions of the Inquisition, by which books are placed on the *Index*, are not in force in England.

[2] September 17, 1881.

—though even from this account it appears that two temperance speeches, at Stockton and at Middlesborough, have been omitted:—"The Cardinal Archbishop is spending his holiday in his own fashion, that is, in work. On Saturday he arrived at the Bishop's House in Salford from Leeds. On Sunday he preached at the Cathedral in the morning, and again in the evening at St. Peter's, Greegate. On Wednesday he attended a great temperance meeting in Manchester, where he spoke for over an hour to a large audience, and on Thursday he attended a similar meeting at Oldham, which was presided over by the mayor. To-day (Saturday) he is due in Liverpool, where he will preach twice to-morrow; on Monday he will preside at a meeting in Father Nugent's Assembly Hall, for temperance; on Wednesday he is to plead at the Philharmonic Hall the cause of Catholic children who are being carried away to Canada and elsewhere by Protestant agents; and the Sunday following he is expected at Wolverhampton, on his way home to resume his regular work after his usual summer—*rest!*"[1]

On the whole, the impression left by a review of this side of Manning's career is that he was a keen-sighted and able administrator, a truly great Archbishop. Nor is it at all to his discredit that, though he can hardly be said to have won the beatitude of those who are

---

[1] It should be mentioned, however, that after Manning had borne alone the burden of the episcopate for twelve years, Monsignor Weathers was consecrated to assist him, and also Monsignor Patterson seven years later. Moreover, a large proportion of the routine work of the diocese is undertaken by the Vicar-General. Without the aid of these dignitaries, and of his private secretaries, Manning could not possibly have taken the important part that he did in public life.

persecuted for righteousness' sake, he at any rate escaped the anathema of those of whom all men speak well. A firm and successful ruler is sure to make enemies, and it is certain that Manning was not always loved by all his clergy, though it is also true that all who were able to understand him were genuinely proud of him. One of his own Canons is indeed reported to have said that the death of Mrs. Manning was the greatest misfortune that had ever befallen the Catholic Church in England; but such post-prandial remarks, even when not apocryphal, must be taken with reserve. In 1883, "after eighteen full years, with the engine always at work," all the priests, secular and regular, resident within the diocese, presented their Archbishop with addresses, on the occasion of his leaving for Rome to pay a canonical visit *ad limina Apostolorum;* and these addresses certainly read as if they were (to quote the *Tablet*) "a spontaneous outburst of admiration and human sympathy. . . . It might have been thought that one engrossed by so ceaseless an activity, and engaged in a multiplicity of works which do not fall strictly within the domain of ecclesiastical duty, might grow hard, unsympathetic and almost mechanical in the discharge of the duties and administrative detail which make up the round of every Bishop's life in his relation to his clergy. Men who are bent on accomplishing certain results, often fix their eyes upon the end, and tread down without mercy, or at least without much heeding, whatever stands between them and the object they labour for. Again, when men grow old, their feelings sometimes grow dull, and the sympathetic chords of nature cease to respond as they did in youth and middle age. . . . We have read from time to time in paragraphs and communications to the press that the Cardinal in correction was harsh and severe; that a gulf divided him from his clergy; that he lived in another region, and was felt only as a *Deus ex machinâ.* . . . The answer to such suspicions and charges is to be found in these addresses."

Manning, as Archbishop, in his care for the poor and needy—to return to that aspect of his work which in this chapter was accounted as first of all deserving of notice—put into practice an ideal which his predecessor, on his first appointment to the see, had sketched out as the true sphere of his duty in Westminster. The British public, genuinely alarmed by the " Papal Aggression," and nothing doubting but that Catholics, with a mysterious foreign power behind them, were capable of anything that might subvert the existing order of things, half expected that Cardinal Wiseman would evict the Dean and Canons of Westminster, cast a spell over the Houses of Parliament, and mark his triumph by a High Mass in Westminster Abbey. In an admirable letter, too little noticed in the dust of the controversies of that day, he had pointed out what, in his judgment, to be Archbishop of Westminster meant:—"The diocese consists of two very different parts. One comprises the stately Abbey, with its adjacent palaces and its royal parks. To this portion the duties and occupation of the Dean and Chapter are mainly confined, and they shall range there undisturbed. To the venerable old church I may repair, as I have been wont to do. . . . I may visit the old Abbey, and say my prayers by the shrine of good St. Edward; and meditate on the olden times, when the church filled without a coronation, and multitudes hourly worshipped without a service. Yet this splendid monument, its treasures of art, and its fitting endowments, form not the part of Westminster which will concern me. For there is another part which stands in frightful contrast, though in immediate contact, with this magnificence. Close under the Abbey of Westminster there lie concealed labyrinths of lanes and courts and alleys and slums, nests of ignorance, vice, depravity and crime, as well as of squalor, wretchedness and disease; whose atmosphere is typhus, whose ventilation is cholera; in which swarms a huge and almost countless population, in great measure, nominally at least, Catholic; haunts of filth which no Sewage Committee can reach, dark corners which no Lighting Board can brighten. This is the part of Westminster which alone I covet, and which I shall be glad to claim and visit as a blessed pasture in which sheep of Holy Church are to be tended, in which a Bishop's godly work has to be done." Manning, no less than Wiseman, might have written these words, for he will perhaps be best remembered as an Archbishop " who lived among his people, and their feet wore the threshold of his door."

CHAPTER VI.

THE VATICAN COUNCIL. CARDINALATE. RELATIONS WITH THE POPES.

MANNING had been Archbishop three years, and was in Rome, one of some five hundred prelates assembled on the occasion of the eighteenth centenary of the martyrdom of St. Peter, when the Pope announced his intention of convoking an Œcumenical Council, none having been held since the dissolution of the Council of Trent, nearly three hundred years before. The Council was formally summoned to meet in Rome on the Feast of the Immaculate Conception, Dec. 8th, 1869. According to Newman, who just at this time was specially sore with both Manning and the Pope on account of the personal snub he had received over the Oxford scheme, this announcement was "thunder in the clear sky." "A Council's proper office is," he maintained, "when some great heresy or other evil impends, to inspire hope and confidence in the faithful, but now . . . . we are told to prepare for something we know not what, to try our faith, we know not how. No impending danger is to be averted, but a great difficulty is to be created. Is this the proper work of an

Œcumenical Council? What have we done to be
treated as the faithful never were treated before?
When has a definition *de fide* been a luxury of devotion
and not a stern painful necessity?" The answer to
this last question was surely easy enough. There was
no "stern painful necessity" in 1854 to define the
Immaculate Conception. If ever a definition of faith
was "a luxury of devotion" it was this one; and yet
Newman had accepted it with gratitude and joy; while,
beyond this, the circumstances of the definition made
in 1854 had involved as a logical consequence that of
Papal infallibility as made in 1870. It was not made
by a Council, but by the Pope himself acting independently, though not without previously consulting the
Bishops. It was to be accepted by the faithful everywhere as an article of faith on the authority of the
Holy See; and there was no suggestion that that authority
depended in this matter on the consent of the Church,
whether given before or after the definition. Whether
therefore it was so intended or not, it was in fact a
sort of "pilot-balloon" which showed that the definition
of papal infallibility might be proceeded with without
risk. Impugners of the truth of the later definition
could be met with an *argumentum ad hominem,* and it
was only left to dissentients to quarrel with the
opportuneness of the decree.[1]

[1] Moreover, in 1862, on the occasion of the canonization of the
Japanese martyrs, over 250 Bishops assembled in Rome had
addressed the Pope in terms which involved their adhesion to
his infallibility. For example :—"You are to us the teacher of
sound doctrine, the centre of unity, the unfailing light to the
nations, kindled by divine wisdom. You are the Rock, the
foundation of the Church, against which the gates of hell shall
not prevail. When you speak, we hear Peter's voice ; when you
decide, we obey the authority of Christ."

It may be assumed throughout that there was no other serious occasion for the convocation of the Vatican Council than the desire of the Pope that this question, which had long been a matter of discussion, should be brought to a definite settlement.[1] It is true that it was not referred to in the Bull by which the Council was summoned, while other things were specially mentioned. The growth of the spirit of rationalism was a grave matter which the Church might well be expected to deal with in an Œcumenical Council, though its method of dealing with it could not fail to be other than it actually was, a solemn condemnation of errors, pre-judged of course as such, and a reaffirmation, perhaps in slightly modified language, of the corresponding positive dogmas of the Church. Sundry reforms were also supposed to be called for—such as a revision of the Breviary—but these were never actually touched ; and, if they were seriously needed, they could easily have been dealt with by small Commissions sitting in Rome, with-out the imposing splendour of a General Council. It might have been said, and indeed it was said, that if the Pope was infallible he could define the dogma himself, without assembling the Bishops from the uttermost parts of the earth to assist him in so doing. But this would have involved some risk of serious opposition, of more stubborn opposition than that which for the most part melted away when the miscontented Bishops were

---

[1] In his *True Story of the Vatican Council* Manning denies that Pius IX. desired the definition of his infallibility, and asserts that there would have been no need for it but for "the small number of disputants who doubted and the still smaller number who denied." The Council, he maintains, was summoned to deal with other matters, and to provide "an adequate remedy to the disorders, intellectual and moral, of the Christian world."

in Rome and under the influence of the *genius loci;*
while, in any case, it was but fitting that so momentous
and far-reaching a decision should be made under circumstances of the utmost possible *éclat;* and these in no
other way could be secured.

It may also be taken as certain that Manning was
entirely in the Pope's confidence in this matter, and
was consulted by him on every step. Every one, at any
rate, is familiar with the reputation he acquired at the
time of the meeting of the Council, as one of the most
strenuous advocates of the definition; and he wrote and
preached continually on the subject. Twenty years ago,
before he had become identified in the public mind with
the causes of education, temperance, labour, and the
like, it was with this matter of Papal infallibility that
his name was mostly connected; and it is not open to
doubt that he never ceased to regard it as a great
external "grace," as one of the chief privileges of his
life, that he not only lived in the days of the Vatican
Council, but was, as Archbishop, in a position to take an
active part in its proceedings, and to hear with his own
ears an important doctrine defined as a part of divine
revelation. Nor can any one who was interested in
and observed those proceedings, fail to remember how
grotesque and contemptible they were generally accounted by the English secular press,[1] and how even
many Catholics were restive and resentful of the
ignominious position in which they found themselves
placed in the eyes of their Protestant fellow-countrymen, few of whom had any intelligent apprehension of
the meaning of the Pope's infallibility, while nearly all
were disposed to regard it as a ridiculous and impious

[1] Again with the sole exception of the *Spectator.*

pretence. It thus becomes necessary, if **Manning's** action in this matter is to be defended, as it ought to be, no less than his secession from the Church of England, as courageous, consistent and honourable, to regard the matter from his own point of view, and to show precisely what the Vatican Council did or did not do.

Infallibility, real or fictitious, provisional or enduring, is a necessary assumption of all government, civil, military or ecclesiastical; and, when that government claims to be nothing short of divine, it is obvious that, *ex hypothesi*, the infallibility must be real, and its utterances not subject to revision. It is not to the purpose to complain that such an infallibility implies the accompaniment of impeccability and of immunity from error in every detail of government, and not merely in defining questions of faith or morals.[1] Consistently perhaps it does; but it is best to leave an imposing claim confined to the limits which it has itself laid down, recognizing with a rare modesty the prudence of being infallible only in a region that is not open to vulgar criticism. A consciousness of some such infallibility has undoubtedly possessed the Christian Church from the earliest period that its existence can be traced; and so, taking that for granted, the question may be narrowed to a discussion of the organ by which that infallibility is to find expression. Anglicans generally would maintain that the organ is "a free General Council"; Gallicans that it is the Pope supported by a General Council. Newman, some years before 1870, expressed the general opinion

[1] The maxim "The King can do no wrong," which expresses the corresponding fictitious infallibility, necessary as an assumption in secular government, extends to the whole sphere of his rule, and, in former days at least, exempted him from accountability to his subjects for his own personal conduct.

of Catholics when he said that the "normal seat" of
infallibility is "the Pope in a General Council," the
question whether his pronouncements were infallible of
themselves, or in consequence of the assent of the
Church, given either before or subsequently, being left
undecided, since that was the very point, and the only
point, on which controversy was possible before the
Vatican Council was held. The tradition that would
make formal Papal pronouncements binding on their
own account has had a long and respectable career,
though of course, like all similar traditions which can
be brought to the touchstone of historical criticism, it
can be challenged to reconcile itself with other reputed
facts. At the Council of Chalcedon, as far back as 451,
the Bishops did not venture to weigh the formal messages
of Pope Leo I., but accepted them with veneration,
exclaiming, "Peter has spoken by Leo!" There is no
very wide gulf between their attitude then and the
"*sacro Concilio approbante*," when Pius IX. asserted his
official infallibility in 1870.

If then it can be affirmed that the question which
the Council was really summoned to hear determined
was a purely domestic controversy that had already
been practically settled in the affirmative, there is no
longer occasion to protest against the idea that the
Bishops who approved of the definition were supporting
a wild and fanatical assumption ; it is clearly only their
prudence that is now in question. Was such a definition opportune or not ? Newman, though he afterwards
denied that he had accounted it inopportune, certainly
acted as if he thought it was so, and had written, "If it
is God's will that the Pope's infallibility be defined,
then it is God's will to throw back the times and

moments of that triumph which he has destined for his kingdom." He had been considering almost exclusively the progress of Catholicism in England, and had been under the impression (probably a mistaken one) that multitudes were ready to submit to the Catholic Church if only this scandal of the Pope's prerogative were not flung in their way. On the other hand, the advocates of the opportuneness of the definition, among whom of course was Manning, recognized in the *prestige* that Pius IX. had acquired during his long pontificate a reason why he should be the Pope to pronounce a decree that doubtless seemed to some extent to trench on the privileges of the other Bishops. The precarious condition of the temporal power was also a matter not left out of sight. It depended solely on the good-will of France; and, with the annexation of Rome to the kingdom of Italy, the assembling of a General Council might become difficult if not impossible. And the sagacity of this forecast was vindicated by the event, when, two months after the definition had been made, the temporal power, to all intents and purposes, ceased to exist.[1] After so much preface, the course of events, and the part that Manning took in them, may now be briefly chronicled.

Before leaving for Rome in November, 1869, the Archbishop issued a Pastoral Letter extending over some hundred and eighty pages, in which he argued for the acceptance of the dogma with considerable skill. His aim was to remove misconceptions, and he pointed out that Papal infallibility, as rightly understood, was

---

[1] Manning would never admit that the Pope's temporal power was finally disposed of in 1870. It was, he said, only the forty-fifth time that the Pope had lost it.

" not a quality inherent in the person, but an assistance inseparable from the office." He selected as his " theologian," to advise him during the progress of the Council, no one from among his own clergy, but an Italian Jesuit, Liberatore. At this early stage of the proceedings a transient controversy sprang up between the Archbishop of Westminster and Monseigneur Dupanloup, the eloquent Bishop of Orleans,[1] who raised certain objections to Manning's Pastoral. These were mainly two:—— (1) That Manning appeared to teach that the opportuneness or inopportuneness of a definition ought never to be counted for anything; and (2) That Gallicanism is more dangerous for Catholics than Anglicanism. The *Tablet* defended the Archbishop's language with considerable vigour, and so incurred the following censure from Dupanloup:—" Bien que tout le monde sache les rapports de Mgr. Manning avec votre journal, je me hâte d'ajouter que je ne puis en rien le rendre ici responsable de tels excès." The *Times*, oddly enough, also defended him at this time, and declared that Manning's argument in defence of the opportuneness of a decision was admirable; adding that in this instance it had " an honest pride in contemplating the more straightforward course of our own countryman "; and even a writer in the *Saturday* admitted that Manning was right in arguing that, if Papal infallibility is a part of Divine revelation, no fear of the possible results ought to be allowed to restrain the Church from its proclamation. Another secular paper, comparing Manning with Dupanloup, said that the former showed " the more heroic faith."

[1] Bishop Dupanloup had proposed to take Newman with him to the Council as his theologian.

Arrived in Rome the Archbishop was immediately welcomed by the Pope with special marks of affection; at the opening of the Council he was placed on the Commission *De Fide*, charged with the examination of questions of dogma; and on an early day he was selected to say the mass *de Spiritu Sancto* before the assembled Fathers. It was stated that he was most unremitting in his labours on the Commission to which he belonged, and that its work was especially heavy. In January, 1870, he suffered for some days from influenza, but was soon active again. At this time the question of Papal infallibility had been formally ruled out of discussion in the Council; but petitions began to flow in (the result, of course, of "intrigues," according to the inopportunists) asking that the doctrine might be defined, two of these coming from the London Oratory and from the Archbishop's own Chapter of Westminster; and accordingly, in March, the matter was added to the *Schema de Ecclesiâ Christi*, and in due course came on for discussion, promptly and entirely eclipsing every other question that was before the Fathers in Council. Manning spoke on it (of course in Latin) towards the end of the month of May; and, though no report of it has ever been made public, it is certain that his speech, which lasted nearly two hours, made a distinct impression, and it was spoken of in Rome at the time as "one of the most masterly that had been made." He devoted a good deal of time, as was to be expected, to a criticism of one of the arguments of the inopportunists, to the effect that the definition would throw back a large number of Anglicans who were believed to be approaching the Church. In his judgment such conversions, conditional on not being called upon to hold a doctrine that was almost universally believed in the Church, would be but nominal and worthless.[1]

At the opening of the Council in December, 1869, it had been reckoned, judging from the signatures appended to sundry petitions, that 450 bishops were in favour of the definition and that 120 were more or less opposed to it, of whom only five, at the outside, rejected the doctrine as untrue.[2] Ultimately, when the decree was passed, at the fourth public session of the Council, July 18th, 1870, 533 voted in favour, and only two against; but to these two should be added 55 who absented themselves, being unwilling to vote either way. The scene, which in itself must have been dramatic enough, had its effect heightened by a storm of

---

[1] The reasons against the definition urged by the inopportunists are given at full length in Manning's *True Story of the Vatican Council*, pp. 101—103 ; and he does not deny that in the course of the debate " representations of history were made which could not be easily squared with the infallibility of the Head of the Church."

[2] It may be convenient to give the text of the definition :—
" Itaque Nos, traditioni a fidei Christianæ exordio perceptæ fideliter inhærendo, ad Dei Salvatoris nostri gloriam, religionis catholicæ exaltationem et Christianorum populorum salutem, sacro approbante Concilio, docemus et divinitus revelatum dogma esse definimus : Romanum Pontificem, cum ex cathedrâ loquitur, id est, cum omnium Christianorum Pastoris et Doctoris munere fungens pro supremâ suâ Apostolicâ auctoritate doctrinam de fide vel moribus ab universâ Ecclesiâ tenendam definit, per assistentiam divinam, ipsi in beato Petro promissam, eâ infallibilitate pollere quâ divinus Redemptor Ecclesiam suam in definiendâ doctrinâ de fide vel moribus instructam esse voluit : ideoque ejusmodi Romani Pontificis definitiones ex sese, non autem ex consensu Ecclesiæ, irreformabiles esse.

" Si quis autem huic Nostræ definitioni contradicere, quod Deus avertat, præsumpserit ; anathema sit."

The precise wording of the last clause in the definition, *ex sese, non autem ex consensu Ecclesiæ*, in which lies all that can be accounted novel in the decree, was understood to have been suggested by the late Cardinal Cullen.

thunder and lightning which prevailed at the very
time that the *Constitutio dogmatica prima de Ecclesiâ
Christi* was being recited. Inopportunists saw in this
an expression (somewhat inadequate perhaps) of Divine
indignation. Opportunists recognized it as a hostile
demonstration of the powers of darkness. The question cannot be settled until we know whether stormy
weather has any transcendental source. What was
more to the purpose was the declaration, the very next
day, of war between France and Germany, which rendered impracticable any co-operation between the
dissentients Darboy and Dupanloup, Archbishops of
Paris and of Orleans, and their German allies. Perhaps in any case there would have been no secession of
any Bishop from the Church; but the triumph of the
majority could hardly have been as complete as it was
without the adventitious aid of the outbreak of the war.[1]

Manning, whose joy at the result was spoken of as "too
great for words," certainly used his victory with moderation. There were among English Catholics a few, some
of them of high station, who repudiated the definition

---

[1] Mgr. Darboy, Archbishop of Paris, has generally been accounted, on the authority of an anonymous chronicler in Dr.
Friedrich's *Documenta*, a disbeliever in the Pope's infallibility.
But in June, 1871, Manning wrote to the *Times:*—"I am able
to attest that the resistance of the Archbishop of Paris to the definition did not touch the truth of the doctrine but the expediency
of defining that truth. I make this statement, not on hearsay,
but on personal conference with him in Rome." When Pius IX.
heard of Darboy's tragic end, he said:—"He has washed away
his defects in his own blood, and has put on the martyr's robe."
The writer of these pages was in Paris, in 1876, and had some
conversation on the position held by Darboy with the blind
Ultramontane ecclesiastic, Mgr. de Ségur. His reply to a representation that the late Archbishop might be accounted at any
rate a martyr in the cause of religion was emphatic :—"Pour la
religion, peut-être ; mais pour la foi, non, non !"

and yet refused to regard themselves as on that account outside the Church, forgetting that obedience to authority is of the very essence of Catholicism, and that no one can be a Catholic on his own terms. Manning avoided the scandal of the formation of an "Old Catholic" body in England by leaving these dissentients very much alone. Privately no doubt they were excommunicated, and could only obtain the sacraments by concealing their opinions or their identity; but no public act ever gave them occasion to become formally dissociated from the body of the faithful; and by this time they have pretty nearly died out.

On the whole the effect of the definition was distinctly unitive. The necessity of accepting it brought the minimizing school of Catholics into line with the Ultramontanes, while the more exacting theologians among the latter, who had been accustomed to ascribe infallibility to almost every Papal pronouncement, found that a definition is strictly what the term implies—a limitation—and that they could no longer claim authority for covering so wide a field with their favourite doctrine. Nor did the definition make practically any difference to the average Catholic priest or layman. They were stared at for a week or so by sturdy Protestants, who expected to see some token of shame on the faces of those who had been called upon to believe a monstrous and blasphemous absurdity—not a bit more monstrous or absurd, however, than the unenlightened Protestant's belief in the infallibility of the letter of Scripture—but no good Catholic was conscious of any change of faith. No doubt, in the case of professed canonists and theologians, there was a little difference; certain texts needed accommodation and explanation;

and scientific students of history, of the German
school, found themselves, as they had feared, with
awkward facts to face. But, what Newman had said
of the definition of the immaculate conception, was also
true of the definition of infallibility, that no priest
left the Church on account of it but would probably
have left the Church sooner or later on other grounds.
The fact of a definition having been made at all led
some men to reconsider the whole question of the
grounds of faith, and to recognize those grounds as
insufficient; but on the whole it may be said that the
definition was a success, and that no similar dogmatic
decree ever obtained more easily an almost universal
acceptance. Even Protestant Englishmen, distasteful
as the whole matter was to them, did not grudge some
admiration to the policy of "thorough"; and Manning
was never thought much the worse of because of the
part he had played in the affair. About seven years
later he put forth his *True Story of the Vatican
Council*, intended as a reply to certain untrue stories,
as he accounted them, which had obtained some credence.[1] The authorities on which he relied were unex-
ceptionable, one being Cecconi, afterwards Archbishop of
Florence, the official historian of the Council, and another,
Fessler, Bishop of St. Pölten, who was the Council's
Secretary. Certain of his statements were criticised by
the "Old Catholic" Professor Friedrich,[2] and it is difficult,
no doubt, to credit his declaration that "Pius IX. had

[1] Such were the writings under the name of "Pomponio Leto,"
ascribed after his death to Cardinal Vitelleschi, but explicitly
repudiated by his brother; and the *Documenta ad illustrandum
Concilium Vaticanum* (2 vols., 1871), and other writings of Professor Friedrich.

[2] *Contemporary Review*, March and June, 1878.

L

neither desire nor need to propose the defining of his infallibility." But it is a case in which, in accordance with the *dictum* of Aristotle, persuasion depends, not on the arguments which either side may adduce, but on what we think of the combatants and of their cause.

The interest, one might almost say the excitement, aroused by the memorable decree of July 18, 1870, has made men neglect other definitions of the Council, in which Manning, as an active member of the Commission *De Fide*, had a shaping hand. They are so decidedly opposed to the growing temper of the times that they are likely to attract more attention hereafter. Newman, who, for some unintelligible reason, resented the definition of the Pope's infallibility as if it had been directed against himself, was really more hardly hit by a canon which set aside the intuitional doctrine of faith, and made it to be, so far as the existence of a personal God is concerned, a process of pure reasoning;[1] and the canon concerning Scripture is also somewhat hostile to the mildly liberalizing views concerning inspiration and the integrity of the sacred books which he put forth in his later years.[2] And a third canon puts out of court those who, in view of modern science and criticism, would give an ideal significance to ancient dogmas, and make a delightful poetry of the faith.[3] With nothing of this

[1] "Si quis dixerit, Deum unum et verum, Creatorem et Dominum nostrum, per ea quæ facta sunt, naturali rationis humanæ lumine, certo cognosci non posse ; anathema sit."—*De Revel.* § 1.

[2] "Si quis sacræ Scripturæ libros integros, cum omnibus suis partibus, prout illos sancta Tridentina synodus recensuit, aut eos divinitus inspiratos esse negaverit ; anathema sit."—*De Revel.* § 4.

[3] "Si quis dixerit, fieri posse, ut dogmatibus ab Ecclesiâ propositis, aliquando secundum progressum scientiæ sensus tribuendus sit alius ab eo quem intellexit et intelligit Ecclesia ; anathema sit."—*De Fide et Ratione*, § 3.

had Manning the slightest sympathy. To assert, to condemn, always with authority, never caring to enquire into the reasons for or against, never taking into account the ethical or spiritual significance of that which was doomed to anathema, this was in accordance with his mind, and, for that matter, in accordance with the mind of the Church; nor inconsistently, considering what her pretensions to a divine commission are.

The part that Manning took in the controversy aroused by Mr. Gladstone's attack on the Vatican decrees must be briefly narrated. The great Liberal statesman from his earliest years had followed the progress of ecclesiastical controversies with eager interest, and had noted with profound misgiving the definition of the Pope's infallibility in 1870, being assured, from his knowledge of ecclesiastical history, that it could not legitimately be made an article of faith. In 1873 he had been moved to something like indignation against the Catholic hierarchy in Great Britain and Ireland—the latter especially—because of the rejection of his Irish University Bill, an attempt to solve a problem that will perhaps remain insoluble until statesmen are prepared to grant demands which the country will assuredly refuse to ratify. The year following, withdrawing for the time from public life, he prepared and published a smart attack on the Vatican decrees, affirming that they were inconsistent with civil allegiance. The moment that this pamphlet, which had an enormous circulation, appeared, Manning wrote a letter to the papers, emphatically denying the assertion;[1] and at a later date he issued a more elaborate reply. Other

[1] See the *Times*, Nov. 9, 1874.

replies, and especially **Dr. Newman's** admirable " Letter to the Duke of Norfolk," **obtained** more notice from the reading public; but **the Archbishop's** rejoinder was not wanting **in force** and dignity, though he did not attempt to meet Mr. [Gladstone on his **own** historical grounds. The controversy occasioned a temporary estrangement between the two—it was even said that one "cut" the other when they passed in the street— but a quarrel is not of long duration when there is magnanimity on both sides ; and from 1875, or there-abouts, onwards, the old friends were on better terms than they had been at any time since the great separa-tion of 1851.[1] Ultimately Mr. Gladstone frankly and

---

[1] In 1868, during the controversy about the disestablishment of the Irish Church, it was stated, on the authority of a news-paper correspondent supposed to be in Florence, that Pius IX. had requested Archbishop Manning to thank Mr. Gladstone for his "attitude" on that question. Manning wrote to deny this ; but a little later the *Standard* insisted on there being some kind of understanding between the Liberal leader and the Archbishop of Westminster. On this Manning wrote to a Mr. Davidson as follows :—"I beg to thank you for calling my attention to the paragraph in which an attempt is made to calumniate Mr. Gladstone by the fact that his eldest son is my godson. This is a mean artifice which can only damage those who use it. The fact is so. Mr. Hope-Scott and I stood sponsors to the eldest son of Mr. Gladstone about 1840. Mr. Hope-Scott and Mr. Gladstone were at Eton and Oxford together, and have been friends during a long life. My friendship with Mr. Gladstone began when we were at Oxford about 1830. We had the same private tutor, and were in many ways brought together. From that time till the year 1851 our friendship continued close and intimate. In 1851 the intercourse of our friendship was suspended by the act demanded of me by my conscience in submitting to the Catholic Church. We ceased to correspond, and for more than twelve years we never met. In the last years public and official duties have renewed our communications. I have been compelled to communicate with many public men in successive governments, and among others with Mr. Gladstone ; with this only difference—of the others most were either strangers or but

fully withdrew his charge against Catholics of impaired allegiance; but the tract in which he did this never obtained anything like the wide circulation of the earlier one.

In a certain sense of course Catholics, who are loyal in things spiritual to the Pope, have a " divided allegiance " —the same indeed is true, *mutatis mutandis*, of every one who recognizes a spiritual authority, independent of the civil power, in any person, or book, or in the moral law itself. But the Vatican decrees can hardly be said to have made any serious change in this matter. Since 1870, no less than before, Catholics are free to resist political dictation from Rome; and in the very narrow

---

slightly known—Mr. Gladstone was and is the man whose friendship has been to me one of the most cherished and valued of my life. To found on this an insinuation for raising the no-popery cry, or suspicion of Mr. Gladstone's fidelity to his own religious convictions, is as unmanly, base and false as the Florence telegram, in which the same political party, for the same political ends, united Mr. Gladstone's name with mine last summer. The indignation you express at this new trick will, I am sure, be shared by every honourable man in the country. I cannot conclude this letter without adding that a friendship of thirty-eight years, close and intimate till 1851 in no common degree, enables me to bear witness that a mind of greater integrity or of more transparent truth, less capable of being swayed by faction and party, and more protected from all such baseness even by the fault of indignant impatience of insincerity and selfishness in public affairs, than Mr. Gladstone's I have never known. The allegation that the policy of justice to the Irish people by removing the scandal of the Established Church has been inspired either by a mere desire to overthrow the Government, or by friendship with me, is imposture; and imposture is the mark of a feeble and a falling cause."

When Manning's godson, Mr. W. H. Gladstone, died in the summer of 1891, among the letters of condolence received by the sorrowing parents, hardly one was more acceptable and none was more worthy of the occasion than that which came from the aged Cardinal.

field in which a definition *de fide vel moribus* is possible, matters affecting civil allegiance can hardly find a place. Should, for example, the Pope define the Assumption of our Lady as an article of the faith, so that it would cease to be, what it is now, merely an universally received opinion; or should he decide, against the teaching of earlier theologians, that a man may put his money out at interest without sin, no Catholic would in consequence become a less loyal subject of her Majesty. Decisions such as these might have been made before 1870, or they might be made now. In the latter case they would have to be accepted as infallible *ex sese*; in the former case they would by some have been accepted as infallible only *ex consensu Ecclesiæ*, which would assuredly not have been withheld. The difference is neither striking nor far-reaching in its effects.

It will be convenient to include in this chapter, which deals especially with the Roman side of the Archbishop of Westminster's career, some notice of his elevation to the Cardinalate, and of his relations with Popes Pius IX. and Leo XIII.

On March 6, 1875, it was announced that Manning was to be invested with the Roman purple, an honour that his laborious episcopate of ten years' duration and his special services to the Pope had amply deserved and won.[1] He had left London the previous day,

---

[1] It was noted at the time by the Roman correspondent of the *Tablet* that the Pope "made no communication to the British Government of his intention to create Archbishop Manning a Cardinal. Since the withdrawal of Mr. Clarke Jervoise [who had informally represented the Court of St. James at the Vatican], Cardinal Antonelli has had no direct means of holding diplomatic intercourse; and the Pope would have nothing to do with Sir A. Paget, who was accredited to the Quirinal."

accompanied by his nephew, the Rev. W. Manning, and, travelling *viâ* the Riviera, reached Rome on the evening of the 10th, being met at the station by Mr. Hartwell de la Garde Grissell, one of the Pope's *camerieri segreti,* and Dr. O'Callaghan, Rector of the English College, where he resided during this visit, which lasted till the end of the month.[1] The Consistory at which he was "created" took place on the 15th, and the formal announcement was conveyed to him at the English College, where a considerable company had assembled. He said a few words only. "I do not affect to think lightly of the great dignity conferred upon me without any merit of mine. It is truly an honour to be associated with the Sacred Council immediately around the Vicar of our Lord, and to share his lot in good and evil. Indeed, I would rather that this dignity fell upon me, as it does, in the time of danger than in the time of safety. It is, as it were, being told off to the 'forlorn hope' in the sight of the world; but it is a 'forlorn hope' which is certain of victory. I feel that your presence this day is a representation of England, especially of those in England who have preserved unbroken the tradition of the faith, and that your kindness to me proceeds from love to England; and I feel assured that on returning to our country I shall meet with the same kindness and affection."

The day following the new Cardinals took the oath in the throne-room of the Vatican, and received the *biretta;* and on Easter Monday (March 29th), at a public Consistory, the final ceremonies of investiture

---

[1] Characteristically he employed his leisure in giving a "retreat" to the students of the College.

were performed.[1]   Considerable interest was attached
to the church assigned by the Pope to Cardinal Manning
as his title.   That of SS. Andrew and Gregory on the
Cælian happened to be vacant, and was appropriately
selected.   The monastery attached to the church had
been originally the private residence of St. Gregory the
Great, and from its walls had proceeded St. Augustine
of Canterbury and his companions, when they were
sent forth to evangelize England.   At the close of the
Consistory Manning took possession of this church, and,
in the course of a long address, remarked that now for
the first time an Englishman held it; and that from
that monastery had proceeded not only the first Archbishop of Canterbury, but also the first Bishop of
Rochester and the first Archbishop of York.   A week
later he was back in London; and on April 13 he made
his first public appearance as Cardinal in England,
opening a new Church of St. Thomas at Canterbury.
One who was present on the occasion recalls the quiet
simplicity of his sermon on the words, "The good
shepherd giveth his life for the sheep," spoken with
his customary gravity and air of authority, as he leant,
sometimes with both hands, on his crozier, and looked,
vested in cope and mitre, and with his familiar clear-
cut ascetic features, as if he were some stained-glass
representation of St. Augustine himself come to life
again.   What only detracted from the effect was a
restless rolling of his deep-set eyes, and an occasional
nervous twitch of the eyebrows; apart from which

---

[1] The last ceremony of all, the imposition of the hat, was not
performed until the last day of the year 1877.   Pius IX. was
at that time in bed (in his private library), and within six weeks
of his death.

there could hardly be portrayed a more satisfying picture of the ideal Catholic ecclesiastic.

Questions about the Cardinal's precedence were mooted in the *Tablet* as soon as he had returned from Rome. Two years previously there had been some remonstrance about the position accorded to him as Archbishop at the dinner held at Oxford to celebrate the fiftieth anniversary of the foundation of the "Union"; and in the autumn of 1889 similar objections were raised to his name appearing above that of "F. Londin." in some documents emanating from the Mansion House Strike Committee. What however was more important, as apparently possessing official sanction, was his signature being appended to the report of the Royal Commission on the Housing of the Working Classes below that of the Prince of Wales but above that of the Marquis of Salisbury, while, in the report of the Royal Commission on Education, it preceded those of the Earls of Harrowby and Beauchamp and of the Bishop of London. In the former case it was understood that the two distinguished personages named had previously considered the matter and had agreed that it should be so; and certainly the general impression was that personal considerations had been taken to justify the precedence accorded to the Cardinal.[1] It was due, it was said, to his "tact and judgment that had made such a position his own." On the other hand, Mr. Bodley, secretary to the first-named Royal Commission, wrote to the *Morning Post* stating that on such a Commission "precedence accorded to courtesy is unknown. The order of the

[1] Mr. Gladstone also wrote, in July, 1890:—"Cardinal Manning, so far as I am aware, is not possessed of any temporal rank, whatever precedence may be accorded to him by courtesy."

names is decided by the most formal rules, and no courtesy rank is accorded to venerable years, to high personal character, or to conspicuous public services." If this be so, it would seem to follow that the Prince of Wales, who may be taken as a final arbiter in such a matter, decided that the princely rank of Cardinals shall henceforth be recognized in this country, as it is in most European Courts.[1] It is easy to exaggerate the importance of a matter like this, but it cannot be said to have no significance. And, as to Manning's own action in the matter, it must be borne in mind that a Cardinal is by his oath bound to maintain, so far as in him lies, the dignity of his position; so that neither would personal ambition be fairly ascribed as the cause of his putting himself forward, nor could he have permitted his courteous instincts as a gentleman to claim for himself a lower place.

Reference has already been made (p. 87) to the close relations which Manning, in the first years of his Catholic priesthood, had with Pope Pius IX. Those relations continued no less close to the end. In November, 1877, Manning left London to perform one of his canonical visits to Rome. He was taken ill with bronchitis in Paris, and remained there nearly six weeks. The Pope wrote to dispense him from his visit, and bade

[1] It may be doubted, however, whether the British public would tolerate, apart from an exceptional case, a Roman Cardinal ranking before all the British aristocracy. Manning, it was said, had " acclimatized the idea of a Cardinal in England," and, as a result of his unremitting philanthropic labours, he had come to be regarded as almost as indispensable in any good work as the Lord Mayor himself. And there was a kind of romance associated with the idea people had of Newman that would have allowed him a similar freedom. But what would be thought of a Cardinal Walsh taking precedence, as such, of the Duke of Westminster?

him return to England. But other letters from Rome told him that the Pontiff's strength was "visibly declining," and urged him to come with the least possible delay. Accordingly, he reached Rome on December 22, and saw the Pope the next day on the sick-bed which he never afterwards left. Pius IX. died on February 7, 1878, in the presence of Cardinals Manning, Bilio, Howard and Martinelli. When Manning returned to England in April, 1878, after an absence of more than five months, he was presented with an address from his clergy, and in the course of his reply he made the following reference to his relations with the late Pope :—
" You will forgive me if I seem to imply too much that is personal to myself in what I add. I say it now because it is the first and will perhaps be the last time I may ever so speak. During the last twenty-five years I have had the happiness, and as I account it the blessing, of being admitted by Pius IX. to an intimacy which had no cause but his paternal kindness. . . Never at any time, such was his undeserved goodness, had I the sorrow of hearing from him a word of disapproval, nor did any cause of displeasure ever lessen or overcast his paternal affection. During those long years, while his health and vigour of life lasted, I had sometimes the privilege and sometimes the duty of speaking with him on matters of great anxiety. But in the last five weeks of his protracted life no subjects of such a kind ever passed. I had the happiness of sitting by the side of his sick-bed to console his last days. No subject of his manifold and great anxieties was ever spoken of ; no business, however slight, was ever introduced. I felt that the sick-bed of Pius IX. was sacred, and that all affairs and interests of his great office belonged to those

whose direct responsibility it was to treat them; that I had the happiness of conversing with him only on such thoughts and things as were consoling and cheerful and free from all anxious thought. More than once in those five weeks I was able, as I hope, to bring before him some momentary solace; and I thank God that my lot was so ordered that I stood beside the Pontiff, whom we have so revered and loved, in the last days and in the last moments of his great and glorious life."

Manning had, not unnaturally, acquired an immense admiration for the predecessor of Leo XIII. Four or five years earlier, speaking at the opening of the Church of St. Dominic, at Newcastle, he had said:—" I believe that when the history of the pontificate of Pius IX. shall be written, it will be found to have been one of the most resplendent, majestic and powerful—one that has reached over the whole extent of the Church with greater power than that of any other Pope in the whole succession." But it must be confessed that Pius IX. was not a Pope to win the admiration of the mass of Englishmen. His lapse from the Liberalism of his earlier years; his continued insistence on the prerogatives of his office; his ceaseless lamentations over the gradual shrinkage and ultimate loss of his temporal power; his alliance with the least respectable among the crowned heads of Europe; his wholesale condemnation of modern progressive ideas,—and so forth,—all this made him as unwelcome a factor in European politics as his successor has, for the most part, been the reverse.

Cardinal Manning, in the Conclave, throughout supported the election of Cardinal Pecci, who has since become, one may say, famous as Leo XIII. Newspaper correspondents at the time would have it otherwise. He was "the leader of an intolerant and fanatical minority," "a discomfited dissensionist in the bosom of the Conclave"; and the theory was that he was endeavouring to secure either his own election or that of Cardinal Bilio, who was spoken of—whether justly or not —as "an intransigent Ultramontane," "an impassive, truculent monk." The Cardinals, it would appear, enjoy the privilege of reading the daily papers during their incarceration; for, on his return, Manning remarked with kindly humour that his brethren had daily condoled with him over his misconduct. He added, "I think it is a duty to the Sacred College on my part to say, and I think you have the right to know all that I can make known without infraction of my oath . . . and I violate no obligation in making these two statements; first, that no proposition of mine was so much as contested by my colleagues; and, secondly, that I had the happiness to be always united to the majority, I may say to the all but unanimity of the Sacred College."

It cannot of course be pretended that after February, 1878, Rome could be the same to Manning that it had been during the lifetime of Pius. That presence was removed that had been his inspiration for more than a quarter of a century; and, however much he might venerate the office in the person of Pius' successor, it could not be quite the same thing. Nevertheless, it is beside the mark to speak, as some have done, of his making unwillingly his stated visits to the throne of Leo XIII. On the contrary, there is much evidence to show that a strong and genuine sympathy soon closely united the two, and that the new Pope was ready to confess that he owed much to Manning's counsel and support. And this special regard continued during the twelve years that the two were thus associated. Visitors to his Holiness so recently as 1890 have reported that his face brightened at once with pleasure when they were able to report that they knew Cardinal Manning. As the preacher at his funeral said :—"Our Holy Father loved him and leaned upon him." Probably in those last words is contained a reference to a matter about which it is impossible yet to do much more than specu-late—the origin of the Papal policy in relation to labour. That Manning had to do with Leo XIII.'s recent Encyclical on that subject is undoubted. One sentence in it—a characteristic one—was almost ascribed to him as if it came from the Cardinal's own pen :—"There is a dictate of nature more imperious and more ancient than any bargain between man and man, that the remuneration of the wage-earner must be enough to support him in reasonable and frugal comfort."

But all this is only bordering on a great subject which will need sympathetic treatment by a competent pen hereafter. Manning we know—and the details will be given somewhat fully in subsequent chapters—emphatically believed in "the people." That was his belief as an Anglican as well as in his later years. During the lifetime of Pius, who thought salvation might still be found in the *ancien régime*, it would have been beside the purpose to suggest the thought that Catholicism, "broad-based upon a people's will," would have a more secure foundation than when it put its trust in princes, who cared for it only on grounds of political expediency. Probably it is due to Manning that Leo XIII. has acquired, and is proud to have acquired, the title of "the workman's Pope": it is not impossible that hereafter it will be recognized that from Manning the Papacy obtained the first idea of a bolder and more popular policy, that may have effects more far-reaching and more calculated to secure the permanence of Catholicism than the policy which he had supported with such ardour during the pontificate of Pius IX.

CHAPTER VII.

TEMPERANCE. EDUCATION. IRELAND.

THE first important movement in the direction of social reform with which Archbishop Manning became connected, and the one with which his name will always be specially associated, was that of Temperance, or, as he came to understand the term, of Total Abstinence. There is nothing to show that during his life as an Anglican clergyman, or subsequently as a priest at Bayswater, he had taken any markedly strong view about the evils of drunkenness, or about the best methods for their suppression. But shortly after his promotion to the see of Westminster it is clear that he came to recognize it as *par excellence* the deadly foe of all social progress, no less than the cause of nine-tenths of the poverty and misery which weighed down the major portion of his flock. His first steps were, however, cautious and tentative, and he had been Archbishop nearly seven years before he fairly gave himself away to the movement.[1] In 1866 he appointed a committee which

---

[1] The writer desires to record his obligations for much interesting information concerning Cardinal Manning's career as a temperance reformer to a valuable communication from the Rev. Dr. Dawson Burns, Metropolitan Superintendent of the United Kingdom Alliance.

recommended the formation of a temperance society with a few simple rules, one of which would bind to total abstinence only those who had given way to drinking habits. The year following, when St. Patrick's Day came round, in view of the degrading scenes to which its celebration had given rise among the poor Irish of London, he issued an appeal for a "Truce of St. Patrick," promising an indulgence to all those who tasted no intoxicating drink on the days during which it was customary to protract the festival. Another pastoral invited men and women to take a pledge not to enter a public-house on Saturdays or Sundays throughout the year. He now associated himself with the "permissive prohibition" policy of the United Kingdom Alliance, and in 1867, and the year following, spoke at its annual meetings in Manchester. In 1871 he addressed for the first time in London a meeting, in support of Sir Wilfrid Lawson's Permissive Bill, held in St. James's Hall; where for full forty minutes an organized body of roughs caused such persistent interruption that his voice could not be heard. His patience however was inexhaustible, and ultimately his speech was made. The year following he signed "the pledge," being driven to it, as he explained, because he was anxious to advise a meeting of working-men in Southwark that he had been asked to address, to be content with nothing short of total abstinence, and he did not see how he could urge this on them unless he could say that he had done the same himself.[1] To this pledge—

---

[1] It was to Dr. Dawson Burns that he told the following story, fully appreciating its humour :—Passing along the street he saw an Irishman, evidently the worse for drink, and, hoping to be able to do him some good, he stopped and remonstrated with him on his disgraceful condition ; but all to no purpose. At last he

apart of course from the modicum of wine which every
priest consumes daily in the mass—he held absolutely
for twenty years; that is, until his death; and on two
occasions, besides in his brief last illness, he entirely
declined to take any alcoholic stimulant, though strongly
urged to do so by his doctor.

Having once set his face to this work, he devoted
himself to it with characteristic resolution and earnestness. In March, 1873, he presided over a crowded
meeting in Exeter Hall, where a new Temperance
Association was formed; and in the course of his speech,
which was cheered enthusiastically, he said :—" The last
act of Father Mathew (the Irish apostle of temperance)
was to receive the pledge from those who gathered round
his death-bed. I desire no better end for my reverend
brethren around me; no better end for myself." At
the close of the meeting he proceeded to Trafalgar
Square—this was of course in days when Londoners
had not lost the right of public meeting in the open air
—and addressed some 1500 men assembled there. The
" Total Abstinence League of the Cross " he had already
formed, in conjunction with Father Nugent, of Liverpool;
but, speaking of its foundation, many years later, he
said :—" I acknowledge that in those days my eyes were
only half opened. I saw the need of a great effort to
save those who had actually fallen into the horrible
bondage, . . . but it was not till later that I saw we

---

thought of urging him to take the pledge, adding, as an incentive,
that he had done so himself. The Irishman looked up with a
jocular expression and replied—recognizing that his interlocutor
was a priest, but not recognizing his Archbishop—" *Perhaps your
riverence had cause !* "

It is said that drunkenness in a priest was the one vice towards
which he showed no mercy.

had something more to do than to reclaim those who had fallen." [1]   Having recognized the importance of open-air meetings, he made use of them indefatigably. In 1874 he addressed three such meetings, each of them attended by thousands of men, on Clerkenwell Green, at London Fields, and on Tower Hill.   It was a singular sight, this ascetic denizen of another world, as he seemed to be, fitter, people would have thought, for the courtly ceremonies of the Vatican than for his present rough surroundings, standing bare-headed on some railway van or costermonger's cart, which served for platform, appealing earnestly, yet not without occasional touches of humour, to the dense and motley crowd by which he was encompassed.   It proved indeed rather too rough work for him, for the people pressed upon him, with no unkindly intention, so as almost to cause him bodily injury; and, to meet this difficulty, a year or two later some enthusiastic young men formed themselves into a " Cardinal's body-guard "; and the association grew rapidly in numbers, so that the " guards," wearing a distinctive sash as uniform, formed quite a notable spectacle in later demonstrations.   In this year, 1874, was also held the first *fête* of the League of the Cross at the Crystal Palace; [2] and the annual recurrence of

---

[1] He often humorously protested against the notion that the League of the Cross was "a confraternity of penitent drunkards." "Don't say that; I am its president and its chaplain."

[2] The *Standard*, which was usually hostile to Manning, cordially recognized the value of his work on this occasion :—" The League has been formed mainly by the untiring exertions of that great apostle of temperance, Archbishop Manning, who has never ceased to strive for the cause, not only of temperance, but of total abstinence.   That he has been to a great extent successful may be judged by the fact that the League now numbers many scores of thousands throughout the United Kingdom ; and that in London

these meetings, in preparation for which the members, numbering many thousands, used commonly to assemble with bands and banners on the Thames Embankment, impressed on Londoners the greatness of the work which the Cardinal had in hand. The League had also meetings in the spring at Exeter Hall, at which proposals for temperance legislation then before Parliament, such as the Sunday Closing or the Permissive Bill, were sure to receive enthusiastic support, Manning being equally sure, if within reach, to be present. Nothing indeed sufficed to keep him away. In August, 1881, being then seventy-three years of age, he appeared punctually on the scene at an open-air meeting on Clerkenwell Green, though the rain was pouring in torrents; and it was only after he had opened the meeting with a few words that he was willing, at the earnest solicitation of friends present with him on the platform, to withdraw; and in April, 1886, he attended an evening meeting of the League, though, under medical advice, he had not previously been out of doors after dusk for months. The mere record indeed of his speeches at temperance meetings, both in London and

alone their 28,000 members shows that the association has done good work amongst the humbler classes of the Catholic population of the metropolis. Very many of these have now taken the pledge, and have kept it most firmly. Thus habits of temperance become, as it were, inoculated and habitual. Of the value of such a League, no man who has seen the evils arising from intoxication can doubt. Yesterday the proceedings were of a semi-religious character, for there was a large meeting held in the opera-theatre at which Archbishop Manning presided. After five o'clock the Archbishop addressed a crowded meeting in the gardens, where he urged, with a homely eloquence that at times was real pathos, the evils of intemperance both mental and bodily. Certainly the cause of abstinence has never found a more able advocate, and we wish his Grace every success." (Aug. 25, 1874.)

in the north of England, would be tedious reading; enough has been said about them to show how devoted he was to this cause, which every one must respect, though not every one feels able to go the lengths that he did in regard to it.

For those lengths were very considerable. Doubtless there is much to be said in commendation of those who, although habitually temperate before, undertake total abstinence from alcoholic drinks, in order to encourage the habitually intemperate to take the same step. Doubtless too in the case of children, especially among the poor, there are good reasons for discouraging an expensive and unnecessary taste; and one would not quarrel with the aged Cardinal, when, for example, at Blackburn, in September, 1886, he "administered the pledge" to more than a thousand children. And there is truth in what he wrote in 1888 to Father Flood, of Athlone :—" I hope all fathers and mothers will bring up their children in total abstinence. It is not only a guard against many and the deadliest temptations, but it is a counsel of a higher life,[1] which teaches temperance in all things, and lifts our will up to desire and to do better things." But yet it is difficult to deny that, from the point of view of those who do not reject as of diabolic origin the "wine that maketh glad the heart of man," or even more vulgar potations, taken in reason and moderation, Manning's teaching on this subject must be accounted as not far removed from fanatical. What is to be said to his bidding, in April, 1878, an

---

[1] This phrase, "a counsel of a higher life," became a favourite one with him; apparently as suggesting, though without the authorization of the Church, a fourth "counsel of perfection." Equally without authority, surely, was his description of temperance as "one of the virtues that St. Patrick loved most."

audience of poor children at Spitalfields "*never to sully their character* by taking intoxicants"? Surely there are already in the world enough entanglements for a sensitive conscience, without leading people to suppose that a purely innocent action has, on account of some possible but very remote consequences, the nature of sin. It may even be doubted whether such teaching is not, from the Catholic standpoint, approximate to heresy, as involving a kind of Manichæan notion that certain substances are evil in themselves. At any rate, there had been murmurings to that effect among Manning's suffragans and clergy; and, in the summer of 1884, a smart controversy arose on the subject. At a Temperance Congress at Liverpool Manning had recently said: "Do you not feel that it is a burning shame on the Christian world and upon the Christian name that we Christians are the only men on earth that are stained and shamed by the manufacture and consumption of intoxicating drink? . . . The great Indian, Oriental, Chinese and Mahometan populations, which I may call four great worlds of men, by their law and their religion are bound not to drink intoxicating drinks. I know indeed that many of them break their law and trample on their religion, . . . but the great mass of them do not; the great mass of those men, whom we regard as unenlightened in this respect, know and practise a rule of mortification, self-denial and self-command which is an example to us." No one complained that what the Cardinal had said was not true; they only complained, some of them, that it was untheological. Special note was taken of a protest signed by "Senex," who turned out to be the Catholic Bishop of Nottingham; and the *Tablet* was filled with letters, some for and some against the line that Manning had adopted. To one of the former—a priest who afterward left the Roman communion and eventually joined the Church of England— he wrote in terms disclosing unwonted excitement, but interesting, as showing how entirely his heart was in the cause, and how he believed it to be making way among his own clergy:—" I thank you much for your letter, and more for your letter in the *Tablet* of last week. The letters of last week were in a majority good; what this week, like to-morrow, may bring forth, I cannot tell. But do not be out of heart. If we were ever on God's side in a battle, it is now, when we are using, *i. e.* giving up our Christian liberty for the salvation of souls. If others think to save more souls by using their liberty to drink wine, let us wait for the last day. I have borne years of reproval and shame in this matter, and I often say, ' I am a fool for Christ's sake.' Why should you or I be afraid? *Si hominibus placerem, non essem servus Jesu Christi.* I am so deliberately, maturely and calmly certain of every reason and principle involved in what we are doing, that I look on this *Tablet* work as part of our gain. I had heard before, but I will not believe it, that 'Senex' is one of my colleagues. Lest it should not be so, I will not write in the *Tablet*; lest it should be, I hope next month to have many opportunities of saying what is necessary; and we must not complain. And now, do not fear. When I began, only two priests in London helped me. Now there are about forty. And the young ones from St. Thomas's have for years been attending our meetings, and almost all are doing something. Everything is going onward. God forbid that we, Catholic priests, should be left

behind in self-denial for the love of souls by those
who are not in the unity of the truth. 'I will provoke
you to jealousy by that which is not a nation; by
a foolish nation I will anger you.' This is a sharp
rebuke. Write on and work on, and may God be
with you."

He was as good as his word about what he would do
"next month." It was his summer "holiday," and he
was absent from London three weeks, in the course of
which he visited Chester, St. Helens, Manchester,
Liverpool, Warrington, Preston, Leeds and Sheffield,
at each place "carrying on," as the *Tablet* somewhat
contemptuously expressed it, "a teetotal temperance
crusade." That was his only answer to his critics. Nor
did he let the matter drop when he had returned. In
October he lectured on intemperance at Reading, and
four days later at the Town Hall, Kensington,[1] where
he quoted Baronius as authority for the statement that
"many of the Apostles were total abstainers." Against
such an advocate the gods themselves would strive in
vain.

And his zeal for this cause was unabated to the last.[2]
In his eightieth year, preaching at the Oratory on behalf of the establishment of an East-end Home for Girls,
he said incidentally, "I have for years (I say it openly
and boldly) been 'a fool for Christ's sake' in the matter
of intoxicating drink, and so I hope to die." The year

[1] At this meeting he made a feeling reference to the death of
Mr. A. M. Sullivan, M.P., whom he thought he would find it
difficult to replace as a helper in the cause of the League of the
Cross.

[2] The withdrawal of the Government's scheme for compensating
dispossessed publicans (1890) was reckoned as due in great measure
to the imposing forces that Cardinal Manning was able to marshal
in opposition to it.

following he said to Dr. Dawson Burns, "Nothing in my public life has given me greater satisfaction than my connection with the temperance movement"; and from the same authority we learn that he did not confine his labours to his own Catholic poor, but took also a warm interest in the London Temperance Hospital, speaking twice at its annual meetings, and was further devoted to the object of protecting native races from the ruinous temptations to which they are exposed by the action of the traders who seek to extend among them a traffic in alcoholic liquors.[1] For twenty years of his life he laboured, in season and out of season, on behalf of the strictest temperance, and we cannot quarrel with his consistency when, on his death-bed, he strictly enjoined his doctors to administer to him no kind of alcoholic stimulant. It is an impressive chapter in the life of a strenuous, earnest, strong-willed, if one may not say wilful, man.

Reference has been made above to some aspects of Manning's work in relation to education, both in the Anglican and Roman Churches. In all it extended over nearer sixty than fifty years, and there was a marked unity of idea and of purpose running through it. There was also, advocates of more liberal ideas than his must confess, an ultimate triumph for his reactionary cause,

---

[1] Consistent with his views about temperance was the interest he took in the question of the London water supply. On this he wrote to the late Mr. James Beal, in July, 1890 :—"My conviction that the water supply of the metropolis ought to be no longer in the hands of private companies is greater than ever. I am glad to see the movement, in which we worked together many years ago, more widely and, I hope, more successfully taken up by public authorities."

a triumph mainly due, beyond all manner of doubt, to Manning's perseverance and sagacity. From the date of the first Reform Act there has been in England a movement, modest enough in its first inception, to make public education a public concern under the direction of elective bodies, and so freed from exclusively clerical control. This movement has been warmly supported by many of the ablest and most active men of the day, statesmen, philosophers, scientists, educationists, *littérateurs*, and the like ; and it obtained (by submitting to a compromise) a partial success in 1870, after about thirty years of active propagandism, during which the whole strength of the Nonconformist element was ranged upon its side. Its progress was hotly contested step by step by the clergy of the Established Church, and by none of them more strenuously than by Manning, during the years 1838-50 ; and, after a period of fifteen years, when he was more or less out of sight, he resumed the leadership of the opposition in 1865, on becoming Archbishop, and retained it until the passing of the Free Education Act in the autumn of 1891, within six months of his death. Although the passing of that Act has not been claimed as a triumph for the cause of clerically-controlled education—for indeed it would not be politic to do so—there can be little doubt as to the fact.

Manning had not been Archbishop a year when he issued a Pastoral on the needs of Catholic elementary education in his diocese, in which he estimated that there wanted provision for at least 7,000 children.[1] In

[1] The estimate was a very rough one. In 1874 the Archbishop estimated the Catholic population of London at 200,000, so that there would be about 33,000 Catholic children, of whom only

June, 1866, he presided at a meeting, which was practically the first of the annual meetings of the " Westminster Diocesan Education Fund," at which he boldly
asked for £7,000 a year for ten years, to meet the
emergency, and received immediate promise of annual
support to the amount of £3,000.[1] He was in Rome,
attending the Vatican Council, during the discussions on
Mr. Forster's Education Bill in 1870, otherwise he
would certainly have been assiduous in attendance at
the House of Commons' lobby, and might perhaps have
secured some modification of its provisions. He held
however a meeting of all the English Bishops at the
English College to consider the bill immediately on its
appearance ; and, so far as he could from a distance, he
worked for the maintenance of the established voluntary
system side by side with the new system of Board
Schools.

Two years later, although the attendance at the
Catholic schools had increased enormously since he
became Archbishop, he issued a Lenten Pastoral, some-

25,000 were on the books. Some 1,200 of these were however
known to be in Poor Law schools, and about 4,000 were reckoned
as belonging to the upper and middle classes, who might safely be
counted on as being educated in convent or other Catholic schools.
Catholics of the middle class have especial advantages in this
matter, many convent schools on the Continent providing board
and education at annual fees of which £20 is not the lowest.
    [1] The Catholic aristocracy gave him prompt and liberal support.
The trustees of the fifteenth (the present) Duke of Norfolk contributed £10,000, and Lord Howard of Glossop, who succeeded the
Hon. Charles Langdale as chairman of the Catholic Poor Schools
Committee in 1869, subscribed £5,000, and obtained £10,000
from his son-in-law, the Marquis of Bute. Throughout the country
it was estimated that 70,000 scholars were added to the Catholic
schools, at a cost of something like £350,000, raised for the " Catholic
Education Crisis Fund."

what desponding in its tone. He lamented the secu-
larization of the Universities, and the growth of the
belief that education was the business not of the Church
but of the State. " The higher culture of England has
ceased to be Christian, and those trained at the Universities will henceforth hold, as part of their political
creed, that the Church ought to be separated from the
State, that the school ought to be separated from the
Church, and that the education of the people belongs
to the civil power."   A little later however, at the opening of some new schools on Tower Hill, he took occasion
to thank the London School Board for the manner in
which they had dealt with every question relating to
Catholic education; thanks which he repeated in 1877
and 1884.

A peculiar interest attaches to a Pastoral on the same
subject issued in 1881, as it was to be read in the
churches on the Sunday on which Cardinal Newman
preached at the London Oratory; and he prefaced his
sermon by reading a passage insisting on the principle
that the education of Catholics should be controlled by
the Church, to which he added "a graceful compliment
to the powerful expression of this truth by the Cardinal
Archbishop, and the greatness of the work his Eminence
had done in the matter"; a tribute that was all the
more handsome, as the work, so far as the education of
the poor was concerned, was one in which he took no
practical interest himself.

About this time, recognizing the greatness of the
burden laid on the clergy, the lay supporters, and the
poorer classes of parents in maintaining their own
schools, in face of the competition of rate-supported
Board Schools, to many of which parents in far better

circumstances than most Catholics were able to obtain admission for their children free, Cardinal Manning made a proposal which seemed at the time impracticable and bold even to audacity. It was that the voluntary schools should have a share of the support from the rates which hitherto the Board Schools had enjoyed exclusively. Even Catholics, who would have rejoiced to see such a proposal adopted, thought it chimerical, and were unwilling to give it their support. The Archbishop however was not to be dissuaded easily from his project. He was urgent in his endeavours to win members of Parliament over to his side, with scant success, it must be owned; and he began (in 1884) to act in union with the "Voluntary Schools Association," thus making common cause in the matter with the Church of England and the Wesleyans. For some years yet his scheme remained in abeyance; but meanwhile he did not relax his efforts on the main work of securing efficiency, and so permanence, for the Catholic schools. In June, 1885, he held a meeting at Archbishop's House in furtherance of a plan to improve the position of the masters and mistresses of the schools in his diocese, and he urged their claims again at a meeting of the Westminster Diocesan Education Fund. It was the position of the masters that most required amelioration; for the mistresses, being mostly nuns, had a sure provision for old age in their convents. He recurred to this important matter again; indeed it was upon a schoolmasters' superannuation scheme that he was engaged when struck down by his last illness.

In October, 1885, preaching at the Pro-Cathedral on "The Future of the Schools," Manning quoted French and American writers to prove the failure of the secular system of education in those countries. A witness from New York was referred to:—" If ignorance were the mother of vice, and if the public school system were what it is set up to be, the fruits of the latter would by this time be manifest and plainly visible to the whole world in our moral advancement. But as a matter of fact, our large towns are filled with idle, vicious lads, and our rural districts swarm with tramps." The Archbishop urged his people not to be misled by imposing statistics, but to hold firmly to sound principles. In this year also (1885), so keenly alive was he to the gravity of the crisis, and so clearly did he recognize the fact that the Liberals were committed to a policy of secular education under popular control, that he departed from his usual course of keeping politics and religion distinct,[1] and informally, through an article in the *Nineteenth Century*, reprinted in pamphlet form, called on Catholics to support the Conservative candidates; which it must be concluded they did, though the effect of their vote was not so marked as might have been anticipated.

The year following he was rewarded for his labours in the cause of religious education by being given a dignified position from which he could exercise the greatest influence in the direction that he had always at heart. The Queen appointed a Royal Commission to enquire into and report upon the whole subject of primary education, and second on the list of those whom she summoned was " our trusty and well-beloved, the

---

[1] In reply to an elector who asked on which side he should vote when both candidates supported the claims of the voluntary schools, he replied, " I hold myself officially bound to neutrality, and leave my clergy and my flock perfectly free."

most reverend Cardinal Archbishop, Henry Edward
Manning, Doctor in Divinity." It is not necessary to
refer to the details of this protracted enquiry. It issued
volumes of evidence, and in the course of its sessions
its *personnel* was considerably changed. Throughout a
majority of its members were favourable to the maintenance of the voluntary system ; but it is clear that,
beyond this, the influence of a commanding and
venerable figure among its members had the pre-
eminence, so that the Commission might almost be
called his Commission, and its Report his Report.
At any rate, when the latter appeared, it contained,
to most men's astonishment, the very recommendation
that Manning had urged some eight years before,
that the voluntary schools should be supported out
of the rates.

The Government, though it doubtless sympathized
with the object of this proposal, and though it had a
strong majority at its back, did not venture to introduce
any legislation to give the Report effect; and the
scheme shortly receded into the background, though
Manning supported it manfully, publishing *Fifty Reasons
why the Voluntary Schools ought to share in the Rates*,
and an article to the same effect in the *Fortnightly
Review*. But the scheme was not really dead; it was,
behind the scenes, taking an even more favourable
shape; and when, in 1891, rumours of "assisted
education" were in the air, there were also rumours of
negotiations in which the Duke of Norfolk, as representing Catholic interests, was asserted to have taken
part; and the event gave to these rumours every
appearance of truth. For the Free Education Act of
1891, with its new grant of 10*s.* per child in average

attendance to replace the fees, was, beyond all, a boon to Catholic schools. Thousands of Catholic children had been perforce admitted free before the passing of the Act, each of whom would now earn the new grant; while many thousands more had paid only penny fees, amounting barely to 3s. 6d. per annum, who would now be good for 10s. This Act was in fact a triumph for the Cardinal's cause—for no doubt the Duke was acting for the Cardinal—so far as such a cause could possibly achieve a triumph. It was even better than the proposed sharing of the rates, for that could never have been worked without much friction with the local authorities, and local supervision as well; whereas now there was no shadow of new interference with the management, and the grant in lieu of fees would come in the welcome shape of a money order from Whitehall.

It was a splendid example of the victory which organization and quiet persistence in a definite policy are able to gain over forces that in themselves are distinctly superior. If Manning had done nothing else for the cause of Catholicism in England, he would deserve the grateful remembrance of Catholics for what he did in this matter. For the arrangement, although it is altogether inconsistent with the principle that education supported out of public funds should be under public control, is not unlikely to be a permanent one, anyhow so far as Catholics are concerned. John Bull is always disposed to respect the system in possession, and this system will have been in possession some time before any political party will find leisure to attack it; and, when it is attacked, the Catholic vote is likely to be able to turn the scale in its favour. And indeed it is not the Catholic schools with which the advocates of universal popular control are most disposed to quarrel. Catholics, like Jews, are regarded as a class apart, whose views are peculiar and difficult for outsiders to meet, and who are best left to manage their own affairs in this matter. It is the exclusive management of the village school by the village parson that most provokes hostility; Catholic schools, that are seldom to be found save in towns where there is plenty of choice of other schools within easy distance, are reckoned less open to objection.

Nowhere in Catholic countries on the continent of Europe does the Church possess the freedom in this matter, coupled with very substantial State support, that she enjoys in England.[1] And it is only fair to add that neither is that freedom abused nor that support undeserved. A vast amount of useful educational work is efficiently performed in the Catholic elementary schools, not without considerable sacrifices on the part both of those who support them financially and of those who devote their lives to teaching in them.

[1] In the summer of 1882 the writer of these pages was at Autun, and had some conversation with Monseigneur Perraud, the Bishop, and sundry of his clergy, on the position of Catholic education in England. All expressed their astonishment at the liberality of a Protestant Government in contributing about three-fifths of the cost of the education of each child, while the management was left almost unfettered; and contrasted it with the conduct of their own Government, which had just been expropriating, in some cases even by violence, the religious orders. The battered door of the convent of the Marist Fathers, only a few yards distant, was a witness to the truth of what they said. At that time there was some prospect that legislation in England would not uphold the existing state of things; but the only changes that have been made in ten years have been to render the official inspection less trying to the teachers, and to increase the public support from three-fifths to four-fifths.

They are, of all such schools in the country, the most economically managed, and their suppression would result in a formidable increase to the charges on the rates. Moreover, whatever may be thought as to the truth of the dogmas inculcated in these schools, the moral teachings, with which those dogmas are always intimately associated, cannot fail to be a social force for good; while the existence of guilds, confraternities, and the like, membership in which is almost a matter of course with the senior pupils in Catholic schools, has considerable influence in retaining their allegiance to something at any rate of what they have learnt, when the time comes for them to leave; and herein they have the pull over the secular system established by their side, which, as things are now, seldom makes any attempt to train or to secure the loyalty of the pupil's feelings. Some years ago there were Catholics—there may be a few still—disposed, in view of the expense, to discontinue the struggle for their separate schools, and to be content with leave granted by the Board to the priest to teach the catechism in a class-room at certain hours. To all such suggestions Manning ever turned a deaf ear; and it can hardly be denied that his policy of no-surrender has been well justified by the event.

Every Catholic Bishop in England must of necessity be more than half an Irishman if he is to rule his flock with sympathy and success. Manning had not a drop of Irish blood in his veins;[1] he was English with an

---

[1] In October, 1878, Mr. John O'Hart, of Ringsend, Dublin, sent the Cardinal a book in which the Manning pedigree was traced to Ireland. The reply that Manning sent is amusing:— " I rejoice to see that I may claim kindred with your faithful race,

admixture, if any, of Italian blood; but it is nevertheless certain that the close relations with the Irish which
his position necessitated, won him wholly round to their
side. He grew steadily in his conviction of the
importance of that race as the great Catholic factor in
the British Isles and in the British Empire; and the
natural tendency of his heart to go forth in sympathy
towards those who are poor, those who suffer, those who
have been wronged, drew him so powerfully towards the
cause of Ireland—the cause, that is, as it is understood
by four-fifths of the population of Ireland, and by the
Catholic Irish with complete unanimity—that they on
their part, to quote the words of Mr. T. P. O'Connor,
"responsive to his evident fondness for them, gave him
a confidence and affection that almost approached to
worship."

In his earlier years Ireland seems to have hardly
entered into his thoughts. The horrors of the Irish
famine in 1847 had indeed drawn from him a cry of
sympathy that has already been referred to ; [1] but it was
not until he had been brought into contact with Catholic
Irish ecclesiastics in Rome, during his first residence
there, 1851-54, that he had any formed ideas on Irish
questions. On St. Patrick's Day, 1857, he preached in
St. Isidore's, Rome, the church of the Irish College, a
sermon to which he afterwards referred with satisfaction,
as the first expression of his love for Ireland; but some

if not descent from King Fiacha. Hitherto I have been afraid
that you would count me among the Saxons of Henry II., for
the name is a tribal name of the Frisians, and is settled in Sussex,
Kent and Norfolk. I am glad however to know that it is, like
the name Catholic, a bond with old Ireland."

[1] See above, p. 44.

years had yet to elapse before he understood and appreciated the true character of the national cause. Speaking
at the Birmingham Catholic Reunion in 1867, he used
a phrase which the *Tablet* thought it necessary to apologize for at the time, and again in 1872 :—" Show me
an Irishman who has lost the faith, and I will show you
a Fenian." He did not mean, it was explained, that
every Irish nationalist was necessarily an infidel, but that
every so-called Catholic Fenian was, *ipso facto*, no true
Catholic.[1] The Fenians had, in short, been condemned
as a secret society by the Holy See. He was beginning
however to realize that to drive popular disaffection
underground was the surest way to make it dangerously
explosive ; and in a letter to Earl Grey, written in
1868, he protested against the narrowness which, in
spite of the more liberal tone prevalent elsewhere
throughout the Queen's dominions, made political partisans at home still speak contemptuously of the Irish
race and of the Irish faith :—" We have become an
Empire of many races and of many religions, and the
worst enemy of civil and religious peace could devise no
surer policy of discord . . . than the attempt to keep
alive the ascendancy of race over race, of religion over
religion, of Church over Church." He was not however
so shortsighted as to suppose that the mere disestablishment of the Irish Protestant Church could satisfy the
legitimate demands of Ireland ; and he gave a spirited
definition of what he understood by the more pressing
" land question " :—" It means hunger, thirst, nakedness, notice to quit, labour spent in vain, the toil

---

[1] Some five-and-twenty years after this speech he said humorously to Mr. T. P. O'Connor, " Remember, I am not only a Home
Ruler, but even a Fenian."

of years seized upon, the breaking up of homes, the miseries, sickness, deaths of parents, children, wives; the despair and wildness which spring up in the hearts of the poor when legal force, like a sharp harrow, goes over the most sensitive and vital rights of mankind."

The growing affection with which he was regarded by the Catholic Irish in London is well evidenced by an account that appeared in the *Cork Examiner*, of a sermon preached by him on the Irish national festival at the Church of St. Patrick, Soho, in 1872:—" Each year the Irish of the metropolis are becoming more and more self-respecting and circumspect, especially in the celebration of the festival of their patron saint. To the influence of the Catholic clergy this state of things is largely due, and mostly to the influence of the Archbishop, the wisest and best of spiritual fathers. . . His sermon was the feature of the day, the thing to be thought over and remembered. . . It was the simplicity of gold, and that of the purest ore. From first to last there was not an oratorical passage, nothing artificial, nothing elaborate; it was a stream of bright, clear, living water. Robed in a splendid cope, crowned with the archiepiscopal mitre, and holding in his left hand the crozier, the emblem of his pastoral authority, his right hand was free for such chaste and almost severe action as best harmonized with the character of his discourse, which was above all things paternal, fraught with the tenderness and sympathy of a friend and father. And it is by this sympathy that the Archbishop's influence is so powerful for good over his Irish flock. Stung too often by taunts arising from national jealousy, the Irish lavish their love and confidence on

those who treat them and their country with respect.
This is what the Archbishop does, and the result is
witnessed whenever he summons a meeting of what
are styled 'English Catholics,' five-sixths of them
being really Irish either in birth or origin. . . The
Archbishop's sympathy is ever free and genuine. He
never forgets what the children of St. Patrick have
done for the Church in England, that to them is due
the practical restoration of the faith in his country.
And, acknowledging as he does this inestimable service,
he seeks to elevate the moral *status* of the Irish in
London rather by words of tender admonition than by
stern or harsh rebuke.   One might witness in the
brightening glance, at times flashing through rising
tears, and in the quick flush of the cheek, how his
simple words went home to the deepest feelings of his
audience; and how in the calm grave countenance
might be read the acceptance of his advice—advice a
hundred times more effective from its being affectionate.   One might say without exaggeration that,
as he thus stood on the altar steps, bearing on him
the emblems of his office, he looked as St. Patrick
may have looked, and spoke as St. Patrick would have
spoken."

Manning never actually set foot in Ireland.   He was
to have been present at the consecration of the new
cathedral at Armagh, in August, 1873, but was prevented from going by the unexpected prolongation of
his own Provincial Synod of Westminster.   He sent
instead a long letter addressed to the Primate of
Ireland, which is in some ways remarkable, and especially
as showing that he was genuinely one of those whose
numbers are now increasing with such remarkable

rapidity, who " were Home Rulers before Mr. Gladstone."
With singular political foresight he advocates what
really amounts to " Home Rule all round," and " Imperial Federation " :—" England and Scotland will not
claim to legislate for Ireland according to English and
Scotch interests and prejudices; and Ireland, when it is
justly treated, will have no more will than it has now
to meddle in the local affairs of England or Scotland.
The three peoples are distinct in blood, in religion,
in character, and in local interests. They will soon
learn to ' live and let live.' They mean to manage
their own affairs with a great extension rather than
a hair's-breadth of diminution in the freedom of local
government."

In July, 1875, on the occasion of the O'Connell
centenary, Manning, writing to Peter Paul McSwiney,
Lord Mayor of Dublin, described O'Connell as " the
man whose prudence, firmness, eloquence and devotion
won for the Catholic Church in these realms its liber-
ation from penal laws " ; adding, " I believe it will be for
posterity fully to appreciate the work which he accomplished." But he spoke of him only as a benefactor to
Catholics, and not especially to Ireland; a limitation
which would seem to imply some want of familiarity
with O'Connell's life. Indeed it was not until ten
years later that he publicly associated himself with any
definite proposal to establish in Ireland a legislative
body empowered to deal with national as distinct from
imperial affairs; and, when Mr. Gladstone's Home Rule
Bill of 1886 was published, he expressed the fullest
sympathy with its general principles and its drift, but
dissented no less frankly from some of its provisions.
The exclusion of the Irish members from Westminster

was, in his judgment, a fatal blot. Others objected
to this exclusion as inconsistent with the principle of
no taxation without representation; others, again, because they hoped the establishment of a Parliament in
Dublin would lead to a wider scheme of imperial
federation, in which all the provinces of the Empire
would have a representation in an Imperial Parliament
at Westminster. The Cardinal was not insensible to
these considerations, but, as a Catholic first, he objected
strongly to the loss of the Irish members, as involving
the loss of a Catholic leaven in the central legislative
body. He did not make any answer to the counter-
objection that it passed the wit of man to conceive
how Ireland could be represented by her best men in
Dublin and in London simultaneously; but on the
question raised by a Mr. Hurlbert—an American who
was somewhat incautiously accepted as an ally by the
opponents of Home Rule—as to whether religious
liberty would not be imperilled in Ireland, he wrote a
long letter, in which he maintained that "the Catholics
of Ireland have never persecuted their Protestant
neighbours in the matter of religion, and have been
always the conspicuous examples of respecting the
liberty of conscience which has been so cruelly
denied to them. The children of martyrs are not
persecutors."

Considerable as his influence was in Rome, it was
not enough to put a stop to efforts that had been made
to utilize the Pope against the Home Rule agitation.
Together with the Irish Bishops, however, he succeeded
in reducing the action of the Pope to a mere condemnation of certain acts, such as boycotting, where those acts
became inconsistent with the moral law. Doubtless it

was as fortunate for the Pope as it was for Ireland that
no bolder step was taken; for an Irish schism would
hardly have been avoided if Rome had, apparently
under English guidance, dictated a policy unacceptable
to the national sentiment.

The cordial feeling of Irishmen—and not of Catholic
Irishmen only—towards Cardinal Manning was well
attested on the occasion of his "silver jubilee," the
twenty-fifth anniversary of his consecration as Bishop,
in June, 1890. An address to him was signed by all
the Nationalist members; and fifty of them, including
Mr. Parnell, went to the Archbishop's House to present
it.[1] It was read by Mr. Sexton, and the Cardinal was
evidently touched by many kindly allusions to his
efforts on behalf of the Irish poor. His reply was
barely audible at times, but one sentence was heard
with close attention, and was remembered by those who
heard it :—" My present feeling is one of the most profound hope. Ireland has entered into the most intimate
and cordial union with the English people. If I know
anything, I know the working people of England; and
I know at this moment that the hearts of the working
people of England have turned to Ireland in true and
perfect sympathy." At about this same time he wrote
to Mr. W. O'Brien :—" The day of restitution has nearly
come. I hope to see the daybreak, and I hope you will
see the noontide, when the people of Ireland will be

---

[1] At this time Manning knew nothing of the case against Mr.
Parnell as it was shortly afterwards to appear in the courts of law.
When that became public he wrote :—" For many years I have
held that a judicial record such as that in Mr. Parnell's case dis-
qualifies a man for public life. From the moment of this deplorable divorce case I have held Mr. Parnell to be excluded from
leadership, not on political but on moral grounds."

re-admitted, so far as is possible, to the possession of
their own soil, and shall be admitted, so far as possible,
to the making and administration of their own local
laws, while they shall still share in the legislation which
governs and consolidates the Empire." And on St.
Patrick's Day, 1891, he wrote to Mr. Justin McCarthy:
" I see Ireland rising and re-organizing itself, after a
passing obscuration, upon the old and only lines which
have unfolded its noble life throughout the world." No
wonder that the writer of such sentences should be
spoken of as " an Englishman beloved in Ireland"; nor
any wonder either that his proceedings in this matter
should be regarded with misgiving by those who hold
that the grant of a national Parliament to Ireland is
but the first step towards the dismemberment of the
British Empire. Certainly Manning desired no such
result. It was always Catholic Ireland that he spoke
of as " pre-eminently the martyr-nation," whose wrongs
he would fain see remedied. Questions of race or of
political arrangement were to him subordinate; but the
catholicizing influence of Ireland throughout the British
Empire was in his judgment so obvious and so precious,
that any privilege might be reckoned to have been
fairly won by the nation to whom it is mainly due that
the Queen counts among her subjects some ten millions
of Catholics, under the spiritual rule of twenty-eight
Archbishops and one hundred and thirty other Bishops
or Vicars Apostolic. So far from desiring the separation
from the British Crown of any member of this family,
he would doubtless, had his loyalty to the Crown permitted it, have desired a still more widely-extended
British Federated Empire, in which the United States
of America, with their eight millions of Catholics, would

have found an honoured place. The faith and the sufferings of Ireland—these are what won him, stranger as he was all the time to the country itself; and the cordial response which his expressions of affection and sympathy evoked gave him a position as Archbishop of Westminster which his successor will find it hard to obtain.

CHAPTER VIII.

So familiar have we become in late years with the spectacle of a Cardinal of the Holy Roman Church taking part in Mansion House Committees, presiding at philanthropic meetings, and acting as conciliator between the rival parties in a strike, that it requires almost an effort of the imagination to realize that these things are but of yesterday, and that five-and-twenty years ago no dignitary of the Establishment and no conspicuous Nonconformist minister would have been willing to appear on the same platform with a Catholic ecclesiastic, nor could any such ecclesiastic have taken a useful or an influential part at meetings summoned to promote some social reform. He would have been reckoned out of place and superfluous.

It goes therefore without saying that the position to which Manning had attained in 1889, as a recognized and indispensable leader in the grave questions affecting labour that were so prominently before the public mind in that year, was only gradually reached. It was the relief of the starving poor in Paris at the end of the siege in January, 1871, that first called him on to a

Mansion House Committee to co-operate with his fellow-citizens of whatever creed; and perhaps the fact of his being a Catholic rather favoured than otherwise the passing of a resolution requesting him to draw up an address to the Mayor of Paris expressive of the sympathy of the people of London. He had been among the originators of the movement, and had preached at the Pro-Cathedral on its behalf.

His next appearance at a public meeting of a philanthropic kind was as president of the International Prison Congress, held in July, 1872. He made then a somewhat laboured and perhaps unnecessary apology for his position as the advocate of a cause that was not distinctively Catholic:—"When I was called upon to preside over this meeting, I felt it my duty to do so as neutrally as possible. That is to say, holding a profound conviction that, on all those occasions which lay on my conscience a public duty, I am bound to be as outspoken, I may say as explicit and determined, in expressing what I believe, as my office requires; so, on all other occasions, when I am not bound to make these declarations or to bear these testimonies, I desire to identify myself with the majority of those whom I love and respect. But outside the circle and the pale of that one subject, I know of no other relating to our political, our public, our social, our industrial welfare, in which it is not in my power to work with the same energy and the same entire devotion of heart and feeling as any other man in England. . . It is the constant desire of my heart to work with my countrymen in everything that can promote the welfare of our people, or that will, like this Congress, world-wide in its character, promote those sympathies which bind

Christian nations together." The chief speaker at this meeting was Dr. Bellows, an Unitarian from New York, whose views on Prison Reform Manning eulogized, adding his own opinion, that criminals should be treated singly and as children, and that due spiritual provision was no less necessary for them than some redress of their material hardships. In December this same year Manning took an active part in promoting the "Hospital Sunday" scheme for London, which has, together with its younger brother "Hospital Saturday," done so much for the sick and suffering poor; though it can hardly be accounted more than a temporary make-shift until such time as the hospitals are provided for by law. He attended and spoke at several meetings at the Mansion House on its behalf, and also ordered an annual collection for it throughout his diocese.

But far more important, both in itself and as a "new departure" in the cause of labour, was his presence at a meeting held in Exeter Hall on December 10, 1872, in the interests of the newly-established Agricultural Labourers' Union. Mr. Samuel Morley presided, and the Archbishop's other companions on the platform were Sir C. Trevelyan, Sir C. Dilke, Sir J. Bennett, Mr. Mundella, Mr. T. Hughes, Mr. Bradlaugh, Mr. Odgers, Mr. Potter and Mr. Arch. Manning moved the first resolution, and explained that he would not have been there had not those who had conferred with him on the subject undertaken that they would work only in a law-abiding and a God-fearing way. But he thought it was a subject on which he had a right to speak. "For seventeen years I sat day by day in the homes of the labouring men of Sussex, and I knew them all and their children by name as well as I knew the scantiness of their means of subsistence." He complained—a bold complaint to have made twenty years ago, though its reasonableness is almost universally admitted now—that men were too much dominated by "the illusions of political economy"; he complained further that the report of the recent Royal Commission on Agricultural Labourers had found no expression in legislation; and he showed that, while the land laws were in process of amendment in Ireland, little or nothing was done for England. The taking of land at thirty shillings an acre and re-letting it as "allotments" at four times that figure, should, he thought, be made illegal; and he pleaded for "a reconstitution of the domestic life of the labouring poor" as a necessary condition of any satisfactory reform. According to the *Times*, the only passage in his speech that was not loudly cheered was a reference to the interest the Prince Consort had taken in the welfare of agricultural labourers.

To some remonstrances addressed to him for having at this meeting "fanned the flame of agrarian agitation," he replied, "To couple my name with that of Mr. Arch gives me no displeasure. I believe him to be an honest and good man. I believe too that the cause he has in hand is well-founded; and I confide in his using no means to promote it but such as are sanctioned by the law of God and the law of the land. I was sorry that the meeting at Exeter Hall was diverted from the purpose for which it was called, and for which I intended it." The last sentence seems to imply that he had been one of the original promoters of the meeting; and this is likely enough, for he had watched the movement throughout the autumn with sympathy, and had been anxious to assist it. They who thought at the time that his appearance on the platform was merely histrionic, knew as little of the man's real mind as they did of the part he was destined to play in labour questions during the next twenty years. What will strike more kindly critics is his remarkable foreshadowing of some of the ideas with which rural conferences have recently made men familiar.

Beyond presiding at a meeting of the Society of Arts in February, 1874, when the subject of "Thrift, or the outdoor relief test" was discussed, and addressing the Society of St. Vincent de Paul the year following, expressing his regret that their numbers were so small,[1] Manning took no further part in labour questions until March, 1876, when he gave a lecture on the " Rights and Dignity of Labour," which was re-written and printed some ten years later. It contained nothing that is not now a commonplace. He expressed his approval of guilds and trade unions as legitimate " protective societies "; [2] he denounced the sending of young children to work in factories, before their bones were strongly set or their education nearly sufficient; and he maintained that wives or mothers, who gave fifty or sixty hours a week to work at a distance from their homes, were acting in disobedience to a law higher than any human law, which claimed those hours for

---

[1] The Society of St. Vincent de Paul is an association of Catholic laymen who visit and relieve the poor under the direction of the clergy of the district. At the time referred to it numbered only 150 members.

[2] It was a favourite expression of his that " labour *is* capital," and he claimed for it precisely the same rights to protect itself, by trade unions, &c., as any other form of capital might claim for itself.

their husbands and children. Such a practice he thought was "an injury to the community at large, and a particular source of misery to the working classes." In 1880, in a Lenten Pastoral, he spoke of the great and growing contrast between poverty and wealth in this country :—" In no country and in no age has the world ever yet seen such commercial activity and prosperity as that of England. But in the midst of immeasurable wealth is a want which the poorest country of Europe scarcely knows. We have in the midst of us, not poverty alone, which is an honourable state when it is honest and inevitable, but also pauperism, which is the corruption of poverty and the debasement of the poor. The inequalities of our social state, and the chasms which separate classes, the abrupt and harsh contrasts of soft and suffering lots, unless they be redressed by humility and charity, sympathy and self-denial, are dangerous to society and to our spiritual welfare. In London all these inequalities and evils are before us."

In July, 1881, a deputation waited on the Cardinal in the interests of the agricultural labourers, with especial reference to the Irish Land Bill then before Parliament.[1] In reply he stated that his heart had always been with the Irish labourer, and that, ten years earlier, when the fact had been brought before his notice that a strike among artisans always involved immediate and acute suffering among the labourers, he had approved and had supported in every way he could the formation of a Labourers' Union. To the Land League also he had given his approval, "so long as it

---

[1] This matter is referred to here instead of under Ireland, as it is one that is of more than local interest.

operated within the limits of law, human and divine."
But he thought it open to grave doubt whether the
Land Bill then before Parliament could be expected
to include and to settle the question of agricultural
labourers. "I am no politician; I speak as an independent pastor of the Church. But this I know, that
the Bill is so large, so unwieldy and so complicated,
that it would be impossible to introduce into it so
awkward a subject as that of Irish agricultural labour.
. . . I believe the question of landlord and tenant is
sufficient to engage a session; and that therefore the
subject of labour should be entirely reserved for the
future. I think that a Royal Commission should be
issued for the purpose of taking evidence on the state
of the labourers only. . . I decline to enter into the
question of political economy; but this I will say, that
it is quite obvious that a certain amount of land being
left to any individual, he is entitled to live upon it and
to live by the proceeds. I believe further, however,
that, when there shall be local county government on a
larger scale, there should be a sanitary commission, and
a law to compel all those who possess an interest in the
land to provide proper houses, in which the labourers
should be able to live in comfort. . . There is not a
mouth in Ireland that might not be fed, nor a hand
that might not be occupied. I know that many of
those who have lived on the soil have been compelled
to seek a livelihood elsewhere. But I would not have
one man leave Ireland until the soil entrusted to him
has been carefully tilled."

The references thus and on other occasions made by
Cardinal Manning to the need of legislation to secure
better provision for the housing of the working classes

had pointed him out as one qualified to advise on such
legislation,[1] and no one was much surprised when he
was named a member of a Royal Commission to enquire
into the subject in March, 1884. Sir Charles Dilke
was chairman of this Commission, and the two were
thus brought into close and friendly relations; indeed
it was said that the Report, a very substantial one
issued as "of great urgency" in 1885, was in great
measure their joint work. On this Commission also
sat the Prince of Wales, Lords Salisbury, Brownlow
and Carrington, Mr. Goschen, Sir Richard Cross, Sir
George Harrison, Lord Provost of Edinburgh, Bishop
Walsham Howe, the Hon. E. Lyulph Stanley, Mr. Dwyer
Gray, Mr. Torrens, Mr. Broadhurst, Mr. Jesse Collings,
Mr. George Godwin, and Mr. Samuel Morley. Cardinal
Manning also signed a supplementary report in favour of
Leasehold Enfranchisement, and memoranda appended
by Mr. Broadhurst and Mr. Jesse Collings, excepting,
from the latter, a suggestion for the formation of a
system of representative municipal government for
London. Speaking at a Mansion House Conference on
the dwellings of the poor, three months after the Com-

---

[1] In his essay on the "Rights of Labour" he made a very
sensible discrimination between the poor, but in many ways not
unattractive, dwellings of the agricultural labourers, and the
sordid misery of the London labourer's home :—"I saw in my
early days a good deal of what the homes of agricultural labourers
were. With all their poverty they were often very beautiful. I
have seen cottages with cottage-gardens, and with a scanty but
bright furniture, a hearth glowing with peat, and children playing
at the door : poverty was indeed everywhere, but happiness
everywhere too. . . But the homes of the poor in London are
often very miserable. The state of the houses with families living
in single rooms, sometimes many families in one room, a corner
apiece. These things cannot go on ; these things ought not to
go on."

mission had been appointed, he said that the subject was one that "bristled with difficulties," and pointed out that one necessary preliminary was that the poor should be "elevated up to an understanding of what was necessary for the sanitary condition of their houses." He admitted that Royal Commissions were often enough shelves on which to stow away difficult questions, but thought that such was not the temper of those who sat round the board with him. Its Report, however, though it might prove satisfactory to contending interests, would be futile unless there were further legislative power to carry it into effect; and legislation itself would be useless unless there were "dynamic power" among the people themselves. The real cure for the evils would, he thought, be in the people's hands if local self-government were extended to every parish; for there were already on the Statute Book Acts adequate for the repression of the evils complained of. "But we are baffled by the interests of those who own the houses, and baffled by the inertness of those who ought to put the statutes into force. . . If only those in London who have heads and hearts to care for the condition of the poor, and who have been aroused within the last six months to the consciousness of an intolerable evil, would continue and sustain this movement by their own self-denying efforts, I believe there would be found the dynamic force that would put the law into operation; and then gradually and with patience, with those kindly and generous modes of treatment with which alone human affairs can be governed, we shall find a full and complete remedy for these sufferings of the population." At a subsequent meeting of the same association, in January, 1885, he advocated the public registration of ownership as a remedy for the existing difficulty of finding out who was really responsible for the disgraceful condition of the poorer class of houses in many districts; a prohibition to the water-companies to cut off the supply from the houses of the poor in consequence of the non-payment of the rate by the owners; and a reform in the system of vestry-elections, the vestries themselves to be re-constituted, with a central authority over them to see that they did their work.

On the whole, it may be said that it was this question of the Housing of the Poor that placed Manning definitely before the public eye as a wise and competent social reformer. He made a marked impression on all his fellow-members on the Commission by his assiduous attendance and by the serviceableness of the questions he asked the witnesses, though he was by no means a frequent examiner. That the report of the Commission has, as yet, had little practical result was no fault of his.

Another matter in which he interested himself at this time was emigration as a remedy for the congested and half-starved populations of the great towns at home. He was unable to attend a meeting at which a scheme for federating the various emigration societies was proposed, so that they might co-operate without friction in a common work, but he wrote an approving letter to Mr. Arnold White, the promoter of the movement; and, in May, 1886, he took part in a meeting of the National Association for Promoting State-directed Colonization, and backed up its main principle with no uncertain voice :—" I have come to the conclusion that the emigration of people one by one is a feeble way of doing a work which requires energetic action at the

present day. I support the view that the right way
of colonization is by sending out a population to form
the nucleus of new settlements in various parts of the
empire. The efforts of individuals and of societies are
unequal to this task, and I therefore hold that the State
should aid the aims of those who would relieve the
mother-country of the evils of overcrowding in the great
cities here. This is the problem before us :—We have
a limited area with a rapidly-growing population, and
land not able to grow grain enough for more than a
third of the year. Under these circumstances it is right
to find for some part of this population a home across
the seas; a home that would become to them what
England is to an Englishman. This is a great empire,
and it is by colonization that it legitimately increases.
In such united communities lies the best security for
peace. Great empires, though powerful to destroy, are
less warlike than a number of separate communities."

There is in this speech a decided ring both of im-
perialism and of socialism; but the true explanation of
it all lies in the speaker's acute sense of the miseries to
which the poor are subjected in the slums of our great
towns, in his recognition of the slowness of the only
remedies that individuals can apply, and in his ardent
belief, justified to some extent by the facts, that under
freer conditions beyond the seas the Catholic leaven can
more effectually work.

Against another evil that afflicts mankind, though
no longer within the limits of Western civilization,
Manning made an eloquent and impassioned protest
at a meeting held, under the presidency of the Prince
of Wales, at the Guildhall, in August, 1884, to celebrate
the jubilee of the British and Foreign Anti-Slavery

Society. After regretting the absence (through illness) of Lord Shaftesbury, " who would have been the one solitary person present who, in the year 1833, took part in the great act of our Legislature by which slavery was abolished," he congratulated the meeting on " the presence, in his venerable old age, of Sir Harry Verney, who, with so signal a devotion, made himself aware of what the ' middle-passage ' was, and who now gives his testimony, and thanks God for the achievement of that work." Admitting that it was a difficult and a delicate task to call on foreign governments to abolish slavery, he made an exception in the case of Egypt, " the centre of the Mahometan world, and the centre too of this abominable traffic," which was under such obligations to England, and so far under English control, that some little urgency on our part could hardly be without effect. " There are tracts on the eastern coast of Africa where no diplomatic delicacy that I know of need bar our passage. At all costs the slave-trade should be made impossible, and it can be made so by the urgency of Christian chivalry. It should never be suffered that the paths of the sea should be polluted by the horrible traffic of these man-stealers, who in God's Word are classed with man-slayers, and with the murderers of fathers and the murderers of mothers. Our cruisers have long ago cleared the west coasts of Africa, and they can blockade the eastern. . . We are told that Living- stone, whose name cannot be mentioned in this hall, or anywhere, without awakening the sympathy of all Christian men, has left it on record as his belief, that half a million of human lives are annually sacrificed by this African slave-trade. This horrible traffic runs in three tracks, marked by skeletons, from the centre of

Africa towards Madagascar, towards Zanzibar, and
towards the Red Sea. Also we are told that, of those
who are carried away by force, some are so worn out by
fatigue as to die, others falling by the way are slaughtered
by the sword, so that of this great multitude only
one-third ever reach their horrible destination. It
would seem to me that never in the 'middle passage'
was murder and misery so great. And again, what was
the market supplied by the 'middle passage'? It was
our West Indian islands and the plantations of America.
And what is the market supplied by these three routes?
It is the countless millions of the whole Mahometan
world, which reaches from Morocco to our Indian
frontier. The demand is in Cairo, in Constantinople,
and throughout the East. I will not enter into its
abominations, . . . but I may say that this slave-trade
is marked by elaborate and exquisite outrages and
violations of the laws of God, which were never known
except in some accidental enormity in that old slave-
traffic for which England was responsible. . . I know
no people on the face of the earth so bound by strict
obligations to give freedom to men as we. We are
bound by the liberty which is an heirloom from our
ancestors, the liberty of our own land in which slavery
became extinct, and serfdom could not survive ; on the
coast of England if a slave set his foot he was free.
We are bound by the great federation of our Christianity,
which binds us in sympathy, not only with Christians
but with the whole human race. We are bound by the
wrongs that we have done in the past, by the deep and
indelible memories of the wrong which England has
inflicted on the African race in centuries gone by ; we
are bound by the memory of the reparation which

England has nobly made ; and lastly, by the responsibility of the great Empire which has been entrusted to us—for imperial power is a stewardship—laying on us the obligation to serve all peoples and nations with whom we come in contact.   If these things be so, then we are above all men bound by the strictest obligations which bind a civilized, a Christian, and an imperial race."

But while Manning could be thus eloquent on behalf of the uncivilized black slaves in Africa, he did not forget another kind of slavery among the civilized whites at home ; a slavery which, preventing healthful recreation during the hours of daylight, and involving prolonged periods of standing, with constant and anxious attention, wears out the health and strength of young men and women, and prepares the way for an enfeebled posterity.   In May, 1886, he spoke in St. James's Hall, at a meeting of the "Shop Hours League and Trades Parliamentary Association," and said :—" I am rejoiced that there is a prospect of a legal enactment enabling the local authorities to close all shops at an earlier hour on one day in the week.   Where a general coercive law is impossible, power given to a locality to put an Act of Parliament into force will operate as an example to the whole country.   I first interested myself in this movement for the shortening of hours in the case of shepherds and ploughmen ; and I am now continuing it amongst the overworked of London ; having no desire nearer to my heart than to see your lot, which is heavy indeed, lightened and brightened by any effort that can be made."

A few months later Cardinal Manning expressed his willingness to receive a visit from Mr. Henry George, the well-known American advocate of land nationalization, and was favourably impressed by him. " I was much pleased by the quiet earnestness with which he spoke and the calmness of his whole bearing." At that time he had read Mr. George's *Social Problems*, but not his *Progress and Poverty ;* and in the former book he had not noticed anything that deserved censure as unsound. Being aware however that his visitor was credited with holding doctrines that were irreconcilable with the holding of private property, he began the conversation [1] by saying :—" ' Before we go further, let me know whether we are in agreement upon one vital principle. I believe that the law of property is founded on the law of nature, and that it is sanctioned in revelation, declared in the Christian law taught by the Catholic Church, and incorporated in the civilization of all nations. Therefore, unless we are in agreement upon this, which lies at the foundation of society, I am afraid we cannot approach each other.' I understood him to reply that he did not deny this principle ; that his contention was mainly, if not only, on the intolerable evils resulting from an exaggeration of the law of property, meaning, in fact, the old dictum, *Summum jus summa injuria.* He added that the present separation and opposition of the rich and poor were perilous to society, and that he saw no remedy for them but in the example and teachings of Christ. He spoke fully and reverently on this subject." [2]

[1] As reported by himself in a letter to the *Brooklyn Review.*
[2] On the publication of the above in New York, the editor of the *World,* with enterprise characteristic of the nation, sent a " cablegram" to Manning (reply of any length prepaid). " Do you apprehend that the labour movement led by Mr. George will extend to dangerous proportions ?" Manning replied (it may be assumed, not without a sense of the humour of the situation),

In March, 1887, he expressed himself as strongly in favour of a defence of the American " Knights of Labour " which had come from the pen of Cardinal Gibbons.   The letter is interesting as a clear declaration of his ideas on the " democratization " of the Church.   Some laymen had previously denounced the association to the Pope.   " The Holy See will, I am sure, be convinced by the Cardinal's exposition of the state of the New World.   I hope it will open a new field of thought and action.   It passes my understanding that officious persons should be listened to rather than official.   Surely the episcopate of the whole world is the most powerful and direct instrument in the hands of the Holy See for gathering correct local knowledge and enforcing its decisions.   Who can know the temper of America, England and Ireland as they who have their finger upon the pulse of the people ?   Hitherto the world has been governed by dynasties ; henceforth the Holy See will have to deal with the people ; and it has Bishops in daily and personal contact with the people.   The more clearly and fully this is perceived, the stronger Rome will be.   Never at any time has the episcopate been so detached from civil powers, and so united in itself and with the Holy See.   Failure to see and use these powers will breed much trouble and mischief. . .   The Church is the mother, friend and protector of the people.   As the Lord walked among them, so His Church lives among them."

" I do not, so far as England is concerned.   The strongest desire of the working-man is to possess a house and garden of his own. When Mr. George was here, it was the working-men in the towns who were chiefly attracted to him.   The working-men in the country said, ' If you nationalize our land, let us have fair play, and equalize our wages.' "

Nothing in fact came amiss to him that served to illustrate this favourite teaching of all his later years, that the Catholic Church is the Church of the people; and so recognized by this time had his position become as a friend to all movements that had in view the bettering of the state of the working classes, that not only was he invited to take part in schemes originating with the philanthropic and the well-to-do, but working-men themselves came to him to ask a kind of blessing on proposals and plans of their own. Thus, in September this same year, he received a deputation from the "London Co-operative Clothing Manufacturing Company," an association of English, Scotch and Irish artisans, which he expressed his willingness to assist in any way he could; waiting however first to hear the opinion of Lord Ripon on the project, as he had been closely associated with and thoroughly understood the co-operative movement. "It is," the Cardinal said, " one of the saddest and most shameful features of our social system, that in the midst of such vast wealth so much misery should abound. . . I approve of your proposal, because it will lead to the material and moral benefit of the workers, and to the production of honest work. Mr. Herbert Spencer has written strongly on the positive insincerity and dishonesty which now cha-racterizes British manufacturers, and is destroying the British character. That is a painful fact; for formerly the English name was a sufficient guarantee of good work all over the world."

The time was now approaching when the existence of exceptional distress among the poor in London was to bring the philanthropic Cardinal very prominently before the public eye, and was to win for him the reproach of being a socialist and a revolutionist. On the first day of February, 1888, he headed a deputation to Lord Salisbury from Earl Compton's Committee on the Distress in London, and asserted that it was the unanimous testimony of his clergy that there existed in their respective neighbourhoods an exceptional lack of employment, and consequently unusual poverty. He complained that the temporary expedient employed in former years to meet such a crisis—a Mansion House Relief Fund—had now been discredited in the name of political economy, and that a proposal made by the Bishop of Bedford and others, to provide work for the unemployed, had been similarly killed off by the assertion that the giving of alms was demoralizing, and that the giving of work was only giving alms in another form. He quoted and denounced as " heartless and headless" a proposition in that morning's *Times*, to the effect that " the only way to make more work for the unemployed is for the employed to produce as much profit as they can, that is, as much surplus as they can over the cost of producing ; for all that profit must be spent on employing somebody in some way or other." [1] He pointed out the weakness of the argu-ment,—perhaps no surplus might be made ; perhaps those who pocketed the surplus might be unwilling to lay it out afresh in employing labour ; perhaps they might do so, but at a distance from the spot where the surplus had been made ; in which last case the working population would have to " lead a nomad life, going to

[1] The proposition was contained in a letter signed "G," and was commonly understood to be from the pen of the eminent economist and statistician, Mr. Robert Giffen. Manning's full reply to him is best studied in three long letters to the *Times*, Feb. 2—7, 1888, reprinted in *Merry England* for July, 1891.

and fro, and hunting after the surplus they had made."
Yet it was by such arguments as this that the two
propositions of raising a fund and of giving work had
been killed off. He referred next to the failure of the
Poor Law to meet the crisis, and expressed his preference for the wider action of the original Poor Law
of Elizabeth, which had made provision, not only for
chronic poverty but for temporary lack of employment;
and he added his opinion that it was the method of
administering the Poor Law, usually harsh and niggardly,
though in no two adjoining Unions uniform, that more
than anything else went to make criminals.[1]

A declaration made at this time by Manning, to the
effect that "every man has a right to work or to bread,"
was very widely denounced as communistic, socialistic,
anarchistic, and generally dangerous to society. So
doubtless it would be if the practical interpretation
given to it were that the storming of bakers' shops
by starving men is no offence against law and order.
Catholic theologians, it is true, do condone the taking
of enough to support life by a man who would other-

---

[1] In the *Tablet* the "convert Cardinal" was sharply called to
account because, while praising the Elizabethan statutes, "the
feeble Tudor substitutes for the ancient tithing system of bene-
volence," he had "studiously avoided any mention of the fact
that they were rendered necessary by the ruthless suppression of
the monasteries in the preceding reign, which for the first time
threw the English poor upon the mercies of the laity." Of course
Manning's position was that the poor need be thrown on no
"mercies," either clerical or lay, but that by proper legislation
the recurrence of crises of poverty might be avoided. The idea
of the writer in the *Tablet* apparently was that there should be
in the East of London a score or more of monastic establishments,
well supported by the wealthy in the West, and that at the gates
of these convents comfortable friars should ceaselessly ladle
out soup to crowds of pious and grateful but starving poor.

wise die of want. But the case is an extreme one, and
has no relation to the combination and violence of a
crowd of hungry men, temporarily unemployed, but in
a position to obtain by legal means sufficient sustenance
for themselves and their wives and children. Manning's
declaration is precisely the principle that underlies the
existing Poor Law, that the destitute have a legitimate
claim on the community for support; and it would
hardly have attracted attention, and certainly would
not have encountered alarmed and indignant denunciation, but for the anxiety existing in London at the time
on account of the unsolved problem of the unemployed.[1]
He defended himself in an article contributed to an
American magazine,[2] which he concluded as follows :—
" I have committed *lèse majesté* by rudely reminding
some who rule over public opinion in London of the
fresh mother earth, and of the primæval laws which
protect her offspring. I was unconscious of my
audacity. I thought I was uttering truisms which all
educated men knew and believed. But I found that
these primary truths of human life were forgotten, and
that on this forgetfulness a theory and a treatment of
our poor had formed a system of thought and action,
which hardens the hearts of the rich and grinds the

---

[1] Again an enterprising American editor made capital out of
the occasion, and sent a circular round to a number of judges,
lawyers, divines and laymen, asking, (1) Whether the Cardinal's
position is justified by the higher law ? and (2) Whether the
recognition of such a right by statute would be wholesome ? A
number of replies were published in the *Chicago Sunday Times;*
and it was noted as a singular circumstance, that while the judges
mostly favoured Manning's declaration, the "divines" were
generally opposed to it.

[2] "The Law of Nature, Divine and Supreme" (*American
Catholic Quarterly Review*, May, 1888).

faces of the poor. I am glad therefore that I said and
wrote what is before the public, even though for a time
some men have called me a socialist and a revolutionist,
and have fastened upon a subordinate consequence, and
neglected the substance of my contention in behalf of
the natural rights of the poor."

During the anxious month of February, 1888, the
Cardinal was questioned by the Hon. Percy Wyndham
as to whether he did not think a solution of the problem
might be found in " Fair Trade." He replied as follows:—" For the last many years I have been afraid
that we have passed the highest point of our prosperity,
which seems to me to have been the result of transient
causes, such as (1) the invention and application of
machinery to production; (2) the application of steam
to the making of machinery, and of machinery to all
industry; (3) the use of steam for transit by land and
by sea; (4) the manual skill resulting from these powers.
In all this we had the start of all nations. We took
away all their staples,—silk from France, cloth from
Germany, glass from Bohemia, steel from Spain, &c.,
—and we made it their interest to buy of us, thereby
making the whole Continent our market. This is all
reversed and can never return. They have our inventions
by machinery and by steam, and the skill resulting.
They are supplying themselves and shutting us out of
their home market. The *Times* of yesterday shows that
all nations are rising relatively to England, and notably
Germany. I have never been able to understand the
enormous excess of our imports over our exports. It
is not paid for either in money or in kind. Is it
accumulating debt? I had some correspondence with
the late Mr. Newmarch, and conversation with Lord

Beaconsfield about it.   But neither accounted for it.
The land and all the moral relations of social life
founded on it are gone.   We may eat bread as long as
we command the sea.   But our relative superiority is
very slender.   The condition of the labour-market is
depressed; and, if neither in agriculture nor in manufacture labour is demanded, I do not see the remedy.
Capitalists have had a run of prosperity, but agriculture
is unremunerative, and our continental market is closed.
If our colonists do not save us, capitalists will suffer
next.   I do not venture to suggest remedies.   Our vast
population is always increasing; our land is a fixed
quantity.   Its productiveness has never been ascertained. . .   The Lords' Committee on Land, &c., some
years ago reported that not more than one-third of our
land is adequately drained.   But I am going beyond
my depth. . . I have believed in Free Trade all my
life, and Mulhall's *Fifty Years of National Progress*
seems to justify it.   But *basta che duri;* my fear is that
it will not last.   It prospered when all its conditions
were in our favour; but this does not prove that it will
prosper when they are, if not altogether, at least ex-
tensively, changed.   As yet this has not been tested.
The next ten years will show if trade will revive; I am
afraid land will not.   I am afraid that neither pasture,
nor ' our wondrous roots,' as Lord Beaconsfield called
them, nor even jam, will restore the value of land and
the employment of our agricultural population."

But it was the famous "Dockers' Strike" in the
latter part of the summer of 1889 that most profoundly
impressed the country with regard to Manning's exceptional powers as an advocate of the rights of labour and
as a patient and skilful diplomatist.   It was certainly

P

a great occasion, and one in which his influence was
seen at its best. The Labourers' Union, of which the
secretary was a working man, Benjamin Tillett, had
during the two previous years held meetings to protest
against the hardships of the lot of the dock labourers;
but the strike itself, which began in the middle of
August, was sudden and unexpected. What was even
more unexpected was the sympathy which the skilled
artisans now for the first time showed with unskilled
labour; the effect of which was that, when the strike
was at its height, between forty thousand and fifty
thousand men were idle, of whom it was reckoned that
only about one per cent. were genuine dock labourers.
These men had been accustomed to receive only five-
pence an hour, with the chance that, when engaged,
the job might last only one hour, or even less. Their
demands were for sixpence an hour, with not less than
four hours' employment; eightpence an hour overtime;
and the contract system to be abolished. Probably
there never was, nor ever will be again, a strike
obtaining wider public sympathy. The clergy of all
denominations were on the side of the men; so were
the people of the middle class, usually so apathetic in
the cause of the poor; so were such of the upper classes
that had not left town for their holiday; so, it was
said, were the shipowners. Only the Dock directors
opposed them; and they soon saw it would be wise to give
way. There would thus have been little or nothing
left for Cardinal Manning to do, the victory being
almost certain from the first, had it not been that the
very brilliance of the victory made it difficult to bring
the strike to a close. Sympathy with the dockers was
expressed warmly in Australia; and out of the very

large total of £48,000 contributed in support of the
strike, more than £30,000 came from the Australian
colonies. It thus came to pass that, after the strike
had lasted a little less than a month, and grave fears
were being entertained as to the permanent injury that
would be inflicted on the trade of the port of London if
it continued much longer, a serious prospect of an
indefinite prolongation arose on the question of the
date when the new scale of payment, which had been
conceded, should come into operation. The day fixed
and provisionally accepted was Jan. 1, 1890; but this
was repudiated at a midnight meeting of the Strike
Committee, who demanded that the date should be
Oct. 1st; that is to say, in a fortnight's time. Other
minor points were at issue, and the prospect of an
amicable and speedy settlement was apparently lost.
At this crisis Cardinal Manning, the Lord Mayor, Mr.
Sydney Buxton, the Bishop of London, and others—the
last-named almost immediately giving up the task in
disgust—endeavoured to find some way of conciliation;
and various proposals were patiently discussed and
carried backwards and forwards from one side to the
other. At length Cardinal Manning succeeded in per-
suading the strikers to propose the first Monday in
November as a compromise. They were unwilling to
make any concession, since funds were plentiful—
there remained in fact a balance of £5,000 in the hands
of the Committee when the strike was over—and the
directors had been signally unsuccessful in their efforts
to import labour from outside. A graphic account was
given of Manning's appeal to the Strike Committee
made late at night in the Schools in Kirby Street,
Bermondsey. "He went patiently through the diffi-

culties, point by point, and reviewed the arguments on both sides. Unaccustomed tears glistened in the eyes of his rough and work-stained hearers as he raised his hand and solemnly urged them not to prolong one moment more than they could help the perilous uncertainty and the sufferings of their wives and children. Just above his uplifted hand was a figure of the Madonna and Child; and some among the men tell how a sudden light seemed to swim round it as the speaker pleaded for the women and children. When he sat down all in the room knew that he had won the day, and that, so far as the Strike Committee was concerned, the matter was at an end." [1] Four days, however, had yet to elapse before the directors would accept the proposed compromise; but they could not be indifferent to the pressure of public opinion, and the strike ended on Sept. 16, with what some termed "the Cardinal's peace."

On the whole, and although some months later it was complained that the men were not holding faithfully to the terms agreed to, and that the Cardinal and those who had worked with him were unable to command fidelity, it was a great and beneficent interposition in a truly deserving cause. Subsequent attempts similarly to interfere and to obtain better terms for the men were not equally successful. With the strike of the South London gas-stokers there was far less public sympathy. The dispute between the directors and the men turned rather on questions of

[1] The account is here given as narrated at the time ; but the fact that the Kirby Street Schools are not Catholic Schools, as the reporter stated, but Board Schools, seems to throw a doubt on the miraculous Madonna incident.

freedom of contract than of insufficient pay, and there
was nothing like the "docker's tanner," that had
seemed to every one so intelligible and reasonable a
demand. So that, when the Cardinal endeavoured in
this case to plead the workers' cause, Mr. Livesey, who
was the spokesman for the other side, declined to be
lectured as if he were something of a wrong-doer; the
interposition collapsed, and the strikers were ultimately
vanquished. And since that day the working-men,
though not grudging to the Cardinal his meed of
praise, have been steadily coming round to the opinion
that strikes are clumsy and wasteful contrivances
to bring about results that should rightly be obtained by the calm action of the Legislature. With
this view Manning fully sympathized. He won his
reputation as a socialist—a reputation to which professed socialists denied that he had any right—by his
advocacy of a policy in relation to labour and the poor
that could only be permanent and effective when
expressed in laws. He was least of all a *doctrinaire*
socialist; it was the visible presence of poverty that
stirred him to make proposals that may at times have
been crude, but were certainly prompted by a warm
and sincere heart. There is little if any evidence to
show that he carried with him his suffragan Bishops,
or any number of his clergy. They were rather be-
wildered by his proceedings, suspected him of posing
before the British public, and complained that he
neglected the service of God to serve tables. But
among a section of the Catholic laity of France, whose
leader is the Comte de Mun, and whose organ the
Vingtième Siècle, he has had considerable influence;
while his ideas flourish among the Catholics of North

America, who are not hampered by aristocratic traditions; and they have borne fruit in the Vatican itself.

Among the working-men of London, however, he will not quickly be forgotten in this his character of advocate of the cause of labour. There was not one but on the morning of the Cardinal's death was conscious that he had lost a tried and faithful friend. The delegates of the London Trades' Council, at a crowded meeting held in the Memorial Hall, Farringdon Street, a night or two after his death, passed a resolution unanimously, expressing their "keen sense of an irreparable loss," adding that "by his tender sympathy for the suffering, his fearless advocacy of justice, especially for the poor, and by his persistent denunciation of the oppression of the workers, he has endeared his memory to the heart of every true friend of labour." The mover of the resolution, Mr. Bateman, a compositor, said that "English, Irish and Italian workers in London felt that by the death of Cardinal Manning they had lost their very best friend." Such a testimony is probably unique, nor can it be accounted undeserved.

CHAPTER IX.

CARDINAL MANNING has sometimes been spoken of as "a thinker" and "a man of letters," but there does not appear to be sufficient ground for applying to him terms that are fitly enough used in the case of Newman, but are, as applied to the former, flattering and inaccurate. Manning indeed never made any pretence to be either the one or the other; and so the employment of such language about him, however well meant, is in effect unkindly, as it lays him open to a criticism that he himself never invited, and that his writings can hardly bear. It was in regard to social problems that he made the nearest approach to being a "thinker," for he certainly thought about them in his own practical way not a little. But no special element of genius or of insight ever entered into his thoughts; he neither discovered nor pretended to have discovered any epoch-making solution of any economic puzzle, nor was he even the consistent disciple of any particular school, nor an uniform adherent to any distinguishing principle. He was termed a socialist, partly because that is a convenient label to affix to any one who is a hearty advocate of social reforms, but more to throw discredit on his labours in behalf of the poor. If he was a socialist at all, he was a "Christian socialist," a follower of Maurice ; but there is nothing to show that he ever definitely accepted Maurice's principles. It was always *pro re natâ* that he did what he did in the cause of labour ; and, if he acted at times as a socialist, it was because the acts of a socialist—without being so labelled in his mind—seemed to him then and there the best way to meet a present and urgent difficulty. In short, he was guided throughout by his heart, and not by his head ; and that is not the mark of " a thinker." [1]

Again, he entered the Catholic Church with a vague reputation as a champion who, in his Anglican days, had fought deftly and victoriously against infidelity; and this was mentioned as an important qualification when he had been selected to succeed Wiseman. He was supposed to know all about rationalism, and to be able to meet its advocates on their own ground. That he had a way of meeting rationalism, and a not in-effective way, will be shown lower down ; but that he had any idea of meeting it as "a thinker " is again a proposition unsupported by evidence. There is nothing to show that he had ever associated with liberal thinkers,[2] or read their books, or in any other way obtained a knowledge of their ideas ; what he did say about

[1] Cardinal Manning's views on social problems owed much to the influence of Ruskin's *Unto this Last,* which, in spite of the abuse with which it was originally received, has proved a marvel-lous dissolvent of the dry old political economy.

[2] The writer has seen it asserted, but on what authority he does not know, that Manning was once a member of the Sterling Club. If so, he would have shown a very transient sympathy with the ideas of Arnold, Connop Thirlwall, and other pioneers of the Broad Church School.

rationalism while Archdeacon of Chichester rather suggests that he regarded it as a thing not to be handled or even glanced at by Christian men. Certainly we look in vain in Manning's works for that intelligent scrutiny of rational principles, and those ingenious subterfuges from rationalist conclusions which we find in the writings of Newman. No, Manning was not "a thinker," and he never claimed to be one.

Nor can he be fairly described as "a man of letters," unless all those who indefatigably use their pens, and who print works that run into several editions, are to be so described. His bibliography shows that he was a voluminous writer, and that many of his works in defence of Catholicism have proved so acceptable as to have been translated into foreign languages. But this has not been on account of their value as literature; it is due to the fact that in Manning's own particular field of didactic popular theology he had few equals, either in this country or on the Continent. It has been maintained by some that he might have been a man of letters had he so wished, but that he surrendered the position when he devoted his life to the practical work of a Churchman. This again is hardly accurate, nor is it complimentary to him to imply that he wrote carelessly because he wrote as a priest. If literary genius had been innate in him, it would assuredly have manifested itself in spite of his surroundings. No doubt, in his later years especially, he wrote hurriedly, and as the occasion demanded, and gave little thought to the finish of his compositions. But in his earlier works, when his time was more at his command, and he was daily gaining prestige as an eloquent divine, there are precisely the same charac-

teristics that are noticeable in his magazine articles of
the last ten years; and among those characteristics is
not the vital spark that gives immortality to true
literature. It is not even recorded of him that he had
at any time a marked literary taste. He was not
ignorant, of course, of our greater poets, or of our standard
prose writers; but it does not appear that he knew
them better or cared for them more than the average
man who makes no pretence to be a man of letters;
and the lack of poetic instinct and power which distinguished him from other prominent figures in the
Oxford movement, a lack which perhaps necessarily
involved the want of style in his writings, is sufficient
of itself to place him outside a circle, within which, it
is only just to himself to repeat, he never professed that
he could claim a place.[1]

Having made these limitations, we are in a better
position to determine what is the position to be assigned
to Cardinal Manning as a writer and preacher; and it
will appear that it is in the latter capacity only that he
can claim any pre-eminence. In the early forties of
this century it is said that only three preachers could
fill St. Mary's Church at Oxford on a week-day, and
those three were Newman, Goulburn, and Manning.
How the first of these three had that power there is no
need here to explain, for it has become a commonplace to speak of his sweet, silvery voice, his thoughtful and restrained manner, and the keen searching
analysis of human character, which made each hearer

[1] In one of his last years some one suggested to him that he
should write a novel, as Wiseman and Newman had done. But
he humorously put the notion aside; admitting that he had
materials for such a work, though conscious, doubtless, that his
lack of imagination and his didactic method disqualified him.

think that the great Tractarian leader had somehow
acquired precise information about his own private life.
Manning's eloquence was of a different but not less
attractive character. It was less scholarly, but more
emotional; it showed less piercing insight into the
motives of human action, but it was more pleading and
more persuasive. Some words might be accounted
ill-chosen and inaccurate, some sentences might sound
slipshod, and sundry arguments, if scrutinized, would
assuredly have been condemned as inconclusive. But
the earnestness of the speaker, his quiet dignity, his
evident conviction of his own authoritative mission, the
richness of his picturesque diction, and—most of all—
his insistence, almost exclusively, on considerations that
warm the heart and bend the will, rather than on
such as force the intellect to assent,—in all this doubtless lay the secret of his power ; for power as a preacher
Manning certainly had, and that long before he was
able to speak in tones more authoritative still. Those
four volumes of Anglican sermons, or five, if the University sermons be counted in, which he was never
willing to reprint, though the price now asked for them
shows that it would in one sense have been worth his
while,—they amply bear out the reputation that contemporaries report he had obtained. They are full of
eloquent passages, full of vigorous appeals; and, as
compared with the contemporary sermons of Newman,
they are distinctly more devout and more "affective."
Manning was at his best in the hortatory style ; if he
attempted to be argumentative, he failed ; but so long
as he had hearers well disposed to didactic paternal
discourse, he could not but attract and satisfy. Critics
at the time made the same exception that readers of

these sermons do now, viz. that an excessive richness and sweetness of diction serves to cover a thinness and poverty of thought; but it may be said in reply that such has commonly been a characteristic of pulpit eloquence, and is perhaps inseparable from it save in the rarest cases.

A testimony to the genuineness of Manning's spiritual power is to be found in the fact that more than one little manual of devotional literature has been compiled from his sermons, and that these books have proved so acceptable as to have passed through several editions. It may be taken as an unfailing test of the sincerity of a man's utterances on religious topics that they can be read again and again with pleasure by other religiously disposed persons no less sincere. The Christian world will have been reduced to a low ebb when a hypocrite can write a book of devotions that will sell. That Manning was no hypocrite may be held to be proved by the fact that *Thoughts for those that Mourn, Devotional Readings* and *Towards Evening* are widely known among and are valued by those who do not hold all that he held as true. And it may be taken as a not improbable forecast of the future of his voluminous works, that only his devotional writings, including *The Eternal Priesthood*, one of his latest, will some years hence survive. Nevertheless, it would be unfair to treat as undeserving of notice the many able and laborious works he issued during the forty years of his life within the Catholic Church, and all the more so, since many who may be sufficiently interested in him to read his life, are likely enough never to have the opportunity, or never to take the trouble, to read anything that he himself wrote. To such however as may be disposed to learn from Manning himself his views on a great variety of topics, but who may be unable to obtain the more important volumes named in the bibliography, a book entitled *Characteristics from the Writings of Cardinal Manning* may be recommended, as a well-arranged and adequate manual of selections from his works.[1]

What will strike the reader of the above-named volume is that, though its contents are divided under the heads of " Political," " Philosophical," and " Religious," they could really all be appropriately placed under the last category. Manning was so unmistakably and before all things a Churchman, that, whatever it was that he spoke or wrote about, he was pretty sure in the end to come round to the same place, and to insist on the " Divine authority " that in his judgment should regulate intellectual and civil as well as ecclesiastical things. The curious reader will also ascertain with interest that, so uniform was Manning's teaching on the subject of " the Church," that many of the extracts referring to questions of ecclesiastical polity or practice are taken from the sermons of the Archdeacon of Chichester, and find their place side by side with extracts from the sermons of the Archbishop of Westminster, the difference between the two being so slight that, apart from the reference to the source of the quotation, a reader might fairly remain in doubt as to which period of Manning's life the passage belonged. Thus, the paragraphs headed " The Church and the World," " Revelation and Science," " Divine Philosophy," " The Intuition of Faith," " The Philosophy of Fasting,"

[1] Edited by Mr. W. S. Lilly. London (Burns and Oates), 1885.

"The Invisible Kingdom," and "Hear the Church," are
all taken from the Anglican sermons.

There is thus not that marked distinction between
Manning's Anglican and Catholic sermons that the
most careless reader cannot fail to detect in the case
of Newman's. The latter's two volumes entitled
Sermons Preached on Various Occasions, and *Discourses
to Mixed Congregations*—containing all the sermons of
his Catholic life that he carefully wrote out and thought
worthy of reproduction—display a fervour of eloquence,
a liveliness of manner, and a warmth of devotion that
would be looked for in vain in the classical Oxford
volumes. Manning's Catholic sermons, like Newman's,
were almost invariably unwritten—the most notable
exception being the sermon he preached at Newman's
requiem at the London Oratory, in August, 1890—and
when afterwards written out for publication, they retain
the thinness which characterized them as spoken; and
they certainly lose much of their power when disunited
from the gracious presence and the dignified manner of
the preacher. The conscious air of authority with which
he spoke, his recollectedness, the ease with which an
appropriate word or phrase came to his lips, the slight
and not ungraceful action, the forefinger being at times
slightly raised and then, in emphasis, pointed down-
wards,—all this being absent when the sermons are at a
later time read, there is nothing to distract attention
from the fact that, though the words are well chosen,
and many of the phrases happy and well to the purpose,
the argument, if flawless, is slight and unconvincing; it
is to assertion and not to reasoning that you are expected
to bow, and the conviction grows upon you that the
preacher has never really touched the "bottom facts"

of the case. Nevertheless, taking the standard of pulpit utterances at what it is, every fair critic must admit that Cardinal Manning's sermons were always far above the average, were always interesting and always worth hearing, though one cannot add that they are always worth reading.

These criticisms apply, *mutatis mutandis*, to the more formal treatises, not strictly sermons, which Manning put forth in defence of Catholicism. The earliest of these, *The Grounds of Faith*, was published in 1852, and is valuable as a full exposition of the process of reasoning which led its author to embrace Catholicism. Other apologetic works in the same field are, *The Temporal Mission of the Holy Ghost*, published in 1865; *England and Christendom*, 1867; *The Fourfold Sovereignty of God*, 1871; *Four Great Evils of the Day*, 1871; *Cæsarism and Ultramontanism*, 1874; and *The Internal Mission of the Holy Ghost*, 1875. Without professing to have read all or nearly all of these somewhat conventionally able and learned treatises, one is in a position to say of them that, as being the writings of a man who is always in the pulpit, they weary more than they convince. They deserve no doubt respect and praise; many striking passages might be culled from them; there are apt references and quotations, and there are vigorously-drawn conclusions from premisses not equally well established; but a reader cannot for ever sit patiently and be lectured as a catechumen; and it is the prevalence of assertion over every other kind of proposition that must always render these volumes unreadable to the great mass of men. Cardinal Manning was apparently aware of this defect, and in his latest apologetic work, the *Religio Viatoris*, he begins at any rate with an effort to gain his reader's confidence by treating him as if, to some extent, on equal terms. He is almost playful in his repudiation of assumptions; and the thing goes on smoothly for a while; but soon the didactic temper finds its way in; and before the book is half finished, the author is again laying down the law, and is speaking, as he could not fail to speak, considering the force that he believed he had behind him, as one having authority, not to argue but to teach.

On the other hand, when Manning had to deal with controversy touching the relations between Catholicism and Protestantism, he showed a liberality of sentiment, quite in accordance, no doubt, with the formal teachings of the Church, but such as not every Catholic is willing to use. In a letter addressed to Dr. Pusey in 1864, entitled "The Workings of the Holy Spirit in the Church of England," he made such full concessions as to the "grace" obtainable outside the one true fold,— always of course on the assumption of " good faith,"— that he seemed almost to leave the pious struggling Catholic in a worse condition than the honest moral Protestant; and in a later work he extended this doctrine to "Dissenters of every kind."[1]   "They are,"

---

[1] In a later work he wrote about "Bible Christians":—"I sincerely respect zealous and earnest men who, knowing the Bible to be the word of God, and finding it full of light and sweetness, think that it is enough for them to take that divine word alone, and to read it for themselves. They are near to the fountain. . . I sincerely respect all such, and for this reason : they submit themselves with all their heart to every word that they can understand in that divine Scripture ; and, if they could know it better and understand it more fully, they would obey it with all their sincerity and with all their soul. But we must not forget the falseness of the principle in the goodness of these people."

he said, "marked by a multitude of high qualities of zeal, devotion to duty, conscientious fidelity to what they believe. If they are rougher in their language against the Catholic Church, they are more generous and candid adversaries; more vehement but less bitter, and altogether free from the littleness of personality and petty faults which sometimes stain the controversy of those who are intellectually nearer to the truth. For such men it is our duty to cherish a warm charity and a true respect." Of the reality of his own spiritual life within the Church of England he said, "How could any one regard it as a mockery? I have no deeper conviction than that the grace of the Holy Spirit was with me from my earliest consciousness. Though at the time perhaps I knew it not as I know it now, yet I can clearly perceive the order and chain of grace by which God mercifully led me onward from childhood to the age of twenty years. From that time the interior working of His light and grace, which continued through all my life till the hour when that light and grace had its perfect work, to which all its operations had been converging, in submission to the fulness of truth and of the Spirit in the Church of God, is a reality as profoundly certain, intimate and sensible to me now as that I live. Never have I by the lightest word breathed a doubt of this fact in the Divine order of grace." To this autobiographical passage may be added another equally illustrative of the view which he took of the growing tendency of his mind towards Catholicism, while he was still in the Church of England:—"For myself, I am conscious how little I have ever done in my life; but as it is now drawing towards its end [1875] I have at least this consolation,

Q

that I cannot remember at any time by word or act to have undermined a revealed truth, but that, according to my power—little enough, as I know—I have endeavoured to build up what truth I knew, truth upon truth, if only as one grain of sand upon another, and to bind it together by the only bond and principle of cohesion which holds in unity the perfect revelation of God."

These passages are interesting as showing that love for constructive theology was the master-passion of his life, the other passion of philanthropy being always subordinated to this. And consistently, he expressed a preference for the High Church party in the Church of England, as opposed in principle to theological liberalism :—" I have ever regarded with regret the so-called Low Church and Latitudinarian schools in the Anglican Church, because I believe their action and effect is to diminish what remains of truth in it. I have always regarded with joy, and I have never ceased to regard with sympathy, notwithstanding much which I cannot either like or respect, the labour of the High Church or Anglo-Catholic party, because I believe that their action and effect are 'to strengthen the things that remain, which were ready to die.'" But with the later developments of the High Church movement he showed a scanty sympathy. "Ritualism is private judgment in gorgeous raiment, wrought about with divers colours. It is, I am afraid, a dangerous temptation to self-consciousness. I could never understand the passive endurance shown by some when the articles of the baptismal creed were heretically denied, and, at the same time, their intense zeal for decorations and vestments. Ritual is seemly and proportionate as the clothing of Truth; and, when the reality is present, ritual becomes as unconscious as the light of day, or the circulation of the blood. A forest tree is hardly more unconscious of the majesty of its foliage than the Catholic Church of the splendour of its worship. Somebody well said of the Catholic priest, 'Incense is the smell of the garden in which he is trained to work.' But it is to be feared that the artificial perfuming of the garden is no sign of unconscious nature. Every fringe in an elaborate cope worn without authority is only a distinct and separate act of private judgment; the more elaborate, the less Catholic; the nearer the imitation, the further from the submission of faith."[1]

But while he could thus understand and appreciate and criticize with discrimination the religious ideas and practices of those who moved on more or less orthodox lines, he had never any intelligent apprehension of what is meant by rationalism, nor any words for it save those of condemnation and reprobation. A sentence like the following, on the attempt of certain philosophers to find a natural basis for morality, may suffice in illustration:—"These last generations have become fruitful of impiety and of immorality of a stupendous kind; and among other of their impious and immoral offspring is a pestilent infidel school, who,

---

[1] The reserved and appreciative language which Manning invariably used of the Church of England stands in marked contrast with some fierce sentences of Newman's uttered in 1862, when some one had said he was about to return to Anglicanism :—" I do hereby profess *ex animo*, with an absolute internal assent and consent, that Protestantism is the dreariest of possible religions ; that the thought of the Anglican service makes me shiver, and the thought of the Thirty-nine Articles makes me shudder. Return to the Church of England ! No ! 'The net is broken and we are delivered.' I should be a consummate fool (to use a mild term) if in my old age I left the land flowing with milk and honey for the city of confusion and the house of bondage."

with an audacity never before known in the Christian world, are at this time assailing the foundations of human society and of Divine law. They have talked of late of what they call 'independent morality.' . . . This philosophy denies and destroys the foundations of morality itself. I should not turn aside to mention this monster of immorality and impiety if it were not that at this time there is an effort making in England to introduce under a veil this same subtle denial of morals both Christian and natural." This was written in 1874, and in 1875 he added,—"There are none so tyrannical, none so bigoted, none so intolerant, as those who do not believe in the existence of God. They are so sure that the reason of man cannot know God, that they confidently affirm that God does not exist. . . We have come at last to know that there is a fanaticism worse than that which they impute to us. . . The men of the nineteenth century, who profess to be the guides and lights of men, the creators and promoters of pro-gress and modern civilization, are beyond all men intolerant, despotic and tyrannous. . . This clumsy and incoherent philosophy . . . this portentous aberration of the reason," &c., &c.

The explanation of this fierce and blind language lies probably in its being an unconscious imitation of sundry of the encyclicals of Pius IX., which used similarly to breathe maledictions. Atheism on the Continent has from time to time been blatant and aggressive, and has forgotten the respect due to the rights of conscience; but to apply condemnations that were perhaps not undeserved in the one case to the mild, regretful, apologetic atheism of our own time and country, an atheism which would rather call itself by any other name, and is conspicuously fruitful in good works, is to go somewhat wide of the mark. Doubtless in later years the Cardinal Archbishop would have hesitated to use such terms, as his exertions in behalf of labour had brought him into close contact with men and women holding views on the fundamental questions of belief not very dissimilar to those which ten years earlier he had so roundly denounced.

Many other quotations from his writings might be made, showing how completely he was in the dark as to the drift of modern philosophy; but enough has been said to indicate a weakness on which it is unnecessary further to dwell. As a busy ecclesiastic he could hardly perhaps be expected to find time to study so as to master the rationalism which seemed to him so terrible. Indeed there is nothing to show that he had ever really grasped its significance in any of the three branches in which during the last fifty years it has so greatly acquired strength,—the scientific establishment of the uniformity of natural law; the historical account of the origin of the books of the Bible; and the comparative study of the growth of religions. But, while he made official condemnation do duty for intelligent refutation,

[1] But as lately as 1882 he wrote in the *Nineteenth Century* "An Englishman's Protest" against Mr. Bradlaugh being allowed to sit in Parliament, though the two had the cause of the poor and helpless equally at heart ; the main difference being that, while the Cardinal would have supported socialistic measures on their behalf, Mr. Bradlaugh would have opposed such measures, and would have relied on the abolition of privilege. No doubt, so long as Parliament maintains the Act of Uniformity, it is a grievance for Anglicans that atheists, or, for that matter, any persons not members of the Church of England, should be allowed a seat in it ; but Parliament cannot touch the faith of Catholics, who might therefore be content to leave alone the private opinions of its members.

he manifested a spirit not other than liberal in relation
to persons and to sundry details. The words " or
periods" were, with the Archbishop's approval, added
to the Penny Catechism in explanation of the Mosaic
days of creation; and an article by Mr. St. George
Mivart in the *Fortnightly Review*, in which he expressed
his general agreement with the conclusions of the
" higher criticism " in regard to the dates and authen-
ticity of the books of the Old Testament, not only met
with no condemnation, but its author was at a later
date, again with the Archbishop's approval, given an
important post in the Catholic University of Louvain.
It is not easy to explain the inconsistency, and perhaps
it is best to do no more than leave it on record. No
doubt to certain minds the temptation is great to
attempt to reconcile ancient religion with modern
thought; both are so singularly attractive that a man
may be pardoned his desire to be a disciple of both.
But "truth by truth can never be gainsaid," and it is
impossible that all that the Church teaches and all
that the critics and the men of science have established
should be true at the same time. It may be politic to
make, or to appear to make, concessions; but in the
long run it will surely be found that Manning's earlier
method (apart from its denunciations) of holding sternly
aloof from rationalism and all its works is the only way
to secure the permanence of Catholicism.

Two incidental controversies in which Manning engaged are of interest as illustrating the methods which
he thought it his duty to adopt. The first of these was
in September, 1873. Preaching at Bath on the " Sacred
Heart," the Archbishop let drop an unlucky phrase
implying the omnipresence of the sacred humanity of

Jesus Christ—a doctrine which happens to be heretical as well as incredible.   It was in fact originally an assertion of Luther's, used in defence of his doctrine of consubstantiation.   Of course in Manning's case it was nothing but a *lapsus linguæ* ; and, considering the varied and extensive field that is covered by Catholic theology, the wonder is that an active, not to say restless, Archbishop, whose occupations allowed him but the scantiest leisure to read, and who had ceased to study theology systematically for nearly twenty years, should not often make such slips; nor is it a part of the faith to hold that he enjoys an official immunity from such misfortunes; though it is apparently regarded as necessary to explain them away, instead of frankly admitting the mistake.   On this occasion a certain Dr. Nicholson, an Anglican chaplain from Stockholm, who had never been heard of before and was not heard of again, chanced to be in the congregation, and fixed upon the Archbishop's phrase and challenged him about it in the papers.   His criticism was so bitter, and his delight at having caught a Catholic prelate tripping so undisguised, that Dr. Littledale and the late editor of the *Church Times* at once recognized a man after their own heart, and watched the fray with intense satisfaction.   There is no need to add anything further about the controversy, save that several letters passed between Dr. Nicholson and Father Guiron, the Archbishop's secretary, and duly appeared in the *Guardian,* and that at the close the Archbishop congratulated his secretary on the soundness of his doctrine, for "if you had made any slip I should have taken upon myself the full responsibility."   But what should also not pass unrecorded is the fact that Manning, treating the affair as if it were of serious importance, took the singular step of defending himself anonymously, and wrote a pamphlet under the *nom de guerre* of " Catholicus."

The other case was two years later, and was also distinguished by a correspondence prolonged quite out of proportion to the importance of the matter. Lord Redesdale had insisted that the practice of giving communion in one kind convicted the Church of fallibility, because the primitive practice had been to give communion in both kinds. It would have been easy to point out that Lord Redesdale's argument confused the infallibility claimed for the Church in deciding questions of faith, in which case the decision must be uniform and binding for all time, with the authority claimed for her in regard to disciplinary regulations, which must, *ex hypothesi*, always be obeyed, though the regulations themselves may differ at different periods. Instead of this, however, long letters were interchanged between the two, the Cardinal showing himself always courteous to his noble opponent, while the real point at issue between them was never touched; and no one obtained any satisfaction from the controversy, save the editor of the *Daily Telegraph*, in whose columns, during the "silly season," the correspondence appeared.

In his work on the *Temporal Mission of the Holy Ghost* Manning had said, "The appeal to antiquity is both a treason and a heresy," a sentence which he afterwards expanded into, " The appeal from the living voice of the Church to any tribunal whatsoever, human history included, is an act of private judgment and a treason, because that living voice is supreme; and an appeal from that supreme voice is also a heresy, because

that voice, by Divine assistance, is infallible." This
sentence has been given the unauthentic form of an
assertion, said to have been made by him, that "the
Vatican Council triumphed over history." To Protestants
it has commonly seemed dishonest in Catholics to profess belief in a doctrine, like that of Papal infallibility,
which is admitted to be "difficult to maintain in the
face of historical facts "; and it is therefore important
to point out that Manning's attitude in this matter, as
explained in the books and pamphlets which he wrote
and published on the prerogatives of the Pope, is not to
be accounted dishonest, however much it may have been
mistaken. Allowance must be made for the view of
those who have accepted as definitely and irreversibly
true, on grounds superior, as they think, to historical
evidence, a doctrine with which the alleged facts must
be squared, since it cannot itself give way to them.
It may be an irrational position, and one that would
have to be abandoned if the whole circle of facts with
which it is concerned were fairly and fully taken into
account; but it involves no dishonesty in the man to
whom the dogma is certainly and antecedently true.
No one who knew the late Bishop of Lincoln (Dr. Wordsworth) would admit that he was dishonest because in
his commentary on the Greek Testament in one or two
places he set aside facts that are pretty well established
by "human history," because such facts were not easily
reconcilable with the precise letter of Scripture, which
in his judgment was inspired and infallible, and true
antecedently to all evidence for or against its statements that might be adduced from other quarters.
So secure was the text, that it was hardly necessary

to do more than suggest a possible interpretation of
the other documents; some other interpretation might
be the correct one; what was certain was that no
testimony was of any worth that could not be reconciled with the infallible Word of God. Just such an
attitude of mind was Manning's towards historical
objections against Papal infallibility; and when one
recollects what historical evidence is, little else, in
fact, than the survival of sundry partisan judgments
out of a multitude that were contemporaneously
formed and have perished, it will not seem wonderful that it should be regarded as a futile weapon
against a doctrine believed to have proceeded from the
very mouth of God, and to have been handed down by
an unbroken tradition. Historical research only becomes
a reality when the belief in a binding authority has
been set on one side. With that belief it is superfluous,
or is at any rate only of value to illustrate foregone
conclusions. And herein Manning had the advantage of
consistency over his opponents among the "scientific
historical" school of Munich. They admitted a dogmatic
backbone into their scheme of Christian history, while
they insisted on using historical criticism only so far as
it accorded with their theory of an infallible Church
governed by a fallible Pope. Manning of course would
not admit historical criticism at all. But they who do
admit it, should permit it to have its full scope, and
should follow it loyally, even if it leads them to the
conclusion that Christianity, in its earliest recognizable
form, was little else than an ethical movement, an
aboriginal Society of Friends, without a permanent
hierarchy, infallible or otherwise, of any sort or kind.

The lately-discovered "Teaching of the Twelve Apostles" is only consistent with such a view.

No account of the literary side of Manning's career would be complete that did not include some reference to his membership of the Metaphysical Society, which was mainly founded by Dr. W. G. Ward, the editor of the *Dublin Review*. Ward was the only Catholic member of it besides Manning, and it ceased to exist at about the time of his death. Its meetings were held monthly, and among those who attended from time to time were Mr. Gladstone, Mr. Frederic Harrison, Mr. Ruskin, Dr. Martineau, Professors Huxley and Tyndall, Lord Tennyson, and the Duke of Argyll. In such an assembly might have been heard the grave and gentle tones of the versatile Archbishop, weighing with calmness and consideration arguments that had been adduced (say) against the existence of a personal God. Probably in no other country and no other time would so unique a spectacle have been possible. Of the value of his papers read at the meetings of this and of other societies —at the Royal Institution for example—it can only be said that they were not wanting in academic form or in gravity of diction. They were in fact worthy of the occasion. But his hearers did not come away with the sense that a new light had been thrown on points that had hitherto puzzled enquirers. When the meeting was over, the world of knowledge was much the same that it had been before.

In the last ten or twelve years of his life Manning made a new literary departure for a Catholic ecclesiastic, in contributing articles on social and other questions to the secular magazines. In all he wrote some twenty such articles, chiefly for the *Nineteenth Century* and the *Contemporary Review*. It was a policy which seemed at the time, and still seems to some old-fashioned Catholics, of doubtful wisdom; and that because it is an encouragement to Catholics to purchase and to have in their houses a number of a magazine which, for all one can tell to the contrary, besides the article by the Cardinal Archbishop, may contain one from the pen of Professor Huxley, showing up the Flood or the Gadarene swine, or something equally scandalous. Manning had doubtless thought over the objections as much as any one, and had come to the conclusion that they were insufficient. His judgment he had expressed as follows :—" It is necessary for Catholics to prepare themselves on the relation of society and of science. . . . They cannot meet without being forced into the time-spirit. We do not live in an exhausted receiver. The Middle Ages are past. There is no zone of calms for us. We are in the modern world,—in the trade-winds of the nineteenth century,—and we must brace ourselves to lay hold of the world as it grapples with us, and to meet it, intellect to intellect, culture to culture, science to science." [1]

This was a courageous manifesto, and one to which Manning acted up, at any rate in his magazine articles on temperance, education, and the like, in which he showed himself a vigorous and able advocate of no un-certain views. By these articles, more than in any other way, he was brought into contact with the general read-ing public, and many prejudices were thereby removed. If then he can be assigned no honourable place in the world of letters, he must certainly be accounted one

---

[1] *Miscellanies*, vol. i. p. 94.

who used his pen deftly and to the purpose ; and, considering the enormous demands that other and more pressing duties made upon his time, his work as a writer, taken as a whole, was such that English Catholics may legitimately regard for some time to come with no little satisfaction and pride.

CHAPTER X.

ON the occasion of the twenty-fifth anniversary of
the Archbishop's consecration,—his " silver jubilee,"—
the *Tablet* wrote an appreciative article on the work he
had done for the Church in England : [1]—" To Cardinal

[1] On this same occasion the Right Rev. Monsignor Gilbert, the
Cardinal's Vicar-General, published an interesting summary of
the practical work accomplished during the past twenty-five years.
Forty-nine new departments in elementary schools had been
opened, and sixteen additional Poor-Law and Workhouse schools.
The number of priests in the diocese had been increased by one
hundred and forty-nine ; eleven communities of religious men
and fifty of religious women had been founded, and about forty
new churches and missions had been opened. Of the sums presented to him at this time—one was a purse of £7,500—he made
use chiefly to promote good works within the diocese ; but a
portion was set aside for the repairs of his titular church in Rome.
The money presented to him by the trade unions, including
seven industrial societies of men engaged in labour in the port of
London, he used to found a bed in the London Hospital, termed
somewhat infelicitously the "Thames bed." The reply made by
him to the deputation which presented him with the large sum
above-named was characteristic :—" As I am rendering in all like-
lihood my last account to you, I will say two things : First, that
I have never consciously or willingly wounded any man ; secondly,
that in many cases I have been bound by duty to act, not as my
personal will but as my office compelled me. The three works
on which my heart has been set have been the education of our
children, the saving of our people by the Holy Sacraments, and

Manning more than to any man is it due that English
Catholics have at last outgrown the narrow cramped
life of their past of persecution, and stand in all things
on a footing of equality with their fellow-countrymen.
He has been the great leader who has led us away from
the desert places and the time of bondage, and into the
land of promise. Before his words and life and example
the barriers of prejudice have gone down, one after
another, as the walls of Jericho. . . He has helped us
to live down a world of ignorant opposition. A great
philanthropist as well as a great Churchman, the
Cardinal has shown himself a great statesman, and a
statesman at all times superior to the petty politics
of party and the hour. An Englishman down to the
marrow of his bones, he has always thrown himself into
every movement which worked for the greatness and
advancement of England. . . No good cause, from
Imperial Federation to Express Postage, ever appealed
to him in vain."

Nothing can be more just than these references to
Manning as a statesman and as a patriotic Englishman.
The speech that he made in Westminster Town Hall
in February, 1887, at a meeting held to promote the
foundation of an Imperial Institute "as the national
memorial of the jubilee of her Majesty's reign," was
full of enthusiasm for the progress that the country had
made during a period well within his own memory, and

---

the rearing and multiplication of priests true to their Divine
Master. What little in these duties has been begun, my successor
will, I hope, complete. . . Much has passed through my hands
in these five-and-twenty years. Nothing has stayed under this
roof ; all has gone into the work which has been entrusted to me.
My desire is to die, as a priest ought, without money and without
debts."

part of it deserves quotation :—"I lived through the whole of the reign of George IV. and a part of the reign of George III., and I can remember that in those days the effects of the French Revolution were still active in this country. There was discontent among the mass of the people,—a discontent that was not unreasonable. In the reign of William IV. the position of affairs was somewhat mitigated ; but there can be no doubt that that period was one of the most dangerous in modern history. There was sedition and discontent, and there were great inequalities of state and condition, great inequalities of law, and various galling Acts and statutes with severe penalties attached to them. Even the wisest and bravest men were full of anxiety. At that time the Princess Victoria ascended the throne, in age hardly more than a child; and she awakened the spirit of personal loyalty and chivalry towards herself, a spirit which had seemed dead to the time and the people. We owe to her Majesty ·in that sense a greater debt than any historian can ever write. The moral effect of her influence and youthful presence had an effect on the minds of men which reconciled them to bear in patience that which was a galling burden to many, until the time of relief could come. The personal character of the Sovereign from that time to this has been a centre of strength, of strength founded upon that spirit of mutual love which binds a people to their Sovereign and a Sovereign to her people. I believe that no Sovereign has ever opened her heart, her sympathies and her sorrows to her people so fully as Queen Victoria has done. Nor has any people so sympathized with the domestic life and the bereavements of their Queen as has the people of this land. The Queen's

reign has been one in which the liberties of the people
have been extended; so that now there is popular con-
tentment where fifty years ago there was popular discontent, not without reason. Nor has there ever been
a period in which the condition of those working in the
darkness of collieries and factories, of those degraded
in brickfields or suffocated in chimneys, of the lowest
and most suffering of our people, has been so watchfully
tended and so mercifully cared for. . . An Imperial
Institute is perhaps the most fitting memorial of the
Queen's jubilee, because it is in its idea co-extensive
with the Empire. If it had been possible to write
hereafter in history that Queen Victoria had found the
working classes of her people living in hovels and had
left them living in homes, that would have been a noble
jubilee memorial. But it would have been partial and
local and confined within the four seas. The Imperial
Institute will be the centre of the truest form of Federation; for that does not exist in documents of parchment,
but must consist in the unity of intelligence, will, heart
and interest." After the Pontifical High Mass at the
Pro-Cathedral, Kensington, sung by the Papal Envoy,
Monsignor Ruffo Scilla, in honour of the Queen's
jubilee, Manning, who had yielded all other points of
precedence to the Envoy, as representing the Pope,
insisted on acting as celebrant in the intoning of the
first verse of the *Te Deum.* "I could not give up that,"
he explained; "I am an Englishman, and feel it."
There can be no doubt that his loyalty to the Crown
was most sincere, and of the good old-fashioned sort.
With the Queen herself indeed his personal relations
were of the slightest; but she is said to have entertained a genuine regard for him, and she publicly

R

expressed regret at his death. With the heir to the throne he was brought into pretty close relations during a considerable time ; and the courtly old gentleman was as welcome and as much at his ease at a garden-party at Marlborough House as any of the *habitués* of the Royal circle, though he was more perhaps in his element when speaking on temperance to a crowd on Clerkenwell Green.

Although he was "officially bound to neutrality" in matters of party politics, there can be no doubt as to the side with which his sympathies mostly lay. He spoke indeed, more than once, admiringly of Lord Beaconsfield, and he was by no means uniformly a supporter of Mr. Gladstone's policy. But his sympathies were always on what seemed to him the people's side ; and, if he cannot fairly be described as a liberal, still less as a radical, he was certainly, both by temperament and by conviction, a democrat. The building up of social order on the broadest base was his ideal; and, if he sometimes advocated legislation that had a socialistic savour, it was because he was convinced that until the working classes have secured a better economic condition, a condition enabling them to possess comfortable homes, sufficient fare and reasonable leisure, there will always be discontent, upheavals and uneasiness. Such a condition he also believed to be a necessary preliminary to their return to some kind of spiritual life. The abolition of poverty he did not look for, but the abolition of pauperism and wretchedness.

Among his Protestant fellow-countrymen Manning was not without honour, though it is true that there was no general recognition of his greatness until within the last ten or fifteen years of his life, when the prejudices against him, aroused mainly by the prominent part he took in defence of the Pope's temporal power and securing the definition of the Pope's infallibility, had mostly melted away; but as early as July, 1869, the *Spectator* had advocated, not without considerable sympathy throughout the country, that he should be specially summoned to the House of Lords; and, while he was in Rome attending the Vatican Council, the committee of the Athenæum Club elected him a member, under a rule which empowers them to admit, in preference to ordinary candidates, men who are of note in the worlds of literature, science or art, or who are eminent in the public service. The former proposal was of course not carried out,— the maze of old-world regulations, and the jealousy of creating a precedent were fatal to it, though the Upper Chamber would certainly have been strengthened by his presence; but the latter was both gratifying and of service to him; and he used to meet from time to time at the shrine of wisdom in Waterloo Place old schoolfellows and Oxford contemporaries, besides men of mark in almost all departments of thought—Mr. Ruskin, for example,—and no little sunshine was thus added to his life.

In his later years no man was ever more accessible or more courteous to all comers than he; and persons of every variety of belief and unbelief availed themselves of the privilege of verifying Lord Beaconsfield's portrait of Cardinal Grandison and his surroundings.[1]

---

[1] "Above the middle height, his stature seemed modified by the attenuation of his form. It seemed that the soul had never so frail and fragile a tenement. . . His countenance was naturally of an extreme pallor, though at this moment flushed with the animation of a deeply interesting conference. His cheeks were hollow, and his grey eyes seemed sunk into the clear and noble

But not all his visitors were merely curious. Many came because they were sure of sympathy if they were in trouble or disgrace. Others came simply because they found him such a delightful companion. He was in fact "all things to all men," in a way that few can contrive to be without obvious, perhaps even conscious, hypocrisy. The young statesman found no one more interested in politics, and went away with the conviction that, though the Archbishop wore a cassock and a pectoral cross, he was before all things a man of the world, and one who cared for the things of the world. An ardent Nonconformist divine, full of ideas about "the life of the Nazarene," would leave with the conviction that beneath the same externals beat a heart warm with spiritual Christianity, uninjured by its formal surroundings; while a social reformer, somewhat contemptuous of politics and a Gallio in relation to theology, was no less sure that it was the cause of suffering humanity as such that the Cardinal only really cared for.

There can be no doubt that he had a genuine horror of cruelty, as seen in his vigorous protests against vivisection, in his labours on behalf of a society for the protection of children, and in his advocacy (so utterly distasteful to many within the Roman communion) of the efforts made, notably by Mr. Stead, some six or seven years ago to sharpen the claws of justice against offenders who had proved themselves not only vicious but cruel in the seduction of the young and innocent. Doubtless he shared in the somewhat

---

brow; but they flashed with irresistible penetration." The account of the Cardinal's library is also an almost exact picture of that in "Archbishop's House," just off Vauxhall Bridge Road.

exaggerated sentimentality of that day, aroused by the acceptance as veracious of some harrowing and not very decent tales, which proved to be the fruit of a journalist's imagination, employing itself on a questionable escapade of his own; and it is not easy to understand how he was able to go the lengths he did in approving that escapade, since it was not only punishable as a crime, but was surely to be condemned as a mortal sin by Catholic theology, though effected *per manum alius.* Still, in the fierceness of his indignation against immorality and the basest cruelty, a fierceness that betrayed itself in an exceptionally sharp reply to a correspondent who implored him not to issue a Pastoral Letter on the subject, the Archbishop showed up more nobly than his Catholic critics, who bewailed the degradation of the Church in England by its head being reduced to the somewhat ignominious position of one of Mr. Stead's marionettes. Some years later the journalist had his revenge on them for their scorn.[1]

And, in truth, no one who fairly considered the matter could withhold his admiration from the Cardinal for the active and effective part that he played in so many departments of social reform. Though not himself of gentle birth, he was not devoid of aristocratic instincts, the gratification of which was easily within his reach in the position of dignity and authority to which he had

[1] "The English Catholics who represent the old stock . . . are the [English] species of the French Legitimist,—a highly respectable, intensely conservative, utterly sterile set of citizens. From any point of view beyond that of the blameless discharge of their religious duties, and the preservation of their families intact from the incursion of modern thought, they are almost as useless to the Church as they can well be. They are the fossils of the Church; and to such men the advent of Cardinal Manning [was] a sore trial."—*Review of Reviews,* June, 1890.

been raised. The refinement of his manners, the associations he had formed at school and college, and his alliance by marriage with families of ancient lineage, all this must have predisposed him to keep strictly within the sphere of his duties as Archbishop and as Cardinal—arduous enough to excuse any man from undertaking anything beyond them. But, heavily weighted as he thus was,—and beyond what we all are with our traditional ideas of peddling charity, and of antique observance or of frothy sentiment doing duty as religion,—his force of character and his hearty democratic instincts enabled him to pass the barriers and to accomplish work that will not readily be forgotten by the mass of Englishmen, however willing the older-fashioned Catholics may be to let it pass out of remembrance. The breadth of his sympathies was evidenced during the summer of 1890, when congratulatory deputations waited upon him, not only from among his own people—interpreting the term either of Catholics or of the working classes—but also from the Jews of London, on whose behalf he had more than once used his influence ; while, in defence of the Jewish race as a whole, he made his voice heard even in Rome, vindicating them against some ridiculous mediæval charge of cruelty, which appeared to have obtained credence within the walls of the Vatican. To speak of this wide range of his sympathies as liberalism would be rather to misuse the term ; still it is undeniable that Manning did something to infuse a new spirit of tolerance into the Church, and that at Rome itself, in addition to what he did there to bring about a recognition of the democratic nature of Catholicism ; and in Cardinal Lavigerie he made a convert—during

his visit to England—to saner views than are common
among Catholics as to the spiritual and moral condition
of Protestants.[1]

It has been referred to as a deficiency in the generally progressive ideas on social reform entertained by
Manning that he was not an advocate of " women's
rights"; and it is true that he did not support a cause
that would, in his judgment, be injurious to the
womanly in woman, by bringing her into contact with
the dust and turmoil of political life. But he was far
from holding women in contempt in regard to their
intellectual and administrative powers; and, if it had
been possible to pass a law enabling only such women
to obtain the franchise as would freely choose to exercise
it, while those who preferred to be " keepers at home "
should be left undisturbed according to their choice,
and not be urged either to become voters or be can-
vassed for their votes, should they at a later time of
their own free will reverse their decision,—such a law
would not have seemed to him open to objection. His
knowledge of the lives of the Saints, of St. Catherine
of Siena, for example, and of the work of the many able
women who ruled convents within his diocese, was

[1] Cardinal Lavigerie wrote to Manning in 1889:—"I remember
what you told me, how for half a century you lived out of the
Catholic Church without even a single doubt as to the truth of
your belief, and how eagerly you turned to the truth when once
you perceived it, to study it closer, to acknowledge it and to embrace it. I shall never forget how you spoke of your former
brethren, and with what charity. I seemed to listen to St.
Augustine when he said to his African dissidents, '*Illi in vos
sæviant*,' &c. Never shall I forget the day when we were at the
meeting together in Prince's Hall, one on the left and the other
on the right of the chairman, a member of the Society of Friends,
who succeeded to the place of Lord Granville, nor with what
marks of respect and goodwill we were received."

enough to show him that aptness to govern is commonly enough found among women; but still the
exercise of such power in public life seemed to him to
be by rights an exceptional and not the ordinary thing;
and he was unwilling to promote the passing of a law
that would of necessity deal with the matter in the
gross, and so prove, as he thought, detrimental to the
rightful influence of women on society.

Great as was Manning's faith it did not extend to
the medical profession. In regard to " doctors' stuff"
he confessed himself a formal sceptic; and this was
perhaps a little ungenerous of him, as during the course
of his life he had three or four sharp attacks of illness,
from which his escape may fairly be reckoned to have
been helped rather than hindered by his medical
attendants. For the triumphs of modern surgery he
was not without admiration; but for the practice of
medicine, as it now exists, he had none. The impotence
of doctors in the presence of serious disease; their
credulity in regard to prophylactics; and the jealousy
with which they protect, under a barbarous mediæval
nomenclature, their administration of drugs, the effect of
which in any given case is hardly more than a matter
for conjecture;—these were, one may suppose, his
grounds of infidelity; and the last question he addressed to a doctor, within a few hours of his death,
" Is it any use?" may be taken as expressive of the
habitual attitude of his mind on this subject.

Of the friendships that stood him most in stead
within the Catholic Church more will doubtless be
known hereafter, when a selection from his voluminous
correspondence is published. But, in addition to those
with whom he was officially in daily close relations,

it was chiefly with Father Faber, Dr. Ward and Canon Oakeley, among the older generation of converts, that he was intimate, and in his own community of the Oblates, Fathers Herbert Vaughan, afterwards Bishop of Salford, O'Callaghan, sometime Rector of the English College in Rome, Richards, diocesan Inspector of Schools, Dr. Butler, and Fathers Rawes, Bailey, Dillon and Lescher were his contemporaries and his close friends. Outside this especially domestic circle he showed a notable regard and admiration for the late Father Burke, the eloquent Irish Dominican.

His private secretary, Father Kenelm Vaughan, has given some account of a matter of which no outsider could venture to speak, his private and personal religion; and some passages from it must not be omitted here:—"The spiritual presence of our Lord in his soul was to him a great living reality, his ruling principle and the key to his inner life. . . The reign of the Spirit of our Lord within him was the secret of his charity, his peace and self-command, virtues which he ever strove to inculcate on his spiritual children. To one of them he wrote, 'My desire is to see a calm, inward, unobserved, even and exact fulfilment of the duties of our state, and of the devotions we owe to our dear Lord. I am never at ease about a religion which is audible, outward and uneven.' . . . He possessed a profound knowledge and love and appreciation of the beauties of Holy Scripture. This sacred book was his daily companion and his constant friend. It was the first book he opened in the morning and the last he closed at night. . . His favourite books of Holy Scripture were, in the Old Testament, *Wisdom;* among the Gospels, that of *St. John,* which he published

separately and loved to distribute; and of the Pauline
Epistles, that to the *Ephesians,* on which he principally
based all he wrote upon the divine creation of the Holy
Church. . . So intense was his love of God that I
have seen him sob bitterly on hearing that the Divine
Majesty had been outraged by some act of sin. . .
The doorsteps of his house were worn with the foot-
steps of the fatherless, the widow, the poor, the forlorn,
the tempted and the disgraced, who came to him for
comfort in their hour of trouble and sorrow. No one
ever went to him in distress who did not go away
consoled and soothed by the few and burning words
which fell from his fatherly lips. . . As to his asceti-
cism, it was far-reaching and profound; probably no
anchorite or recluse could live a more severe or
penitential life than this Prince of the Church and
accomplished man of the world. His food was of the
plainest; his drink was water; his room was a bare
cell. His thin, emaciated frame bore the visible marks
of the mortification of Christ, and the life of Christ was
made manifest in his mortal body. . . His ardent love
for our Lord, and his perfect detachment from earthly
things led him frequently to converse on heaven, and
to sigh to be freed from the prison of the body, that he
might enjoy there the vision of his Divine Lord and
Master." [1]

To what influences are we to assign the formation of
such a character as that of which the foregoing pages
have given a sketch? Surely he must be accounted
the ripest and best fruit of the Tractarian movement.
Matriculating at Oxford the year that Keble's *Christian*

---

[1] *Tablet,* Jan. 23, 1892.

Year was published, coming under Newman's influence to some extent during his undergraduate life, and much more when he read the Tracts in his quiet home at Lavington, and later, taking the leading part in the great Church revival which was the practical outcome of the teaching of the Tracts, he was faithful nevertheless to their fundamental principle of authority; and, following that out, thoughtfully and self-sacrificingly, to what he believed to be its legitimate conclusion, he found himself within that Church towards which the movement tended. Once there, he devoted the whole of his powers to that Church's service, relaxing his exertions only when he had to succumb to old age and death. His instincts in religious matters were Catholic long before his "conversion." He never knew of any spiritual world but that of which dogma and revelation are the light and life; and in a passage quoted above in which for once he congratulated himself on his work, it was because he believed he had never done anything to unsettle any one's belief in a revealed truth.

A distinction is here noticeable between his position and Newman's. Newman, although he clung to Catholicism so tenaciously, knew all the time that men might lead pure, honourable and useful lives, faithful to family and to friends, and forming units in a secure civil society, without any theological beliefs whatever. He also did much, though not of course intentionally, to undermine faith. In his zeal to throw men back on the authority of the Church he did more, in Tract LXXXV., than any sceptical writer of this generation to weaken the independent authority of the Bible; while Tract XC. certainly promoted the liberalism he so detested, by showing how formularies may be

twisted to mean anything or nothing.[1] To Newman,
not unnaturally, the Tractarian movement[2] seemed
the most important of modern times; but later judges
will probably rate it more truly as no more than a
local offset from a temporary wave of reaction.   Of
course its influence in England has been very marked;
but that has been partly due to the feebleness of the
obstacles it has had to encounter. The real Catholic
reaction is that which has prevailed on the Continent
of Europe against tremendous odds; and the history
of it can be clearly read by those who care to study it,
from the imprisonment of Pius VII. by Napoleon at
Savona, within a few months of the date of Manning's
birth, when the fortunes of Catholicism were at their
very lowest, down to the present day, when the Church
is probably as powerful in Europe as at any previous
period.   That the reaction has been political no less
than religious is clear from the writings of De Maistre;
a reaction, that is, not merely against the profanity of
the great French Revolution, but against the premature
dissolution of the ancient bonds of society which it
involved.   The English reaction, like the English
Reformation, began later, and was in great measure an

---

[1] Manning never got over the dislike he entertained for Tract
XC. It always seemed to him of doubtful honesty. When, in
the autumn of 1845, after his return from his first visit to
Döllinger at Munich, Mr. Gladstone, much perturbed by the
grave series of secessions from the Church of England, asked
Manning if any one principle could be found that would explain
them, the latter said, after reflection, "Yes; *want of truth.*"   At
a much later time he said that he thought he must have had in
his mind the impression of dishonesty produced by the shifty
arguments of the last Tract.

[2] This title is surely to be preferred to "Oxford movement,"
which seems to destine that ancient seat of learning never to
move except backwards.

imitation of that which was taking place on the Continent; and it too was political as well as religious. We learn from Newman's writings how Catholic Emancipation alarmed the old-fashioned High Church-men, though that measure of political justice was really granted rather in pity and contempt for what was regarded as a harmless and moribund sect, than definitely on the principles of liberalism and toleration; and we learn from him further how the French Revo-lution of 1830 aroused fears of a corresponding move-ment in England, which the suppression of a few superfluous Irish bishoprics and the passing of the great Reform Act were thought to justify. It was against this very innocuous progress of liberalism that the Tractarian movement was originally a protest; and, by its appeal to the principle of authority against the progress of liberal ideas, it became a Catholicizing movement, first in doctrine and then in external observance; and we know how during the last sixty years it has completely transformed the religion of the Church of England. But originally the movement obtained its impulse from the corresponding great tide of Catholic reaction abroad, in relation to which it may be regarded as a river tidal wave, such as the "bore" or the "eager," with which we are familiar on the Severn or the Trent at home.

At any rate it was this movement that brought Manning—though he did not sympathize with the teaching of some of its later Tracts—into the Catholic Church, which was his true home; and there he grew to be a living and visible embodiment of what Catholicism is at its best. It is true that not all English Catholics thought so, that there were occasional sneers at "the convert Cardinal," and that some of his priests regarded him as a kind of magnified parson, swelling with authority and not recognizing, as a technically-educated priest would, its precise limitations. It was said, for example, that in the "censuring" of books submitted to him before publication, he would not confine himself to the strict duty of excising passages derogatory to faith or morals, but would mark for omission what seemed to him in bad taste or ill written. But, after all has been said, the Popes must be reckoned good judges of the qualities that go to make a Catholic, and both Pius IX. and Leo XIII. extended their special confidence to Manning as to a faithful child of the Church. He may be compared, not inaptly, either with St. Martin of Tours, or, better still, with his own spiritual father, St. Charles of Milan. Like him, he was a great Archbishop who did much to raise the standard of life among his clergy, and who was zealous in the cause of Christian education; and, like him, he moved amongst the people, not indeed miraculously healing them of the plague, but doing all that in him lay to remedy ills that are hardly less grievous, and are certainly more persistent and injurious in their effects.

It seems not unlikely that the ecclesiastical historian of the future may mark the period of Manning's Cardinalate (1875-92) as that of the zenith of the Catholic revival in England. Within this may be taken the years (1879-90) during which Newman held the same exalted rank; and, if a culminating point is to be indicated in that period of some twelve years, it would be the day (April 25, 1884) when Manning and Newman were both assisting as Princes of the Church at the opening of the new church of the Oratory in London. No doubt, on some future occasion, two or more Cardinals may be got together, but never again two such striking and memorable figures, appealing, by their almost romantic past, and by their great but very different abilities, to the attention and respect of all Englishmen. Neither of them has left any successor. This was commonly said of Newman when he died in August, 1890; and no one would be more ready to admit the truth of the proposition than the thoughtful, kindly-hearted and unambitious priest—a nephew, by the way, of Manning's—who is actually his successor as Superior of the Oratory at Birmingham. But it is not less true of Manning. There will be of course within a few weeks a third Archbishop of Westminster, who may hereafter be created Cardinal. But, whoever he may be, he can never fill for the outside world the place that was occupied by Manning, who touched the life of England at so many points. He has been a "leader in religion" in more ways than one. At the Vatican Council he pursued to its farthest point the principle of authority as the basis of religious faith; and, though in that matter he was treading on ground unfamiliar to and suspected by the mass of his fellow-countrymen, they did not deny to him any more than they have denied in other cases, the approval with which they regard a policy of "thorough." But his lead has been more acceptable in a second field, where he consecrated the forces of the Church to the cause of the people. Of his appearance on the platform in Exeter Hall, at the meeting of the Agricultural Labourers' Union in December, 1871, when he was the only ecclesiastic present, it may be said that it was in itself a courageous act, and one that has opened a new era for all the churches. Since that day the sight of clergymen, especially of Nonconformists, taking part in such meetings has become familiar enough; and Manning himself eclipsed the memory of his earliest public effort in behalf of labour by the success of his similar undertakings in later years, and especially in 1889. But when he is spoken of as "a leader in religion," the first bold step must not be forgotten, nor the earlier memorable words of the Archdeacon of Chichester, "Time must be redeemed for the poor man. The world is too hard upon him, and makes him pay too heavy a toll out of his short life." [1]

Whether, under less noteworthy rulers, the Catholic Church is destined still to gather strength in England, is a matter on which it is easy to express an opinion, but difficult to make any trustworthy forecast. One thing seems unfavourable to the idea, and that is the prospect of the return of a more old-fashioned type of Catholicism to power, a type which would have for its ideal the conversion of the aristocracy and especially of the owners of land, with the anticipation that the mass of the people would then follow suit—a futile notion from first to last. Manning himself it was thought on his first appointment would have proved such an "apostle of the genteels"; but he knew better, and turned to the poor, and especially to the children, with far more practical results. And indeed, if his spirit should survive in his successor, there is one field— a very widely-extended one—in which the Catholic Church in this country might hereafter reap a rich harvest. Manning's sympathy with the philanthropic

[1] *Vide supra*, p. 40.

work of "General" Booth was never disguised, and he
was too much of an organizer himself not to look with
admiration on the order and discipline of the "Salvation Army." The Army has a growing affinity with
Catholicism, and its members, accustomed to an auto-
cratic rule, might very well find in some future Archbishop of Westminster the successor who will surely
one day be needed, if the organization is to be held
together at all. Of course these soldiers and salvation
lasses are far enough from being Catholics at present;
but they have accepted fully the fundamental principle
of Catholicism—obedience; and in other ways they
are really nearer the Church than Dean Stanley's
"three men in green, whom your Lordship will find it
difficult to put down." The ritualists, in spite of
Catholic externals, are mostly liberals wearing blinkers,
in accordance with the fashion introduced by Newman,
and still much affected in polite society. But the
Salvation Army men are not theological liberals, and
wear no blinkers, for they do not need them any more
than Manning did, believing with him that the straight
road before them is the way revealed, and so caring to
look neither to the right hand nor to the left. A
simple, certain faith is theirs,—belief in God, in sin, a
Redeemer, the Bible, judgment, salvation, heaven and
hell; and this simple faith is a far more serviceable
basis, on which to build a permanent structure of
Catholicism, than the clever literary quibbles by which
men better educated are able to persuade themselves
that they hold to the old faith. There is thus here a
promising field for an expansion of the Catholic Church
—unless Catholics themselves shirk the opportunity—
which should be further facilitated by the marked

s

revival of credulity in recent times, and the growing
popularity of ritual and outward show.

But it could only be a partial expansion, not one
that would include the nation. Alongside the growth
of credulity, there is also a growth of a scientific positive spirit that must be taken into account, and an
extended knowledge of the results of biblical criticism.
Oxford itself is moving, is in fact almost taking the lead,
in this last-named department of knowledge; while Darwinian biology is now as firmly established among scientific scholars as is Copernican astronomy; and, as being
more intelligible and coming nearer home, is being far
more rapidly established in the popular mind. These
things are against the growth of Catholicism, for they
meet sundry of its dogmas with a direct negative; and
the Vatican Council decided, no doubt finally, that there
was no prospect of any compromise between the two.
Manning himself, who denounced Darwinian biology as
"the brutal philosophy which says 'There is no God,
and the ape is our Adam,'" would assuredly have
desired no such compromise; though it is true that he
never made clear how far, in his judgment, a man may
accept the results of modern research without ceasing
to be a Catholic.

Ecce sacerdos magnus,—that is the conclusion to which
from every point we come when we review the various
aspects of Manning's life and work. Whatever we find,
either to praise or perhaps to blame, it is always a
characteristic of a great and good priest. Those to
whom the idea of the Catholic priesthood is altogether
unwelcome, and who regard it as the very incarnation of
evil on this earth, can hardly be expected therefore to
admire a man who was always and before all things a

priest. But yet it is true that, whatever may be the inevitable tendency of the teachings of Catholicism towards intellectual obscurantism, it yet remains, and is likely long to remain, the greatest social force for good that the world possesses; and it is true also that, whatever may be the moral shortcomings of a small percentage of its priesthood, and although no man penetrated with modern ideas can permanently remain in its service without a consciousness of intellectual dishonesty which must sooner or later be fatal to the moral sense, the Catholic priesthood is far away the greatest organization that exists on earth of good and able men working for the moral welfare of the human race.

As a priest Manning had lived, and so, as a priest he would die. To those who did not understand the man it must have seemed histrionic and formal, that, when he knew he was within a few hours of his death, he should desire to be duly vested in the imposing full dress of a Cardinal, with rochet, girdle and pectoral cross, surmounted by the scarlet *biretta* and *cappa magna*, and so make a solemn profession of the faith of the Holy Roman Church. But it was all of a piece with the rest of his life—obedience to the prescribed rules;—and, when it was over, and he had given the last kiss of peace to Provost Gilbert and the other Canons, he said, exhausted but fully conscious of all that was passing around, " I am glad to have been able to do everything in due order." He died, as he had lived, with courage and dignity; and the thousands who patiently awaited their turn to see the withered body lying in state in the reception-room in Archbishop's House, or crowded to hear his *requiem* sung and his panegyric

preached, or lined the roads along which he was carried
to his resting-place, were conscious, many of them dimly
perhaps, but not the less sincerely, that in him England
had lost a venerable figure, the Church a great ruler,
the poor a true friend, and the world a prophet of
righteousness.

www.ingramcontent.com/pod-product-compliance
Lightning Source LLC
Chambersburg PA
CBHW020345030726
47496CB00007B/2007